BACKWASHED

- a novel -

PETE GALLAGHER

BEAVER'S POND
PRESS

This is a work of fiction. Names, characters, places, and incidents are either the products of the author's imagination or are used in a fictitious manner, and any resemblance to actual persons, living or dead, businesses, events, or locales is purely coincidental.

Edited by Kerry Stapley
Cover design by Ed DuRose

ISBN 13: 978-1-64343-563-3
Library of Congress Catalog Number: 2024910215
Printed in the United States of America
First Printing: 2024
28 27 26 25 24   5 4 3 2 1

Interior design and typesetting by Dan Pitts.
Minion Pro

BEAVER'S POND
PRESS

Beaver's Pond Press
939 Seventh Street West
Saint Paul, MN 55102
(952) 829-8818
www.BeaversPondPress.com

Visit www.petegallagherbooks.com for more information about the author.

For Louise,
who took a chance to give me a chance.

- 1 -

So by dawn, in the early spring chill, the street was a festival of flashing lights, the pavement overrun with a noisy caravan of people in municipal vehicles that included an ambulance no one had requested (and that the dead man would not need), its curious crew happening upon the commotion while returning to their station after a trip to the grocery store.

Arno St. Albans sat against the rear bumper of the ambulance, considering whether to ask the medics about his eye, as he pushed his left foot into a tall rubber boot provided by the storm sewer crew. When he got the second boot on, along with a yellow raincoat and hard hat fitted with a light, he was ready for the manhole.

A work truck with a winch arm arching from the bed was in position in the middle of the roadway, a narrow steel cage dangling from a cable that hovered over the dark opening to the access shaft. Stuffed into the cage was Tico Tocopilla, a young foreman who gave St. Albans a thumbs-up.

"Sixty seconds?" St. Albans asked.

Tico nodded.

"A second per foot, Sergeant. Like the river over there. One, Mississippi, two Mississippi. Count slow. You'll be down in the tunnel before you know it."

St. Albans turned to consider the open field along the street and the wide lanes of the river parkway beyond, traffic still sparse, as the morning sky struggled toward a hue the color of skim milk. The river was past the parkway, deep below in the valley that curled east into Saint Paul downstream of the Minneapolis divide.

"Rats?" St. Albans wondered.

The foreman smiled patiently.

"See, here's the deal on that," Tico answered. "We're the biggest things down there. Anything that sees us runs the other way."

Tico adjusted his work gloves and switched on the lamp at the front of his hard hat, then nodded toward the winch operator to lower him.

"And if they don't run away"—he pointed to the sergeant—"you can arrest them."

At three Mississippi, the winch motor roaring, Tico was swallowed into the street. After a while, the motor quieted down. There were shouts exchanged between the workers on the surface and Tico down below; then the winch fired again, and the cage came up empty.

St. Albans got in and hung on, making it to eleven seconds or so in his descent before a hint of panic teased the hairs on his thighs.

"Jesus," he huffed out loud.

The concrete cone of the manhole structure soon gave way to damp lenses of cracked green shale close enough to touch, something he had little intention of doing. His arms shivered, and his helmet lamp inflamed the shaft wall where the rock layer ended on a shoulder of buttery sandstone, crystals sparkling in swirls of yellow. At forty feet, he felt his elbows shaking inside his jacket as Tico's light below grew stronger on the wall. Groundwater misted from the shale above.

"Almost there?" St. Albans called, weaker than he would have liked, releasing his grip on the cage just for an instant to push a knuckle into his right eyelid for a quick wink.

Then there he was. The shaft suddenly widened as it breached the tunnel ceiling. Tico shouted up to cut the winch, leaving the sergeant stopped a foot above the wet floor.

"You good, man?" Tico asked, studying him for a moment. "Claustrophobic or anything? Not everybody can handle being down in the tunnels, so give yourself a second."

St. Albans took a couple of short breaths as he stepped from the cage, nodding as his limbs relaxed.

"I'll be okay," he said. "Carnival rides and heights have never been my thing."

The tunnel was a narrow void carved from the sandstone in the shape of an antique coffin, wider at the shoulders than the feet and just tall enough to stand. Bricks embedded in the floor created a gently sloping channel that extended into ominous darkness in two directions. St. Albans peered warily left, and then right. Tico pointed downstream with a strong flashlight, forcing shadows down the cavern. The air smelled like rotting paper.

"The outlet to the river is that way. We go opposite, toward my house."

Tico brushed yellow dust from the sleeve of his coveralls and headed uphill into the tunnel, following his flashlight beam. St. Albans fell into step behind him, rubber-ized footsteps smacking wetly on the bricks.

"You live around here?" St. Albans asked.

Tico answered without turning around.

"My folks still do. Not every Mexican in the city grew up around Cherokee Heights or on the West Side Flats, you know. A few of us always lived over here on the West Seventh Street side of the river."

Then he turned halfway around, talking over his shoulder.

"You?"

"Highland Park. Just off the south bridge."

"Ahh," Tico said in a tone that sounded like he meant something by it.

St. Albans hunched forward as they walked, fitting himself into the contours of the uneven walls, each awk-ward twist of his spine a reminder that he was getting old enough to start thinking of early retirement. A black in-sect, enormous with colorless wings, scuttled along beside him at the edge of the brick floor.

"How'd you find the body?" he asked.

Tico replied that he hadn't found it, that his crew had when they were investigating a complaint.

"The drug treatment house up the block found a hole when they started digging foundations for their new addi-tion," Tico said. "We've got abandoned tunnels and shafts all over this part of the system close to the river. It's like, ancient. So, the gang came down to see if they could figure out what the hole belonged to. See if we should seal it up."

"And it belonged to the dead man," St. Albans said.

Tico slowed his pace a bit. "You know, I've never seen a

body that wasn't part of a funeral."

"You can hang back," St. Albans said. "Getting me here is enough."

Ten minutes of trudging up the incline brought them to an opening in the side of the tunnel where a battered wheelbarrow sat overturned beside a short pile of cement bricks and a dusty sack of mortar. Tico stopped and shined his flashlight into the jagged circle of the small cavern.

"Here we go."

St. Albans looked, thinking that he saw something like a tennis sneaker beneath a mound of glass that shimmered in their headlamps. He pulled his cell phone from his jacket.

"That won't work down here," Tico said.

The sergeant held the phone toward Tico and took a photo.

"Oh."

"Gotcha," St. Albans said, the word tumbling unsteadily from the left side of his mouth. Tico's flashlight was there at once, glaring mercilessly into the sergeant's unblinking right eye. St. Albans quickly reached up his hand as a shield and turned his head.

Tico let the light beam slowly sink between them. "You sure you're okay? I think there's something wrong with your face."

St. Albans sucked in a slow, tense breath and took a step into the side cavern, sweeping pebbles out of the way with his foot as he inched forward, rubbing his paralyzed eyelid. His helmet light painted a bright halo over the end wall, two dozen feet away. On the floor, he saw reflected glimmers from the glass prisms of a chandelier, a tangle of brass chain, and a bloodied mat of curled hair on a gray human forehead.

The dead man was fiftyish, maybe a little older, in sneakers and white dungarees, both spackled with a confetti of faded paint smudges. He also wore an athletic jacket, less blotched, but not new, in the colors of the neighborhood high school. When St. Albans got close, he saw clumps of topsoil spilled around the body's twisted legs. A huge waxy black millipede slithered along the edges of the dirt.

Looking up, the sergeant saw a narrow shaft that threaded high through the overhead rock, a thimble of sky visible up beyond the surface of the ground.

He heard a scraping sound behind him and looked. Tico was moving slowly in from the storm tunnel, his flashlight throwing shadows over the corpse.

"Don't touch anything." St. Albans aimed his phone camera toward the dead man.

"As if," Tico said, and when he got to the body, in a tone that could have meant several things, he added, "Fuck."

When the sergeant turned, his helmet light found the foreman, who, from a couple feet away, appeared to be shining with sweat. St. Albans then realized that he was beginning to perspire himself, burning with a sudden adrenal rush.

"Let me guess," he said, his mouth flattening to a frown on the side where the nerves were still awake. "You know this guy."

Tico stomped on the millipede. "What guy?"

The sergeant's cell phone rang.

- 2 -

Two miles east of the bridge where the downtown express-way spanned the Mississippi, a grim ribbon of road curved along the dredged river channel through a flat expanse of automobile salvage yards and industrial sites.

Where the pavement ended and the rocky lowlands of the floodplain spread downstream, Dion Drury stood just inside a razor-wire-topped chain-link fence that surrounded three acres of vehicles in the custody of the Saint Paul police. The distant drone of early morning traffic on the shoreline parkway drifted from across the river. Dion looked downriver at the scrubby vegetation and then up toward trees that bearded the bluffs along the wide river canyon, gray limbs mossy with new spring buds.

"Smells like cat shit out here," he said.

In front of him, Hefty Von Hanson rose from a crouch beside a sedan with a shattered rear window and an official city insignia on its door. He scratched his stubby finger over the short red hairs that bristled from the edges of the ball cap he wore pulled low atop his ears. His sweatshirt advertised his father's automobile salvage business next door, the lettering a match to the decal on the door of the flatbed tow truck parked behind them in the aisle. He pointed toward holes in the car.

"Bullets, huh, D-man?" he said. "Somebody must have been kind of pissed."

"That's what I said too," Dion told him. "We should be cops, you and me."

"No thanks," Hefty said. "It's weird enough that you're down here clerking for them, you know?"

Dion brushed back his hair with one hand and shivered in his dungarees and police windbreaker. The lights that dotted the lot on overhead poles switched off as the morning sky brightened. He looked toward the office, a concrete cube two stories tall a hundred yards away, beside the road. He saw movement in the big windows on the second floor.

"I'd better get back upstairs," he said. "I don't want Shiner answering the telephone."

"She couldn't sleep last night, huh?"

"She called her dad for a ride," Dion told him. "He brought her down around four. He wasn't exactly thrilled."

"How's she doing?"

Dion shrugged. "Same as always," he said. "Happy enough to make up for the rest of us."

"I'll take her with me when I go," Hefty offered, adjusting his cap. "The cops don't need to be seeing her and me when they show up for the morning shift, you know?"

"Good plan," Dion agreed, climbing into the passenger side of the flatbed, but not closing the door.

Hefty pointed at the wounded car.

"No blood inside?"

Dion shook his head. "I'd say somebody was lucky. Or maybe the thing was parked when it got sprayed. The tow report said it was picked up a little before midnight just off University Avenue, not too far from the Capitol. Plenty of knuckleheads with guns running around up there at night.

Could be somebody was just bored."

"Who's the car signed out to?"

"The records don't show. Just that it's a city vehicle. There were some folders and papers on the front seat, though."

"Clues?"

Dion thought about that for a long minute before answering. "Puzzles," he said.

Hefty came around the front of the truck and pulled himself up behind the steering wheel, the motion harmonized by the great wheezing rattle of his heavy breaths. Key rings jangled from chains clipped to a belt loop on his coverall pants. He brushed an empty fast-food soda cup and straw from the dashboard to the floor, then looked at Dion and grinned.

"Smells like cat shit in here too, huh?"

- 3 -

Arno St. Albans steered his unmarked sedan over the railroad crossing that paralleled Cesar Chavez Street at the southeastern corner of the city. He continued slowly along the barge channel road, following a large wrecker truck that was towing the rear half of an orange school bus. His window was down in defiance of the morning chill, his clothes still smelling like the storm sewer tunnel, but it was not so noticeable now, this close to the river. The wrecker pulled to the side near the gate for Von Hanson's Auto Salvage and Parts. The sergeant veered into the center of the street to pass.

The fence around the police impound lot began a few yards east of where Von Hanson's property line ended. St. Albans braked to a crawl, studying the nearest lanes of impounded vehicles. He saw lights on in the second-story windows of the office. When he reached the electric drop gate beside the building, he didn't try to drive in. He parked along the edge of the road. As he got out and walked around the closed gate arm, he saw a face in the window above watching him as he made his way past the tall garage door to the office entrance.

The steel door opened to a small concrete landing at the foot of a staircase. A closed door to the left led to the big garage. There were two doors to the right, also closed. Behind the nearest one, a toilet flushed loudly. The sergeant started up the stairs, and he heard the toilet flush again.

He reached the upper-floor landing. A small window in the wall to his left looked down into the garage area. A window in a closed door revealed lockers and a kitchen with an office beyond. Turning to his right, St. Albans faced a long service counter behind clear plexiglass with two stations for transactions. A young blond woman on a high stool behind one station refolded a newspaper on the counter in front of her.

"I don't work here," she said, giving her full attention to the comics.

Large windows looked out in three directions to the road and the two dozen rows of vehicles on the graveled ground within the fence. A desk took up the corner where the windows came together. There, a young man with slicked hair sat typing before a computer screen, the same person whom St. Albans had seen watching him walk in from the street. Out the window beyond the young man, the tall buildings of downtown knifed the western horizon. A speaker on the desk crackled with sounds from microphones outside, a police radio beside it droning low exchanges between patrol officers and the dispatch center.

Downstairs, the toilet flushed once more. St. Albans looked at the woman, then at the kid at the desk. Then he cleared his throat.

"I am the egg man," he said.

The young man stopped typing but kept his eyes on the screen. After several long seconds, he responded without turning.

"I am the egg man," he echoed.

St. Albans nodded when the kid finally looked toward him.

"I know you are," said the sergeant. "But what am I?"

The woman looked up from the comics, puzzled. Her eyebrows narrowed, and St. Albans saw then a large white scar on her left temple, a protruding mangle of distended flesh that seemed to cling along her eyebrow like the truncated legs of a starfish. A clock on the wall beside the stairs drummed the silence with ten loud ticks that became the beat to the distantly familiar tune she'd begun to hum.

"I am the walrus?" she decided, not sounding too sure.

"You wish," St. Albans told her.

"It's okay, Shiner," said the kid at the desk. "This isn't about the old Beatles song. This is about me."

The kid turned back toward the screen and resumed typing, talking over the clatter of keystrokes.

"So," he said, "if Honest Mike is looking to collect on a favor, I should probably ask what he wants."

St. Albans nodded, saying, "Lieutenant Walerius wants what every politician wants. To cover his ass."

"So, the shot-up city car is his?"

"You picked up on that fast," the sergeant said. "I'm impressed. He saw it being hauled away, and decided that as a sitting city council member, it doesn't look good when his private life spills over into public view, so he didn't try to stop the tow truck driver."

The bathroom door on the first floor clanged open, and a voice boomed up the stairway, dragging footsteps with it.

"Hey, hey, Miss O'Shea, let's go get some breakfast. And tell the D-man to let his bosses know that they need a new toilet plunger."

St. Albans turned to see a big kid in a Von Hanson's Auto Salvage and Parts sweatshirt reach the top of the landing and suddenly realize that an outsider was among them.

"I don't work here," the kid said, holding up his palms.

St. Albans pointed at Shiner O'Shea behind the counter and said that she didn't either, then felt her staring at him with a focus he did not appreciate.

"There's something wrong with your face," Shiner said.

In the half second he considered telling her that it took one to know one, St. Albans felt something else, brought on by the subtle triumph in her voice at having figured something out for herself.

"Yes," he said quietly. "There is."

Then the other kid, the one at the computer, was talking again.

"Hefty," he said. "Last time I looked, there was a bathroom over at your old man's place."

"Well, yeah," Hefty admitted. "But ours is gross, right? Of course, now yours is gross too."

He pointed at the door to the kitchen. Shiner pushed a button and the doorknob buzzed. Hefty went in and then reappeared through an open doorway behind the counter. He crowded against her stool, reading the comics over her shoulder.

"Knock, knock," he said.

St. Albans saw Shiner smile. "Who's there?"

"Ya," Hefty answered.

Shiner pulled her elbows in close to her ribs, like she knew what was coming.

"Ya, who?"

Hefty grabbed both sides of the stool and began shaking it violently, bouncing her up and down.

"Ride 'em, cowgirl!" he bellowed while Shiner broke into giggles.

The kid at the desk stopped typing and shrugged when the sergeant looked at him again.

"Like they said, they don't work here."

"It's a good thing that you do, then," St. Albans said. "Any way we can make that city car less of an issue for our mutual patron?"

The young man told him that once a tow report was entered into the system, there was no deleting it, raising a slow burn in the sergeant's right eye.

"That's probably not good," St. Albans said, digging into his pocket for his eye drops.

"Sometimes not," the kid agreed slowly. "That's why I haven't entered it yet."

St. Albans breathed out a low chuckle. "Egg man," he said.

"I know you are," the kid answered. "But what am I?"

Shiner and Hefty emerged from the kitchen then, ready to head down the stairs as the windowed door locked behind them. The speaker on the corner desk crunched with the sound of tires braking on the road outside and a vehicle door opening with a squawk.

The sergeant remembered something. "Lieutenant Walerius said there were some papers in the car."

The kid looked out the window. "Were there?"

Footsteps in the speaker grew louder, and then the door at the bottom of the stairs crashed open. St. Albans saw Shiner and Hefty looking down toward the door while he heard a voice from earlier that morning rise toward them.

"Where's the D-man?"

St. Albans leaned over the railing to see Tico Tocopilla, the sewer crew foreman still in his coveralls, looking up at the three of them, one boot suddenly frozen on the first step for the instant it took for him to pivot and head back out the door again. The sergeant turned and looked toward Shiner and Hefty, one eyebrow raised.

"What guy?" said Shiner.

- 4 -

Officer Kady L'Orient stood up in her cubicle in the investigators' offices on the third floor of the public safety building at the north edge of downtown. She watched through her window as rush-hour traffic clustered on the northside interstate freeway a block away, but she was not really paying attention. Instead, she rewound in her mind an inventory of the numerous folders and case files she kept arranged in neat piles across her desk and table.

The stack of dormant case materials on a far corner, busywork to fill in the lulls between assignments, was one murder short.

Kady clambered onto her chair so she could see over her cubicle walls. The big room appeared the same as always, people moving in the aisles and voices speaking into telephones, no one seemingly focused on her. She bit her lower lip gently. Without a note wedged under her stapler, nor a phone message or an email to explain who had taken the file and why, she had to consider the intrusion of her desk space an obvious personal insult.

She climbed back down from the chair. She pulled a facial tissue from a box beside her computer monitor and polished the lenses of her eyeglasses. The plastic inbox tray on the desktop near her cubicle door held some papers. On the top rested an interoffice mail envelope addressed to her, the sender unknown, the line for filling in the last point of origin left blank.

Kady put her glasses back on and unwound the string that held the flap closed. When she peered inside the envelope, the trimmed hairs along her blouse collar went stiff.

"What fucking now?" she said quietly.

She turned the envelope over, and onto the desk spilled a thin copper chain curling from a springy hinged clasp of anodized aluminum she thought very like one on her bedroom nightstand at home.

A nipple clamp.

- 5 -

The story from the police at the scene was that the county medical examiner had recovered what she listed on the official report as the remains of a human male, lifted from a storm-sewer tunnel earlier that morning with the aid of a city maintenance crew. The name of Brillo Ziemer would be withheld from the media pending notification of next of kin, which Dion Drury and Tico Tocopilla both agreed might keep his corpse anonymous for some time.

"I don't remember anybody," Tico said. "Do you?"

Dion did not and said so, adding that he had not recently seen much of the old guy anyway. He looked out the passenger window of Tico's official city pickup truck toward the hedge along the driveway to Brillo's house. Brillo's van sat parked in front of the garage, its roof rack overloaded with painting scaffolds and ladders.

Beyond the hedge, the yard sloped upward toward the uprooted landscape of the Kittsondale Treatment Center next door. Orange cones and yellow tape marked the hole there that Brillo had obviously not noticed in the dark the night before, encumbered as he was with an unwieldy antique light fixture—pilfered, Tico surmised aloud, from the center's dining hall, which was under renovation as part of a larger expansion project.

"I still don't get the logic of the chandelier," Dion said. "What was he going to do with it?"

Tico took a sip of takeout coffee from a paper cup and adjusted himself behind the steering wheel.

"See, here's the deal on that," he answered. "Brillo was pissed about the building addition. The Kittsondale people and the city council kind of rolled over him with their variance to the property line setbacks. He didn't want the construction so close to his house, and they didn't care."

"So, he decides to nick them for an old ceiling lamp?"

"Well," Tico said, "I suppose you could say there was more to it, maybe."

Dion chewed on that for a few seconds, rolling down his window to listen to the traffic on the river parkway nearby. Then he spoke again.

"I could say, or you could say?"

Tico took a long breath before answering, the pause telling Dion that what was coming might be something that neither of them really wanted to know.

"You probably don't remember the partnership, D-man," Tico began. "But my dad stayed painting with Brillo for a few years after your dad died, just until he could put enough money together to go off on his own. He didn't want his reputation as a contractor connected to Brillo or to your old man."

Dion frowned. He had been too young to understand his late father's decorating trade and did not really remember much other than details noted in the news clippings that had been saved along with some old drywall finishing tools. Though Tico's dad and Brillo had stayed in contact with Dion and his older sister over the years, no one had ever given any indication that their father had been anything other than some ordinary, unlucky guy from the neighborhood who managed to get himself shot and dumped along a railroad track on the other side of town.

Dion wanted to know what the old men had been doing back in the day, so Tico told him.

"My dad says that there has always been a market for old house fixtures," Tico explained. "Crystal doorknobs, old-growth wood or marble fireplace mantels, wainscoting, tin ceilings, stuff like that. Bathtubs and sinks. Doors and trim. People restoring old mansions up on Summit Avenue or in Crocus Hill have always been willing to pay through the nose for old authentic shit."

He took a sip of coffee and then went on.

"Brillo and your dad saw pretty quick that there was a lot of cash potential if they could connect people to the materials that were in demand. A lot of side money beyond patching and painting and hanging wallpaper. My old man told me that those two were so good at collecting, it eventually made him nervous. He never knew what things they bought from someone and what things they just went out and boosted from someplace. Once your dad was gone, Brillo just kept on with it, and my dad couldn't stop worrying about getting caught."

The low moan of a towboat whistle sounded from the river channel. Dion sniffed and pointed toward Brillo's van and the building beyond.

"So, you're telling me that Brillo's place is filled with stolen building stuff?"

"Well, not right now," Tico said. "When he started fighting with the city and the Kittsondale folks, he moved it all into my garage in case the construction inspectors from next door came snooping."

Dion looked over at him and laughed.

"And you always talk about Hefty being a doofus," Dion said.

"The man asked. What was I supposed to do?"

"Tell him *no*, maybe?"

Tico shrugged. "Well, I didn't, and that's why I freaked out when I saw that police sergeant down at your office. He was with me in the tunnel, and then he was with you, and I didn't know what that meant."

"He didn't tell me he was a cop," Dion said. "But it wasn't hard to figure out."

"And he didn't say anything about Brillo?"

"No," Dion said. "He wanted to talk to me about something else."

The towboat whistle sounded again, growing fainter upstream. The morning sun warmed a circle on Dion's shoulder. He smoothed back his hair as he spoke again.

"I don't know how much Brillo's stuff might be worth," Dion said, "but I would bet all of it that the next time one of us sees that sergeant, we'll talk about Brillo."

Tico opened his door and emptied his coffee onto the ground.

"I thought it was bad enough when we were in the tunnel to let on that I knew Brillo," Tico said. "Letting that sergeant see me at your office only made things worse. I should have just gone back to work." He shook his head. "I am a doofus."

"I know you are," Dion said half under his breath as he looked out the window. "But what am I?"

"What?" Tico asked.

Dion told him to never mind.

- 6 -

On the fourth floor of the city hall and county courthouse building downtown, the office suite for the Tenth Ward City Council representative overlooked the river. Arno St. Albans stood at one of the two big windows and looked down toward the Wabasha Street Bridge, which connected the business district to the lowland flats across the channel and to the West Side neighborhoods atop the rising bluffs beyond. His eye was smarting as he watched a homeless person having an apparent existential conflict with the large flagpole that sprouted from the sidewalk plaza along Kellogg Boulevard. He could hear garbled shouting in some unintelligible dialect.

The breathy voice of Honest Mike Walerius rose quietly behind him, responding to the muffled uproar outside with a precise, short flurry of words that made English sound something like a pressed tuxedo shirt, starched and folded.

"A loyal constituent singing my praises, might I presume?"

"Or maybe one of your campaign donors," the sergeant answered, turning around, "wanting their money back."

Honest Mike was sitting behind a big maple desk perpendicular to the windows, the elbows of his charcoal suit jacket resting on the desktop. The ceiling lights reflected half-moons on the blue-tinted lenses of his rimless eyeglasses. A tight helmet of silver permed ringlets tufted from his head. He was shuffling through a stack of index cards inside a small metal box, like a historical reenactment of a competitor searching for a reference in the heat of a high school varsity debate in the last third of the twentieth century.

"Young, I believe you have said?"

St. Albans nodded as he dug out his eyedrops, saying, "And a little bit dark. With hundred-mile-an-hour hair."

He swept a hand quickly over his scalp from front to back.

"Supersonic styling, then," Honest Mike said. "And swarthy to some minor degree. Possibly Mediterranean, I am thinking, per your description."

The councilman pulled out a card, frowned at it, and then put it back, saying that he was beginning to remember.

"A youthful Greek fellow who came to the team through my dear wife. I never saw him. He was recommended by one of her compatriots in the Restaurant and Tavern Association. I arranged a civilian placement in the 'Evidence and Property' lockdown at public safety, and then later, I believe, he procured a transfer to a rotating graveyard shift at the impound lot, although I struggle to appreciate the appeal of such an assignment."

"Maybe he's antisocial," St. Albans said. "His friends down there call him the demon."

"Truly?" Honest Mike asked. "That certainly lends to him an element of panache, although no doubt his given name would prove more prosaic, if I could only bring it to mind."

He restacked the cards inside the box and closed it, saying, "No matter. What is the status of the vehicle?"

"The kid said he didn't enter it into the system, so you're clear there."

"What action might we expect him to attempt while resolving the situation in some manner of acceptable finality?" Honest Mike asked.

St. Albans said he had no idea and didn't really care to know, so he hadn't brought it up. "I wouldn't worry too much about it, though," said the sergeant. "The kid seems pretty sharp."

The councilman opened a desk drawer and pushed the box deep inside, thinking out loud.

"Under the current circumstances, that could become a worry in itself," he pointed out. "What did he say of the papers?"

"He showed me the tow report," St. Albans said. "There were no interior contents listed."

Honest Mike slowly tapped one finger against the desktop, digesting this news. St. Albans looked toward the ceiling while hoisting the eyedrops with a slightly wavering hand.

"I would observe that your technique appears to be improving," the councilman said.

St. Albans did not thank him for noticing. When the sergeant lowered his gaze, he looked to the open doorway where staff in the outer offices moved among work areas. One woman in a traditional African wrap for which the sergeant did not know the correct name was not merely moving; *sashaying* was the only word he could think of that adequately described what her hips seemed intent upon communicating as she walked a slow arc between a printer station and her cubicle. He shook his head.

"I'm assuming that the trouble your city car was getting into last night didn't have much to do with your dear wife," St. Albans said. "Has she seen the new sidekick?"

"My better half recognizes my prerogative in selecting a legislative aide," said Honest Mike. "And as a member of a minority community herself, my sweet Corinne would certainly appreciate the effective result of an affirmative action placement. Marnette Sims comes to this office highly qualified from her membership in the Capitol Area Business Owners' League. Should the two ladies ever have the good fortune of a mutual encounter, I speculate they would find one another delightful."

St. Albans reached up to give his eye a wink.

"I have to admit that the action under that dress seems plenty affirmative close up," he said. "But as far as the two of them meeting, it'll probably be over your checkbook in divorce court."

Honest Mike adjusted his glasses.

"You, my friend, have been a tiresome scold since our days patrolling the streets," he said. "And the ensuing decades have rendered you no less tedious."

St. Albans agreed through a short laugh. "I only irritate you because I'm always right," the sergeant replied. "You might be the evil mastermind, but you're also the one who always needs everybody else's help."

St. Albans rubbed his eye again as he watched Marnette Sims glide along the printer in something like a pirouette as she retrieved a paper clip from an adjoining table.

"I suppose having a woman around who looks like she could curl your toes might seem worth the risk," he said.

The councilman responded by raising a hand to pat himself on his permed head, saying, "If you please, any such curling shall be reserved exclusively for my scalp."

- 7 -

A couple of hours before lunch, Dion Drury had his choice
of parking spaces in front of Lauda Aplikowski's Matterhorn. The restaurant was ten blocks up West Seventh
Street from the hockey arena at the edge of downtown.
Instead of stopping at the curb, he went around to the
parking lot in back. A few vehicles were scattered there,
all outshone by a vintage chromed Chrysler convertible
restored by Lauda, which, to hear him tell it, came at great
expense but was worth it to assuage the memory of his late
father's perplexing affinity for mundane Plymouths and
Dodges. A picket of steel bollards protected the rear of the
building from errant drivers and delivery trucks. Locked
with a cable to a bollard beside a pair of large dumpsters
was the bicycle that Dion had expected to find.

The back door to the Matterhorn opened into a dim
hallway in one of the several additions to the building in
the forty years since Lauda had taken over the original
business from his father and uncles. When Dion walked
in, the familiar woody dankness of the paneled walls
brought gauzy memories of wedding receptions for old
school buddies, and bleary happy-hour encounters with
neighborhood girls that he sometimes wished he had tak-
en the time to kiss, and other times wished he had not.
From a speaker in the ceiling drifted soft arpeggios of
strings behind a cool modulated voice.

Tony Bennett, maybe.

Past the restrooms, the hallway forked. One branch led to the kitchen, the other toward the lounge, where Dion found Evan Arcade behind the bar slicing limes. She looked up as he climbed onto a stool.

"Evangeline," he greeted.

"Dionysius," she responded airily. "You're up pretty early, little brother."

"Out pretty late," Dion answered. "I need to go home and get some sleep."

"But you're here."

She held out a fist. Dion made a fist of his own and gave hers a bump.

Evan aimed the knife again, and then her dark eyebrows narrowed. She reached for a towel on the backbar. Her bicep stretched the sleeve of her polo shirt, which she wore tucked into her cargo shorts. Her thighs suggested the pistons of a diesel locomotive. On her feet were a pair of expensive court shoes over athletic socks. Her black hair was held away from her face by a softball visor. A line of small diamond studs shimmered along the curve of her left ear.

"Something going on with Shiner?" she asked.

"She's the same as always," Dion told her. "But Brillo Ziemer isn't."

Evan tilted her head to one side, confused.

"He's dead," Dion said. "Sometime last night, sounds like."

Picking up another lime, Evan voiced a predictable assumption as she polished the skin with the towel, the knife glinting in the recessed lamps above the bar.

"Heart?"

"Hole."

"Huh?"

He told her the story as Tico Tocopilla had told it to him, of the tunnel and the phantom shaft outside the Kittsondale Center and the chandelier that Brillo had died liberating.

"Fell down a hole?" Evan said when he finished. "Or was pushed?"

Dion reached for a lime wedge, saying, "So I guess Tico wasn't lying when he told me about the old days between his dad and Brillo, and our dad too."

Evan shrugged. "I was young, so I don't remember much about what those guys were up to. I figured out more listening to Brillo when he'd hang around here half in the bag, telling me things I didn't really want to know."

"You never told them to me," Dion said.

"You didn't really want to know either."

"My only memory of the painting business is that we were supposed to stay out of our garage," Dion recalled.

"You were just a kid," Evan said. "I wouldn't expect you to know what was going on."

Dion turned atop the stool and looked toward the small stage in the corner of the room, where his mother Elysia and her younger brother Elias had once performed as Ellie and Easy, the Andrews twins, he on piano and accordion and she in the role of chanteuse, taking requests for show tunes and standards from elderly customers who could still remember life before color television. Now, there was only Easy's scuffed piano, the act having long gone solo following Ellie's disappearance in the wake of her husband's murder.

Evan turned the knife over in her hand, thinking out loud.

"It is kind of spooky, when you think about it," she said.

"What's that?"

"Brillo down a hole," she said. "And our father in a ditch. Like bookends."

Dion picked at the peel of the lime wedge. "Don't forget Ellie. I thought there might be something in the news about the two of them. A milestone year thing."

Evan's eyebrows went up then.

"I didn't tell you," she said. "There was a cop in here a few days ago, looking for Lauda about some old case, but Easy found Lauda in the office and the two of them ducked out. I figured they thought it was about our dad."

Dion thought that over, asking if the cop had been an older guy who looked sort of grim.

"No," said Evan. "A younger gal, who looked sort of cute."

"She didn't talk to you?"

"She wanted Lauda," Evan said. "And I don't think she knew who I was."

From the dining room came sounds of chairs scraping across carpet and rising voices, the staff preparing for the lunch rush. Dion tossed the hunk of lime into a trash bin behind the bar.

"So maybe we're not the only ones with the anniversary on our minds," he said.

Evan scraped the cut wedges into a small bowl.

"Oh, it's on somebody's mind," she said. "You're damn right it is. It might be twenty years, but you know there's at least one person out there who still knows something and is holding out. And eventually they'll get theirs."

"Like Brillo got his?" Dion wondered.

Evan gave him a thin smile.

"Like it says in the Bible," she replied. "You getteth what you deserveth."

"Is that what passes for bartender wisdom these days?" Dion teased.

"What can I say?" Evan set aside the knife to wipe up the lime juice that had pooled on the bar. "You get what you pay for. If you want Gandhi, you'll have to go to the library."

She opened a jar of beef jerky and offered him a stick, then took a big bite of one herself.

- 8 -

At about the same time, Arno St. Albans was leaving a neurology clinic just up the street from the state capitol building. He carried a prescription for a medication that the doctors hoped might relieve the nagging pressure behind his right ear. They theorized that a vital canal there, where a hole in his skull allowed a sheath of nerve fibers access to that side of his head, was under attack by a virus, with the resulting inflammation choking off the signals that held some of his facial muscles taut and made others move. Sort of like sleeping with an arm pinned beneath you, they said. You wake up at some point with a numb hand that doesn't want to function.

They told him of similar cases they'd seen before, although none of them were exactly the same. The condition had a name, and they could give him pamphlets to read that would tell him that there was nothing to be done but wait it out, hope for the best, and try not to worry. Most episodes cleared themselves in a couple of weeks. Except, of course, for the ones that didn't.

The sergeant did worry and wondered aloud what happened to the unfortunate patients in those cases. For them, he was told, came a menu of plastic surgeries to shore up flagging features and gold droplets that were implanted into unresponsive eyelids to add enough weight that a minimum muscular effort would force them closed.

Pretty much any procedure was on the table if it might help a person to not look and feel like a circus-sideshow freak for the rest of their life.

The medical specialists assured him he didn't need to worry about any of that because as a man reasonably fit for his age, he was going to be fine. Unless, of course, he wasn't, and anyway, he should imagine how much worse the experience was for teenage girls who suffered through the same mortifying symptoms. As a guy, he could surely take it.

As St. Albans stepped outside into the sunlight, it seemed to him a curious thing that with half his face no longer on speaking terms with the rest of his head, the affected muscles of his cheek all drooped. The eyelid, though, somehow went contrary, receding upward, the socket beneath unnaturally enlarged to expose more of his eyeball. The disquieting ghoulish stare it created, he supposed, was a preview of how he would eventually look as a corpse. Kind of the way people looked at him now.

He scratched at his hair, thinking of what the doctors had said about the numb, fuzzy sensation of a limb that had fallen asleep. His scalp had been feeling that way for several days.

In the car, the sergeant steered toward downtown, thinking about where to go for lunch. He stopped at a red light behind a line of cars waiting to cross University Avenue, where a commuter train on the light-rail line in the median passed leisurely from left to right alongside a truck painted in the insignia of Von Hanson's Auto Salvage and Parts.

St. Albans reached for the speed dial on his cell phone and waited through a series of voicemail options.

"Hey," he said, when prompted by the phone voice. "I think I just saw your city car on a flatbed truck heading west on University."

The traffic signal ahead of him turned green.

"So, I'm wondering," he told the recording, "where exactly does this Marnette Sims live?"

- 9 -

After lunch, Dion Drury was still awake in his bungalow near an old, decommissioned fire station on Randolph Avenue, a couple blocks up from West Seventh Street. Spread before him on his kitchen table were the papers from the city car. He paged slowly through short stacks of old reports, photographs, and news clippings, many of the sheets peppered with square sticky notes emblazoned with recent ink in an artistic script he could readily ascribe, in his mind, to a woman his sister might have judged a few days earlier as "sort of cute."

When he came across printouts of email strings only a few weeks old, the address lines gave him a pretty good idea of the person who had been working the file, but he didn't recognize the name, or even the nature of the name. So then, looking at the penmanship on the sticky notes again, he was embarrassed to realize that his imagination may have been aroused by the jottings of a man. He turned the pages face down on the table.

Across the room, a shadow clouded the window of the back door, and then the door opened with a mild huff of displaced air. Shiner O'Shea came in and closed the door behind her. When she turned around, she reached both hands into the front pockets of her coat.

"I got us lemon bars," she said.

She pulled them out, wrapped in paper napkins, one in each fist.

Dion cleared a spot on the table for them.

"How did work go today?" he asked. "Kids throwing fish sticks around the lunchroom?"

"They were loud." Shiner unzipped her coat. Her white smock beneath it showed multicolored fingerings of food stains. She sat down on a chair. Dion heard a rustle beneath the table as she kicked off her sneakers.

"You're not asleep," she said.

"Pretty soon," he told her. "I've been looking at stuff."

Dion tapped a fingernail on the email sheets, saying, "What kind of a name is Kady, do you suppose?" He spelled it for her.

"I suppose it's kind of a nice name," she said.

He felt a sleepy smile cross his face.

Shiner wondered what all the papers were about.

"I guess it's sort of my family history," Dion said. "At least according to the Saint Paul police. All of this is their take on the case of Cullen Arcade."

She reached for a pile of photos. Dion moved to stop her, but she grabbed the top two images, one a scaled laboratory exhibit of a spent bullet recovered from the body, and the other a print of the body at the crime scene, clothed and prone, face down in some snow and dead grasses, a police officer in a topcoat standing over it.

"Is that him?" Shiner said, pointing at the dead man.

"Yes," said Dion quietly. "My dad."

He reached into the stack then and pulled out an old promotional notice for a floor show at the Matterhorn, an autographed photo of Ellie Andrews filling the top half of the sheet. He slid it across the table to Shiner.

"My mom," he said. "Remember?"

Shiner nodded as she set the photos aside to unwrap a lemon bar.

"Your dad died," she said. "But not me."

"That's right," Dion said. "You didn't. You were a lucky girl."

"My mom says I had an angel."

"Your mom is pretty smart," Dion said, scooping up the photos.

"She says your dad was kind of bad."

Dion took a slow breath and swallowed it.

Shiner aimed a finger toward the policeman in the picture. "Who's that?"

Dion took the print and held it up to the ceiling light to better see the face. "Him? That would be the walrus."

She seemed to think that over for a few seconds while she licked at the edge of the lemon bar.

"I'm a cowgirl," she said.

"You are," Dion agreed. "The only one I know."

"Ya," she said, standing to leave, the lemon bar shedding crumbs onto the table.

Dion made her sit down again, reminding her that food was for the kitchen, not for her room.

- 10 -

Kady L'Orient presented her police identification to a stunning woman in a kente cloth dress at the city council office of Honest Mike Walerius. She was invited to wait for him in the reception area, although the woman could not say if or when he might return. He had apparently received a phone call around lunchtime and left without telling her where he was going.

"He does that," the woman said, before excusing herself to deliver some printouts to a fellow legislative aide down the hall, leaving Kady standing there alone.

Seeing that the door to the inner office was open, Kady went in and did a quick survey of Honest Mike's desk, not really expecting to find the Cullen Arcade cold case materials, but not entirely sure that she would not, since the councilman figured prominently in the file contents, and she had come to his office in the hope he could answer some questions. As she was lifting a folder to look beneath it, a voice behind her gave her a jolt.

"Well, you're not at all what I expected."

Kady turned to see another stunning woman in the doorway, this one more petite than the first. She wore creased black slacks beneath a silver blazer that matched her eye shadow. She stood regally on three-inch heels the same color as her periwinkle blouse, her dark hair swept into a crisp bouffant with teased bangs.

"Don't look so surprised, kiddo," the woman said. "My husband doesn't have a monopoly on what he would call clandestine sources. I've got a few friends of my own."

"Excuse me?" Kady asked.

The woman held up a hand before Kady could say more.

"Look, I know this is awkward," the woman said, "so I'll keep it short. Whatever my husband may have told you about his relationship with me, or with you, keep in mind that he's a guy who tends to look out for himself. He doesn't really care about anybody else, you included."

"Whoa," Kady began, but the woman straightened with a serious breath and talked over her.

"I care about you some, though," the woman said. "Because anybody who dallies with my partner might be a threat to my business, and that business matters to me way more than anything else does, including him."

"You are way wrong," Kady told her, but the hand went up again.

"No, you are," the woman said. "Last night was his car. Next time maybe it's your car, or maybe your front door. Or your cute little ass in your distressed jeans."

With that the woman turned and walked purposefully away through the outer office. The door to the hallway clicked quietly shut behind her.

Kady reset the folder on the desk, her heartbeats high in her throat. She got out of there quickly, not so much interested in waiting around anymore, wondering in the elevator what the deranged lady had been talking about, and thinking that for somebody crazy, the woman for sure knew how to put herself together with an enviable sense of style.

- 11 -

On a side street just off University Avenue near a light rail station, Arno St. Albans and Honest Mike Walerius stood in the narrow shadow of a budding boulevard tree, discussing the appearance of the councilman's official city vehicle, which rested against the curb along a row of renovated townhouses.

"The tow report said that the rear window had been shot out," the sergeant said. "Looks like somebody fixed it."

He searched along the pavement for evidence of broken glass. "Is this close to where you parked it last night?"

Honest Mike nodded, seeming impressed. "Very nearly. The young demon you encountered at the impound lot is evidently gifted with the expansive vision of a seasoned mind. The inspiration to return the machine to the scene of the crime in this way verges on the poetic."

St. Albans squinted and said, "If you say so, but right now, I'm more interested in an inspiration that verges on the lunch special at your wife's place."

The sun flashed brightly in the blue lenses of the councilman's eyeglasses as he turned and smiled.

"I sometimes forget that my enlightened musings are completely wasted upon you," Honest Mike said, and then remembered something. "You say the officer on the scene last evening could not account for the folders missing from the vehicle?"

"She said she didn't notice anything, or it would have been on the report," said St. Albans. "It's more likely that she didn't look too hard or care that much about a bunch of papers. I can tell you that she wasn't tickled with me waking her up when I called her at home this morning."

The electronic whistle of a light rail engine revving itself to speed rang through the air as the train departed the station. Fainter, in the far distance toward downtown, an emergency vehicle siren wailed on the freeway.

"What's in these papers you had?" the sergeant wondered. "Something that somebody could use against you?"

"Quite the opposite," Honest Mike said. "Which is why their loss is at once vexing and worrisome. The folders comprise a dormant case file that one of our junior investigators decided to resurrect and reexamine, a typical endeavor of extra credit for aspiring personalities in the ranks. Her initial inquiries into the reopened review rattled a particular cage to the extent that I was enjoined to intervene, and therein rose an opportunity."

"Opportunity?"

Honest Mike reached into his pocket for his car-key fob as he moved to the driver's door. "In my experience," he said, "there is no person riper for exploitation than a hapless soul harboring ancient secrets."

He allowed himself a shallow sigh at the thought.

"And now I am unsure as to whether my potential target has made a move to neutralize my advantage, or if someone else is maneuvering to seize the moment for themselves. I find this development most unexpected and distressing."

"Count your blessings," St. Albans suggested. "At least you got your car back on the quiet."

"That is no minor triumph," Honest Mike agreed. "I must reaffirm, as always, that I truly appreciate your efforts on my behalf."

The sergeant stepped toward the car and fingered a bullet hole in the trunk lid.

"So, just which cold case are we talking about?" he asked.

"Cullen Arcade."

St. Albans tapped his tongue against the back of his teeth for the long seconds it took his memory to unravel twenty years, and then the name matched a vision in his mind of a railroad ditch just within the city limits, at the farthest edge of the West Side where Cesar Chavez Street climbed a hill that overlooked the barge channel and the wider river. He felt the left corner of his mouth curl itself taut as he recalled the circumstances out loud.

"The guy we left in the snow?"

- 12 -

Tico Tocopilla lived in a house not far from where he grew up, behind the defunct brewery that fronted several blocks along West Seventh Street halfway between downtown and the hills of Highland Park. Dion Drury stood in the backyard as Tico unlocked the service door to the detached garage at the corner of the lot, the sky above them fading toward twilight. Hefty Von Hanson shuffled along the sidewalk from the house and tapped Dion on the bicep.

"Here," Hefty said, reaching out with something in his hand.

Dion turned, and Hefty dropped a metallic nugget into his palm.

"The girl who did the glass replacement on the city car this morning found it in the back seat, you know?" Hefty told him. "It's a bullet."

Dion fingered it for a second before stashing it in his shirt pocket. Tico got the door open, and they followed him inside.

When the lights went on, the space revealed a jungle of wood, stone, and metal that covered the entire floor and was stacked to the height of the lone window. Loose doors, windows of stained glass, disassembled fireplace mantels, and finished trim boards were mixed among piles of ceramic tile. Old plumbing and lighting fixtures spewed tangled pipes and wiring.

"Jeez," Dion said.

"Ditto, you know?" Hefty agreed as he nudged his boot against a small painted iron radiator at the edge of the cluster. "So, if this stuff was Brillo's, and he's dead, whose is it now?"

"Some of it probably still belongs to people he stole it from," Dion said. "But I wouldn't want to have to figure all that out."

"No shit," Tico agreed.

Dion spied on the floor an old dusty canvas satchel with worn wooden handles. The sight of it put a surprised space in his breathing.

"That was my dad's, I think," he said.

Hefty kicked it over to him. Dion looked at Tico.

"Now it's yours," Tico said.

Dion bent and looked inside at a collection of screwdrivers, tinsnips, bolt cutters, hacksaws, pry bars, and hammers of varying sizes. Burglary tools. A limp paper booklet outlining instructions for picking locks was affixed by a rubber band to a small pouch of clear plastic that held several thin metallic blades with multicolored handles of Bakelite.

Tico peered over Dion's shoulder into the bag, then at the array of materials that overwhelmed the garage, and blew a soft, lamenting whistle.

"What the hell am I supposed to do, D-man?" he groaned.

Hefty lifted an object from a cardboard box in front of them, the big kid cradling a large brass door hinge and whistling in admiration of the weight.

Dion straightened up then. When he did, he felt the

spent bullet in his shirt pocket brush against his chest. Spreading two fingers to touch it, he looked down at the satchel again and nodded slowly.

"I know what I'd do," he said.

He picked up the bag.

- 13 -

On the overnight shift, the impound lot settled into a surreal calm. The ceiling fixture in the kitchen was the only light Dion left on. He wanted the service-counter area dim so he could better view the illuminated rows of vehicles outside. Sporadic dispatches from the police radio on the desk droned languidly like the recount of a minor Central American election.

Dion processed towing reports from the few arrivals the previous hour, then slouched on his chair, his heels resting on the desk. It was just after midnight. He locked his fingers over his chest, looking out the windows to the south, where a freight train trundled slowly along a track just beyond the perimeter fence. Up a steep embankment, past the railroad grade, car headlights enlivened Cesar Chavez Street, the blended sounds of lazy motion faint in the outdoor monitors.

He sat there for a long time, letting the wall clock echo seconds to his thoughts, and then took two sheets from the Cullen Arcade cold-case folders on his desk and went to the copy machine in the kitchen. He fed it the ballistics report and the photo of the bullet that had killed his father, their more recent sticky notes still attached. Then he slid the copies into an interoffice message envelope and added the slug from his shirt pocket, along with a sticky note of his own. He inked a destination onto the grid of address lines on the front of the envelope and slotted the envelope into the middle of a stack of outbound mail on the kitchen counter.

After midnight, Hefty Von Hanson, dusty and yawning, stopped by in his flatbed to drop off what remained of a sack of onion rings from the Lebanese cantina on Cesar Chavez Street near the South Robert Street viaduct.

Another tow arrived an hour later from an accident. The owner of the disabled vehicle followed close behind in a taxi and waited patiently at the counter for Dion to sign her in so she could collect some personal items from the car. Her forehead was bandaged and swollen, her eyes wide and red with the unenviable clouded stare of someone slowly rousing from shock to comprehend that their day had just turned to shit.

After that, Dion passed a few quiet hours breaking into various rooms, including the furnace room and the office and desk of the day-shift supervisor. He also sprung open the locks on the fingerprinting-and-processing supply cabinets in the big garage, and the towel dispenser in the bathroom, for more practice.

He was straightening up his desk at sunrise when another tow truck pulled up to the gate. He let it in and went down the stairs to grab the report from the driver. Dion slapped a numbered identification tag onto the windshield of the car trailing behind, realizing that he had seen this car before. Leaning through the open driver's side window, he smelled whiskey. Then he looked at the report.

"Huh," he said out loud.

While the tow truck driver pulled away to deposit the car in a vacant space, Dion went inside to use the office telephone.

- 14 -

The next morning, Arno St. Albans stopped his car at the end of the block where Brillo Ziemer had been hoisted from the storm sewer tunnel the previous day. The city maintenance crew had apparently returned, their winch truck crowding the center of the street beside a pile of cement blocks. The sergeant spotted a familiar municipal pickup truck pulled just off the roadway, an elbow jutting from the open window. He drove up slowly and rolled down his own window as he braked alongside it. Tico Tocopilla jerked against the steering wheel of the pickup when the sergeant called out to him.

"Better not let the neighbors catch you sleeping on city time," St. Albans said.

Tico blinked at him twice. "I was meditating, Sergeant," Tico said. "That's my story and I'll stick to it."

"Meditating?"

"You know," Tico said. "Like, stress relief."

St. Albans looked over toward the river parkway, across the open field along the street, where a pair of squirrels darted back and forth over the grass.

"How much stress can you have before breakfast?" he wondered.

"You'd be surprised," Tico told him.

The sergeant nodded in the direction of Brillo Ziemer's house. "So, tell me about the dead painter and his stolen chandelier."

"Brillo?" Tico asked, rubbing a palm over his forehead. "He was just a guy from the neighborhood, doing what some guys from the neighborhood do when they think they won't get caught. An old West Seventh Street lifer. Everybody knew him."

"Your friend from the impound lot included?"

"The D-man is one of us, yeah," Tico said.

"Which is why you were in such a hurry to get down there and give him the news?" St. Albans said.

"What news?" Tico said. "And who says I was in a hurry?"

Along the horizon above the trees, a silvery low airliner banked into its landing approach to the big airport across the river from Highland Park. St. Albans watched the early sunlight glint upon the wings.

"Well, you sure seemed in a hurry to leave," he said. "Once you saw me, anyway. You left without even telling him about the dead guy."

Tico drew in a long breath through his nose. He let it escape in a low thoughtful burst, seeming to slowly fuel an idea that lifted the pockets of skin beneath his eyes.

"See, here's the deal on that," he said, breaking into a satisfied grin. "I figured you already told him, so I didn't need to."

St. Albans felt a slow heat creeping over his ears as the foreman's smirk held steady and needling.

"Welcome to West Seventh Street," Tico said.

St. Albans released his brake and rolled slowly along the final hundred feet that brought him to Brillo Ziemer's van in the driveway of the house. He got out of his car, reached into his pocket for the ring of keys found on the body, and noticed through the garage window a light burning inside.

He used one of the keys to unlock the van. He found the garage door opener control inside and pushed the button. As the wide garage door rose, St. Albans took a step backward. Measured footsteps scuffled behind him, coming closer.

"Holy shit, Sergeant," Tico said. "I didn't know Brillo was such a pack rat."

St. Albans stood silently, his head cocked to one side as he regarded the jumbled piles of building fixtures and materials that covered the garage floor.

"Yesterday, when I first took the keys off your dead pal, I took a quick look around the place," St. Albans finally said, pointing at the garage. "And none of this stuff was here."

"For real?" Tico moved past him.

At the nearest edge of the stacks rested a box of framed maps and dusty books bound in leather. Tico picked up a volume and spread open the cover, the river breezes riffling the foxed pages.

"I'd say that sounds like a plot twist," he said.

St. Albans thought of something Honest Mike Walerius had said upon the recovery of his city vehicle.

"It sounds," St. Albans corrected, his ears pulsing hotter, "poetic."

- 15 -

Dion Drury got to the Saint Paul Public Safety building not long after the end of his shift. Evan Arcade was already there, waiting in the lobby. She rose from her chair and came over to him when he pushed his way through the glass front doors.

"The desk cop says they'll be letting him out in a few minutes," she said.

Dion opened his jacket. Evan stuffed her fists into the pockets of her hooded sweatshirt. Her gaze was dark beneath the brim of her baseball cap, her hair tucked behind her ears.

"He called you?" Dion asked.

"Right after your call woke me up," she told him. "I thought about calling Lauda, but Easy said not to bother."

"How'd he sound?"

"Kind of slurry."

Dion nodded. "Before I talked to you, I got hold of a clerk I know down here," he said. "The tow report said there was an arrest, and the incident report from the squad said that Easy caused some trouble."

Evan tapped the heel of her hiking shoe against the floor. "He was still drinking at the bar when I went home," she said. "After you came down to tell me about Brillo, I told Lauda what you told me, and Easy was there. They both acted kind of weird about it, but Easy seemed like it bothered him more. He was kind of off all night. I didn't think they even knew each other that well, Brillo and Easy."

Dion pursed his lips. "What I don't get is where Easy was going," he said. "Sounds like the cops followed him out of downtown onto the Wabasha Street Bridge, so it wasn't like he was headed home. He was on his way to the West Side in the middle of the night."

A door opened near the reception desk, and Easy Andrews shambled out, a free man for the moment, slight and rumpled in a light herringbone sport coat and dark dress slacks. He pushed against his sweep of graying hair with one scratched and scabbed hand, rings on his fingers reflecting the ceiling lights, his lower left jaw sporting a bulge that hurt just to look at.

"So, Uncle Elias," Dion asked him. "How many were there?"

Easy huffed out a dismissive grunt. "Just the one, at first," he said. "Big guy. His backups were the cheering section. Not a goddamn sense of humor in the bunch." He winced as he straightened the collar of his shirt. "Dickheads tried to say I was speeding."

"Looks like maybe you didn't agree," Dion said.

Easy chuckled sourly, gingerly touching the welt on his jaw.

"You think?" he said. "How was I to know the sons of bitches couldn't take a joke."

Evan asked what he had done that was supposed to be funny, and Easy seemed to brighten at the memory, smiling as though he did not, at that moment, look and smell like an old car floormat. He didn't tell her, though. Instead, he shook his head, a little more ruefully.

"It was right about then that the band broke into a rumba," he recalled.

Evan reached out, tugging on his jacket sleeve as she nodded toward the exit.

"Good idea," Easy said. "We need to get working on my revenge."

"What you need to get is a lawyer," Dion said as they stepped outside. "You're facing some charges."

Easy blinked into the daylight. "Dionysius, you are steady on the beat as always, but first things first. Doctor, then lawyer. But not doctor just yet. Bartender, then doctor."

He hooked his elbow toward Evan, as though expecting her to take his arm, like a couple in an old movie. "Evangeline," he said. "May I have this dance?"

She shook her head wearily. "I'll get the car," she said.

Before his sister turned to walk away, Dion said he still wanted to know why things had gotten so out of hand between Easy and the police at the scene.

"The cops asked me if I knew how fast I was going," Easy answered, reaching for his jaw as his rasping laugh corkscrewed quickly into a groan. "I told them I couldn't see the speedometer from where I was sitting."

- 16 -

The middle of the morning found Kady typing on her computer in her cubicle at the public safety building, so she did not immediately react when a clerk dropped an interoffice mail envelope onto her desk. When she turned and saw that there was no sender address, her breathing tightened. Fingering the small bulge in a lower corner of the envelope, she gauged by its stiffness and size that she was likely about to encounter another anonymous nipple clamp, and the prospect brought her teeth together in a hard grind.

When she opened the envelope and spilled out the contents, though, what rattled onto her computer keyboard was a misshapen spent bullet, followed by two sheets of paper that she recognized as photocopies of original documents from the Cullen Arcade file, the first a ballistics laboratory report and the second a photograph of the bullet that had killed him, her own sticky notes showing on each of them.

She picked up the bullet and studied it for a minute, then leaned back on her chair and hummed out a slow exhale, glancing at her wristwatch as her computer pinged a chime for a meeting reminder. Then she gathered the two pages.

Affixed to the top of the photograph was a fresh sticky note, with two lines of small digits scrawled tightly over it in dark ink, the hand unfamiliar.

A telephone number and a time.

- 17 -

After leaving his sister and uncle, Dion made another stop downtown before heading home. He parked beside the city hall and county courthouse building and went in. He made his way to the fourth floor where the city council offices were for the Tenth Ward. There was no one at the reception desk, but a woman emerged from a nearby cubicle that displayed the nameplate of Marnette Sims, legislative aide to the representative.

"How may I help you?" she greeted in a voice that shimmered like the animal-print dress wrapped over her torso.

Dion held out a mailing envelope with the return address of Von Hanson's Auto Salvage and Parts stamped on it.

"For your boss," Dion said.

Marnette took the envelope and pushed open the unsealed flap, peering inside. From high up on the wall behind her, a vent blowing recirculated air rattled like Morse code in a hailstorm.

"There's nothing in here," she said, confused.

"The envelope's an invoice," Dion explained. "The first number written on the inside of the flap is what he owes. The second one is the phone number to call once you have the cash."

"Cash?" said Marnette.

"He'll want to pay cash," Dion replied. "The kid you call will be down to pick it up when it's ready."

She studied the numbers. "If the councilman needs to pay with cash, he'll want a receipt," she said.

Dion shook his head and turned sideways to leave. "No," he said. "He won't."

Marnette curled her upper lip in a skeptical frown.

"It's cleaner this way," Dion told her. "No paper trail to worry about later, if people get curious."

She turned the envelope over a few times, still frowning. Dion worried that she might make him take it back, but she finally pressed it to her chest with both hands, her chin angled in a way that suggested to him her slow realization that maybe not all the expected duties of a gatekeeper to a guy like Honest Mike Walerius were noted in a civil service job description.

"All right," she agreed. "I'm new as his aide, so we'll try it your way. If I get yelled at, though, I'm going to be pissed. Who do I say was here?"

"Just tell him an egg man stopped by," Dion said.

"An egg man?"

He was a little surprised that she sounded surprised, so he didn't answer.

"And that will make sense to him?" she said.

Dion held up his right palm in a slow goodbye wave, saying, "More than it makes to me."

At the door, he was stopped by a muffled whistle rising behind him. He looked over his shoulder to see Marnette nodding appreciatively in his direction.

"Nice haircut," she said, and gave him a thumbs-up.

- 18 -

Arno St. Albans felt like Brillo Ziemer's property told a depressing story. The home of the dead painting contractor needed paint itself. The white exterior shakes cracked and flaked, and the green shutters were soft with rot. Scattered over the scrubby yard were bits of landscape edging and empty decorative planters, reminders of plans apparently cut short, or more likely, given the overall condition of the place, never vigorously pursued. Along the twisted fence that abutted the Kittsondale Center property, haphazard stacks of treated timbers thawed in the morning sun. A wheelbarrow with a deflated tire rested on its side nearby, a low mound of dark, icy snow enduring stubbornly in its shade. In a far rear corner of the yard, a collapsing low flagstone wall encircled a wildly overgrown lilac bush in spring bud.

A clatter of voices arose from the open garage, where a trio of investigators from downtown tried to match the objects gathered there with printed lists from previously reported burglaries. St. Albans went back inside the house.

As he wandered among the dead man's things, the dim stillness of the rooms seemed to him a time stamp of a life peopled by ghosts. Most walls were decorated with faded wallpaper, and heavy curtains draped filmy windows. The kitchen cabinets and appliances, the table and chairs, and pretty much all the furniture seemed to be forty years out of date. In the lone bathroom stood a pitted clawfoot bathtub, the toilet beside it a mismatch of a porcelain bowl and a slightly less antiquated tank.

He found one bedroom upstairs arranged as though for a child, with a bare twin mattress and small bureau. The largest bedroom across the hallway was populated with a vintage tiger maple-wood headboard and footboard, nightstands on either side, and a large dresser near the door. Beside the window sat a feminine vanity with a mirror. The sheets and blankets on the bed were askew, framed in hazy sunlight from the window, and the sergeant envisioned, then, a bleak trajectory of the dead man's life from young through done. He'd never left the childhood home and merely supplanted his parents within it, an uninspired adulthood of deterioration in dreary cadence with his musty family possessions.

St. Albans rummaged through the closet. The wall behind the hanging clothes was patched with a rough coating of drywall filler, like a repair had been made following some roof or plumbing leak. On a shelf above, he found photo albums bound in old vinyl. Tucked behind them was an aged metal box with a lock. The box was heavy, the albums not much lighter. He struggled to get all of them onto the bed. He mucked through the dresser, and in the top drawer of the vanity, he found a few tarnished brass keys in a cubby of brooches that also held several chipped tie clips and cufflinks.

The first key he tried opened the box, where the sergeant found the title registration to Brillo Ziemer's van, some savings passbooks from banks that no longer exist-

ed, and a fair number of old postmarked business envelopes stuffed with papers.

"Okay, Mr. Ziemer," he said aloud. "Let's see if we can
figure out who might be missing you about now."

He sat down on the mattress, pulling a few items from
the box to review, and then, without really thinking about
it, he flipped open a photo album.

- 19 -

Just before dinnertime, Dion Drury awoke to slow breaths crossing his forehead. He opened his eyes to see Shiner O'Shea standing at the side of his bed, her hands in the front pockets of her jeans, her chin tucked low in the collar of her hooded sweatshirt. Fading sunlight at the edges of the drawn window shades etched soft lines on loose blond hairs that straggled over her cheek. She smiled at him as he shifted onto his side beneath the blankets.

"What's up?" he asked.

When she responded by clucking like a chicken, he smiled back.

"No problem," he told her, stretching out a long yawn as he nodded toward his open bedroom door. "Give me some space while I hit the shower, and we'll head out in an hour or so."

Ninety minutes later, passing through the rear entrance of the Matterhorn as he held the door for her, Shiner told him that he smelled clean.

"I am clean," he said.

They took seats on two barstools in the lounge. Evan Arcade came down from the other end of the bar and gave them each a fist bump. Shiner giggled and bumped fists with Dion two more times.

Evan poured a diet soda for Shiner, saying, "Chicken wing night?"

"She woke me up for it," Dion said. "I could've slept for a couple more hours."

Evan leaned closer to Shiner, gesturing toward Dion with her eyes as Shiner giggled again. "He's just a peach, isn't he, my little brother?" Evan said to her.

Shiner clucked.

A fair amount of noise was coming from the adjacent dining room, a healthy crowd for that time of evening. The lounge itself was quiet, many of the booths and tables empty. The spotlight over the piano onstage shone white.

"How's Easy doing?" Dion wondered.

Evan fingered their food order onto a touchscreen, looking over her shoulder toward a clock on the backbar.

"He made it here," she said. "He comes on for his first set in a few minutes."

"Did you get his car out of jail?"

"It's at his place," Evan answered. "I told him if the cops catch him driving without a license, he'll be sorry, but you know him."

Dion suddenly sensed someone standing behind him, a hand falling purposefully upon his shoulder. He turned to face Lauda Aplikowski, the old man's waxy face the color of a peeled potato, his body stretching tight an unflattering nylon track suit that smelled of cigar smoke.

"The prodigal nephew," Lauda greeted, then held up a thumb toward Evan.

"Charged water, when you get a chance," he told her. "Tall glass."

Dion felt the fingers tighten over his collarbone.

"It's damn criminal what your cops did to your uncle," Lauda said to him. "He's going to make them pay, by God."

"They're not my cops," said Dion. "I just work for them."

The grip loosened, and the old man patted him twice.

"Good man," Lauda said. "You'll stand up, then, when the lawyers get around to taking depositions?"

Dion nodded. "I'll stand up."

Lauda retreated then and headed for the dining room with his glass of water. At the same time, a soft flurry of triplet notes wafted from the stage piano. Easy Andrews had slipped past without Dion seeing him and was warming up.

The spotlight cast a silhouette of Easy over the back wall of the stage, his head bowed over the piano. Dion watched the shadowy rise and fall of knuckles on his uncle's expansive hands that could stretch across a rolling tenth chord like a bat's wings.

Then Dion saw Easy's swollen ear, the screaming red shade of the old man's right eyeball, and a heavy scab on his puffy lip. After a few seconds, Dion gradually turned his gaze toward his sister, who lowered her eyes as she stabbed a paring knife into a lemon, halving it without looking up, but seeming to sense his thoughts.

"Like the boss said," Evan told him. "The cops are going to pay."

Easy struck the opening notes to his theme song. Dion looked his way again and then back at Evan.

"The guy looks like January dog shit in a March thaw," he said. "How many times did you hit him?"

"The cops broke his jaw," Evan said. "The doctor had to wire it shut. The kitchen staff ran his dinner through a blender so he could suck it through a straw."

"Yeah, but?"

Evan shrugged. "It took a while to get the feel of how much force worked best," she said. "And I had to stay off his chin, which was tough. When the blood vessel in his eye burst, though, that seemed like enough."

She lazily scratched a fingernail over the diamond studs in her left ear.

"Actually, the red eye was kind of a bonus," she decided. "It showed up really strong in the attorney's pictures."

"So, how many times?" Dion asked again.

"I wasn't counting," Evan said. "Maybe five or six. Not enough to be that much fun."

"Lucky for him."

"He'll live," Evan said.

She picked up a lemon half and tapped it playfully against Shiner's nose. Onstage, Easy skittered the low keys into a slow progression of jazz chords. Evan drew in a long breath that sounded pleased.

"You're smiling," Dion noticed.

"Am I?" she asked.

Dion glanced over at the clock on the backbar, climbed down from his stool, and told the others that he would be back shortly and to save some food for him.

- 20 -

There was a lively small marquee over the front door of the Amor Abrasadora on Cesar Chavez Street. Argon lights splashed a yellowish sheen on the pitted concrete walls of the viaduct on the other side of the intersection, which cut a pass up and through the West Side bluffs. The presence of a Lebanese cantina in the heart of a neighborhood where Spanish was a common language had always slightly mystified Arno St. Albans.

He lingered on the sidewalk and watched traffic for a few minutes after parking his car, and then went inside, entering a large room of ranch tables and hanging wagon-wheel lights. There was a bar along part of one wall and booths lining another. A swinging door beside the bar opened to the kitchen. Painted murals on the walls alternated between Mayan ruins and minarets. St. Albans took a chair alone in the back, near a pool table. Just beyond was a hallway that led to the rear entrance and restrooms.

He looked up from the menu at his table to see Corinne Nasseff coming down the hall from her office. When she saw him, she walked over, her three-inch heels tapping on the floor tiles.

"Look what the cat dragged in," she said, resting one palm on the back of a chair across from him. "If the walrus sent you, I don't want to hear about it."

"I'm just hungry," the sergeant said.

With her other hand, she adjusted the collar of her white tuxedo shirt, then the headband that held her hair back tautly from her temples. He could feel her eyes on him and hear her voice soften.

"Face still the same?"

"No change," he confirmed. "And I'm worried."

"You told Honest Mike there are things they can do?"

"Things they say they can do," he answered. "But who knows."

She came around the table and patted his shoulder a couple of times before suddenly digging her nails in.

"I'm mad at you," she said. "You could've told me about his new office toy."

St. Albans stared at the menu like she was not there. "Not my fight," he said. "And I didn't even see her until yesterday."

"I saw her yesterday too," Corinne said. "I went up there to have a look for myself, told her that she'd better watch her back. I think I got my message across."

St. Albans pulled out his bottle of eyedrops and slowly unscrewed the cap. "I'll bet you did," he said. "How'd she take it?"

Corinne paused, seeming to search for the appropriate description. "Stunned," she decided.

"Well, if there's one thing that can't be denied about you, it's that you're stunning," the sergeant said.

Now Corinne rubbed his shoulder, saying he was sweet, but that he might be more help in controlling her husband.

St. Albans held the bottle to his right eye. "Not my job," he said. "I can't stop him from being attracted to exotic women of color. Where would you be if I could?"

Corinne stopped rubbing.

"This chick wasn't dark," she told him slowly, thinking back. "Dark hair, and kind of elfin, but she was a mostly white girl."

St. Albans used a knuckle to wink his eye. "Huh?"

"She was lighter than me," Corinne repeated. "Cute, though."

"Oh," he said after a second, trying not to sound confused. "Right."

She slowly dragged a fingernail across the back of his neck, causing the hairs in his ears to stand up.

"Maybe I shouldn't worry so much about what he's up to and just find a toy of my own," she said. "What are you doing after you've had your dinner?"

St. Albans put the eyedrops into his pocket.

"No plans at the moment," he said. "But I've got to warn you, I probably wouldn't kiss very well."

He felt a subtle tug beneath the collar of his shirt, a pinch between her finger and thumb that sent a static pulse from her hand that crackled down to the pores on his ankles.

"Silly man," Corinne said as she leaned closer, a whispered breath tickling his frozen eye. "I probably wouldn't kiss at all."

- 21 -

Dion Drury was just stepping out the rear door of the Matterhorn when his cell phone rang. He answered, but he did not say hello. Instead, he said that the caller was right on time.

There was no response for a few seconds, long enough to give him a nervous idea.

"Am I being recorded?" he asked.

Then he heard a soft breath, and a quizzical, feminine "hmm" that widened his eyebrows.

"I didn't think of that," the voice said. "Am I?"

"No," Dion answered, glad that Kady was apparently a female name. "I didn't think of it either, until just now. And it wouldn't do anything for me, anyway."

A car passed slowly through the parking lot, tires crunching on the pavement. The woman noticed. "You're outside."

"I am," Dion said. "Behind Aplikowski's place."

The connection went silent. Dion thought back to what Evan had told him about a female police investigator looking to question Lauda a few days earlier.

"I'm following your lead," he said.

He heard the breath again. "Are you a cop?"

"No," Dion said. "But I'm trying to think like one."

"One I know?"

Dion told her that he couldn't say, since he didn't know

who she knew. Then, saying it, he realized that for all he knew she may have left the Cullen Arcade materials in the city car herself. She may have been another minion of Honest Mike Walerius, or, judging by the way her voice was slowly resonating in his ear, she may have been more than that to the councilman. He thought of something.

"Where did you last see the file?" he asked.

"On my desk," she said a little more tersely. "Before you took it."

"I did take it," Dion admitted. "But not off your desk. Someone else did that."

"An accomplice?"

"I work alone," Dion said. "But I can tell you that you and I aren't the only players in this game."

The phone went quiet for a moment.

"So, I started something," she said.

"Somebody sure did," Dion said.

"And what's it to you?"

Another car trundled past, looking for a parking space. Dion followed with his eyes.

"Personal," he said. "You?"

"Just a dormant case I could burn some hours on. But it feels a little personal to me now, after having my desk raided."

He could hear a rustle of papers over the phone.

"By the way," she went on. "The discharged bullet you sent me has nothing to do with the Arcade case. The caliber is all wrong. I could tell just by looking at it."

"I didn't really think it did," Dion said.

"So why send it?"

Dion looked up into the night sky over the building,

lazy traffic passing on West Seventh Street beneath the streetlights and stars, his breaths falling into time with hers.

"Maybe because you have nice handwriting," he said.

This time the phone went quiet with an energy he could hear, and then the woman spoke again.

"You still at the Matterhorn? I could be there in half an hour."

"I could be gone in half an hour," Dion told her.

"But what does that solve?" she argued.

It was his turn to breathe through a pause. He stabbed at the cold asphalt with the toe of his shoe.

"I wish I knew," he told her.

He could hear her again, in the silence over the phone, thinking to herself.

"You got a name?" she asked him finally.

"I do," Dion said. "But I like yours better."

It took half a minute for her to react.

"I'm on my way."

Dion nodded. "So am I," he said.

Then he hung up and went back inside. At the bar, he got back onto the stool beside Shiner and asked Evan for a notepad and a pen.

"If that cop who was here the other day comes in before I leave, give me a nod," he said, inking a message onto the sheet before folding it and adding a name to the outside. He handed it to his sister while a server from the kitchen slid a basket of hot chicken wings onto the bar between them.

"Kady," Evan read aloud before she set the note aside. "Nice ring to it. How did you figure out her name?"

"I stole it," Dion said.

Evan snickered and fished her hand into the basket, pulling out a wing.

"What if she shows up after you're gone?" she asked.

"Either way, pass the note to her but don't let her know who I am," Dion said.

"You're trying to stay a step ahead of her?" Evan asked. "Or just want to scope her out on the sly?"

Dion felt his forehead redden. "Maybe a little of both," he said. "So far, I'm not quite sure what I'm doing."

Shiner picked up a wing and gave its tip a tentative stab with her tongue.

"Nice ring," she said.

Evan looked at her and then at Dion.

"You sound pretty sure that this cop chick is coming," Evan said to Dion.

"She'll be here," he answered. "She's curious."

Up on the stage, Easy Andrews strung out the melody of a slow waltz on his piano. Shiner rocked on her stool from side to side in time with the music, staying on the beat as she chewed.

- 22 -

Kady L'Orient took a quick look around the dining room of the Matterhorn. Not finding a promising contender for the guy she had just spoken with on the phone, she turned her attention to the lounge. An older man there was playing piano on the stage. Another older man in a track suit, carrying a tall glass, was standing nearby, hunched over as he spoke with an elderly couple seated at a table. The sparse crowd among the other tables and booths regarded her with measured disinterest as she stood in the entryway, but she noticed behind the bar an attractive woman, buffed and butch, looking her way. She went over there.

The woman was clearing the dishes of a man and woman on two stools while talking to them. Kady passed behind the pair and stepped up to the bar. The bartender slid over and smiled out a greeting. Small diamond studs embedded in the fold of her left ear glittered in the ceiling lights over the bar.

"You were here the other day," she said to Kady. "You left before I could give you my phone number."

"Your number?" Kady asked.

"I'm teasing," the bartender said with a short laugh. "No need to blush."

Kady blew out a breath to cool her face and said that she wasn't blushing.

"I'm Evan." She wiped the bar between them with a towel. "What can I get for you?"

Kady unzipped her leather jacket, feeling her sweater shift underneath it.

"Is your boss around?" she asked.

Evan said that she'd just missed him, but that he might show up later. She turned around, her toned forearm tensing below the short sleeve of her polo shirt. Evan pulled a slip of paper from the backbar. The couple on the neighboring stools made ready to leave.

"Are you Kady?" Evan asked, handing the paper over. "A guy said someone named Kady might be around asking questions about certain people, and he left this."

Kady unfolded the note and dimly recognized the printing. As she read, she sensed that the blond woman at her elbow was staring. Kady looked downward to see that a fold of her sweater was caught on the underlying lace accents of her brassiere, so she straightened it.

"Nice ring," the woman said, then turned to follow the man, who was already moving away.

Kady felt her face heating up again. Evan called out toward the woman.

"Hey, hey, Miss O'Shea, remember our boundaries with strangers."

Then Evan looked at Kady. "Don't mind Shiner," Evan said. "She didn't mean anything by it. She's a little challenged, if you get my drift, but she's a sweetheart."

The pace of the music stepped up, the old guy on stage sweeping into a medley of Broadway show tunes as Kady turned to look.

"I didn't know piano bars still existed," she said.

Evan reached for a short glass and a bottle of white wine, talking as she poured.

"Easy is an institution down here. Been doing this forever. Every year there's fewer people who remember the old songs, but he doesn't care. He'll die onstage."

"Easy," Kady repeated slowly, thinking of the few days she had spent reviewing the Cullen Arcade file before it disappeared. "Easy Andrews."

"The one and only, and that's more than enough," Evan said.

"Who's his friend?"

Out past the tables, the man in the track suit was dancing by himself, turning haphazard circles in time with Easy's left-hand bass line.

"Him? That's the boss."

Kady gave her a look. Evan shrugged guiltily and took a sip of wine.

"What can I say?" Evan told her. "This is West Seventh Street. The truth takes a little while sometimes."

Evan offered an empty glass. Kady demurred and picked up the note, speaking again.

"So, since this is West Seventh Street, and that means you have to make me think that Lauda Aplikowski is nowhere around when he's standing right over there, I suppose there's no point in asking you for a description of the guy who left this note for me."

"You mean, like, how he looked?"

"Yeah, exactly."

"That," Evan said, tilting back her head and draining her glass with one swallow, "I can tell you."

Kady felt a sudden warmth on her nose as Evan leaned

closer with a breathy grin that was brighter than the diamond studs that cupped her left ear, and twice as sharp.

"He looked curious."

- 23 -

From a dark booth nearest the Amor Abrasadora's front entrance, Dion Drury watched the police sergeant who had sought him out at the impound lot, the older man alone at a table along the game area across the room. Dion had spotted him in the brightness surrounding the pool table when he'd walked in.

Dion could see both the front door and the hallway to the rear entrance as he sat sideways with his back against the wall. A cluster of patrons at the end of the bar jostled noisily in Spanish and a few other languages as they watched a soccer match on a large television.

He turned when Kady L'Orient came through the front door. She spent a second assessing the soccer fans, the green of the televised image reflecting on the lenses of her eyeglasses. Her leather jacket was unzipped open over tight jeans, and her purse hung from a strap over her shoulder. She brushed one hand over her spiky short hair and looked around.

Dion was deciding how to introduce himself when she caught sight of him and walked straight over. His lips went tight.

Kady pulled a slip of paper from a pocket in her purse. She sat on the opposite bench and slid the paper across the table as she shifted over to the center of the seat. Written on the slip were the letters and digits of his license plate.

"Still think my handwriting is nice?"

Dion picked up the paper.

"I thought I'd get here before you," he said. "I guess I didn't."

She dropped her hands out of sight below the table and sat looking at him. He looked back as coolly as he could manage.

"So, what's going to turn up when I call in this plate number to the dispatch desk?" she asked him.

Dion let out a short breath. The fans watching soccer let out a yell at a narrowly missed shot on goal.

"I'd say you've already called it in, and gotten your answer," he said. "You were outside watching for me?"

"You're a thinker," she decided. "I'll give you points for that. I parked across the street and took a couple of numbers from other cars as people came in, but when I saw you, I recognized you from Aplikowski's. Two and two make four."

She slid the purse strap from her shoulder. "What was the idea, luring me over there like that and then lying low, and telling the bartender to cover for you?" she asked.

Dion set the note down and looked away toward the bar.

"I knew I had an advantage over you," he said. "And I knew that I wouldn't have it for very long, so I wanted to get a sense of how dangerous you might be once you caught up with me."

"And now I have."

"Yes, you have."

"And?"

When he looked at her, he could see that she was reading him as best she could, her gaze a mix of cautious aggression and bemusement.

"And I'm going to try to stay on your good side," he said.

He pointed toward the kitchen.

"Want something?"

She seemed to relax slightly, sitting back.

"I'm surprised you're still hungry," she said. "Your date at the Matterhorn eat more than her share of wings?"

"Roommate," said Dion. "She wouldn't know what to make of this, so I dropped her off at home."

Kady didn't change her expression.

"Your bartender friend said the girl was challenged," she said.

"That bartender isn't exactly my friend," Dion said. "But my roommate is challenged. Sometimes she's challenging."

"What's your connection?"

He didn't respond for a second, following the action on the television before his fingertips rested over a spot on his left temple.

"A bullet," he said.

This time he could see a reaction in her eyes and sensed her hands finding her knees beneath the table.

"So, now we both have a name and a face to go with it," Kady said. "What comes next? I'd like to know what's going on, if you don't mind."

Some action in the soccer match brought a multilingual outburst from the end of the bar. Kady turned to look, a pretty profile in the shadowed light of the booth.

"It's like a foreign country down here," she said.

"For a lot of these people, this is a foreign country," Dion told her. "As far as what's going on, I'm not sure I can say yet. But I think I need your help figuring things out. I'm not a cop."

"So you said," Kady recalled. "You're not a cop, but I'm thinking you might be a criminal. In unauthorized possession of a police case file."

Dion felt himself smile, which drew a frown from across the table.

"Depends on how you define *unauthorized*," he said. "And *police* too, I guess." He leaned upward and pointed across the room. "There's another cop here who wants the Cullen Arcade file like you do," Dion said. "He's sitting over there by the pool table. I think he's the number one egg man for Honest Mike Walerius."

"The number one what?"

"Egg man," Dion repeated. "You really don't know?"

"Know what?"

"Anyway," Dion continued without answering, "he's looking for the file because Honest Mike told him to. The lieutenant was one of the investigators on the case, and I think that there was something maybe not on the up-and-up going on back then."

Kady leaned over sideways to see around the corner of the booth.

"His name is St. Albans," she said. "A sergeant working in administration. You'll find his name listed in the file as one of the officers assigned to the case. I don't know much about him, but word around the building is that he's got some physical thing happening with his face that's not good."

Dion told her that he thought something not good had probably happened to Honest Mike's face when she started asking questions at the Matterhorn.

"Then when he lost the file," he said, "it probably got worse."

Kady didn't offer an opinion. Instead, she suddenly slouched lower in the booth. "Shit," she exclaimed in a hushed whisper.

"What?"

"That woman," Kady said. "With St. Albans."

Dion looked over and saw Corinne Nasseff at the sergeant's table.

"That's Corinne," he said. "Honest Mike's wife. She owns this place. Kind of helped me get my current job."

Kady slid her purse strap over her shoulder. "I went to his council offices yesterday, but he wasn't there," she said. "I was going to see what he could tell me about the case, and she showed up. She thought I was somebody else and read me the riot act, telling me to stay away from him. Like the other woman kind of thing."

"Really," Dion said.

"She said the night before it was his car, and maybe next time it would be my car, whatever that meant."

"His car," Dion repeated slowly. "She said his car?"

Kady was halfway out of the booth as she answered. "Yes, she said his car, and I'm getting out of here before she sees me, because she also said maybe my car next time, or maybe my ass, and I don't feel like dealing with her right now. I'm already over my limit for weird encounters for one night."

As she stood, Kady aimed a threatening finger at him.

"You and I need to talk," she said. "Soon. And no more games."

Then she was gone, out the front door.

"His car," Dion said again to himself, watching as Corinne and the sergeant shared a laugh, one of her hands resting on his shoulder, chummy.

The television then erupted in a flurry of sound, the surprise of a scored goal slowly radiating down upon the huddled fans, who broke out in hoots and bellows at the end of the bar.

"And the crowd goes wild," Dion said aloud, watching St. Albans and Corinne as they turned to look toward the noise.

When they turned away again, he got up.

- 24 -

Dion Drury lingered for a minute on the sidewalk in front of the Amor Abrasadora, cell phone at his ear, looking cinematically mysterious beneath the light of the marquee. Kady L'Orient watched him from her idling car across the street. When he walked away and got into his car, she shifted hers into gear.

Tailing him along Cesar Chavez Street and then onto the Wabasha Street Bridge, heading across the river upward into downtown, Kady felt a bit cinematic herself. She had a sense that after her evening of odd conversations, she would not sleep well.

At the top of the bridge, Dion turned onto Kellogg Boulevard toward the hockey arena, where he turned again and drove away from downtown on West Seventh Street. As he neared Aplikowski's Matterhorn, Kady expected him to stop, but he kept going deeper into the neighborhood, past the old brewery and a few blocks more until he steered onto a side street that led to the river.

She watched him pull to the curb a few blocks in, beside the campus for the Kittsondale Treatment Center, where the taillights of his car went dark. She switched off her headlights and parked a few car lengths back to see what he was going to do.

- 25 -

The locks on the back door of Brillo Ziemer's house yielded without much of a challenge. Dion Drury raked them with a pick while Tico Tocopilla shined a flashlight on the brass plates.

"You're sure no one is here?" Dion asked him.

"I checked it out," Tico said. "Looks like there's a light on upstairs, but we should be good."

Dion pushed open the door. In the darkness of the yard behind them, a splatter rose as Hefty Von Hanson wetted down a bush without using water. The kitchen walls offered shadows to the sweep of the flashlight as Tico went in.

"You guys done with me now, or what?" Dion said, following. "I've got to be at work in a couple hours."

"We'll have to lock up again when we leave," said Tico. "So, I suppose you can either stick around or come back."

Hefty came up the concrete stairs, zipping his fly as he looked toward Dion at the door.

"Maybe you can help, you know?" Hefty suggested. "It'll go quicker."

Tico pointed the light at the refrigerator and told Hefty to pull it away from the wall. Then he told Dion to do the same with the stove.

"And we're doing this why?" Dion wanted to know.

"See, here's the deal on that," Tico said, moving to give

Hefty a hand. "When I was telling my dad about what happened to Brillo, he told me that these shady old painters and drywall guys did a lot of work off the books and didn't want that money going through a bank where the tax people could trace it. They'd keep a stash inside a wall in their house. Tearing a hole in Sheetrock or plaster and then fixing it up again was nothing to them."

Tico stretched with his light to look at the wall behind as Hefty eased the refrigerator out a few inches, the vinyl flooring beneath the wheels compressing with an airy gasp of complaint.

"So we're trying to find patching on the walls in places that won't draw attention," Tico said. "Like behind sofas and big, hard-to-move stuff."

"Anything over there?" Dion asked as he tugged against the stove.

"No," Tico said, shaking his head. "This wallpaper is probably older than we are."

He moved closer to aim the light over Dion's shoulder.

"Same thing here," Tico huffed. "And I was hoping this might be easy."

They pushed things back into place. On the rest of the first floor, under the soft glare from the flashlight, they found more walls papered with out-of-style patterns showcasing lots of flowers and stripes. Hefty lingered at a front window, seemingly nervous as the minutes passed. He shifted his weight from one large boot to another, looking out from the darkened room to the darker night outside. Dion could see headlights from the river parkway drifting slow waves of color over the big kid's chest.

"We should go, huh?" Hefty asked. "We've been here long enough."

Tico was already on his way upstairs.

"Apparently not," Dion followed.

In the main bedroom on the second floor, they found a lamp burning dimly on a table beside the bed. Spread over the bed were several old photo albums. Tico reached for one that was open and had a new sticky note attached to a picture pasted to the corner of the page. Dion looked down at the photo, the image showing three young men in painting overalls posed together in front of a small commercial building Dion felt he had seen somewhere before, the youthful faces familiar in a bad-dream kind of way. Tico's finger tapped the page, below each figure in turn.

"Brillo," Tico said, following his hand. "My dad. Your dad."

"You know where this was?" Dion asked.

Tico replied that he did not know. Dion turned to ask Hefty, but found him gone, somewhere down the hallway in the dark. Dion pointed at the sticky note. "Somebody marked this."

"Probably that police sergeant from the tunnel," Tico said. "It must be driving him batshit, trying to figure out who the hell Brillo was and where all the stuff in the garage came from."

Dion was studying the photo when he heard the closet door creak open.

"Ahh," Tico said. "Here's something interesting."

Dion went over. The beam of Tico's flashlight wavered over a wall inside the closet, where ripples on the paperless surface showed evidence of a repair.

"Might have to give my dad a finder's fee," Tico said.

"That's assuming you found something," Dion answered.

Tico switched off the flashlight, saying there was only one way to find out. He turned around and Dion did too, to see Hefty back outside the doorway, in the shadows of the hall, looking more anxious than he had downstairs.

"We need some tools," Tico declared.

Hefty did not say whether he agreed or not, only that he had a different idea. "We need to go, you know?" His thick fingers curled and uncurled in an agitated rhythm at the ends of his jacket sleeves.

"What?" Tico asked.

But Hefty was already moving out of sight, his footsteps loud on the hall floor, growing louder when they started down the stairs.

Tico looked at Dion, puzzled.

Dion said, "I guess he meant, like, right now."

- 26 -

Arno St. Albans left the Amor Abrasadora intending to go home, but instead found himself driving aimlessly around the city for an hour, the lingering memory of Corinne Nasseff and her palm on his shoulder still tingling his knuckles. At University Avenue he headed west, his rear-view mirror sparkling with lights from downtown's skyline. His own reflection taunted him with a slivered view of his drooping right cheek.

Though his doctors could explain the physical elements of his affliction and offer suggestions for coping, the sergeant grimly understood that no one could guide him through those slack moments when he got a feeling that any new burden was only a reiteration of the tepid nature of his life, the closed circuit of his mind coursing with a familiar disquiet that sounded the way a teardrop would if it were made of glass, and anyone were listening.

He turned onto the side street of townhomes where Marnette Sims lived. The city car assigned to Honest Mike Walerius was nowhere along the curb, not that St. Albans expected to see it there, or much cared if he did. The flailing persistence of pointless human events was not at the top of his mind right then. He was wondering more about the unfair quirks of fate that relegate certain people, without them ever really seeing it happen, to the role of side-kick and perpetual bridesmaid.

The car crawled down the street and he went along for the ride, his thumbs damp on the steering wheel, in impassive pursuit of an elusive reckoning that he refused to concede might be forever beyond the reach of both his headlights and his yearning.

As he navigated a corner at the end of the block, he reached tentatively for his balky eye, now wet with an echoing shard that he knew would not be blinked away, which made it that much worse.

- 27 -

Dion Drury was peering through binoculars to check the fences at the beginning of his overnight shift at the impound lot when the outside security speakers grumbled with the approach of a vehicle on the barge channel road. Tires rolled to a slow stop and the engine went quiet. A door wheezed open and then coughed itself closed. At the sound of footsteps, Dion looked out the window to see a petite figure walking through the gate. He heard the groan of the steel door at the bottom of the stairs. When he saw Kady L'Orient coming up, he pushed himself back from his desk and stood.

"I know you said we needed to talk soon," Dion told her as she reached the top step. "Looks like you weren't kidding."

Kady made a slow turn, looking around the office. "You work here," she said.

"Somebody has to," Dion answered. "You followed me?"

"Somebody needs to."

"You said no more games," Dion recalled. "Did you just mean me?"

Kady didn't answer. She pointed at papers on his desk. "Is any of that my Cullen Arcade file?"

"No," Dion said.

He reached for the button to unlock the security door that accessed the kitchen. The lock buzzed, and he invited her in.

When she got behind the service counter, Kady climbed onto a tall stool and peered out a big window toward the rows of vehicles in the lighted yard.

"I haven't been down here since my cadet training," she said. "I thought this was a dreary place then, and that was during the day. I didn't know how bad it got at night."

"Out there, maybe," Dion said, sitting down again while he studied her. "In here, I'd say things are looking up."

"Who's playing a game now?" Kady asked.

"You're on my turf," Dion reminded her. "So, my rules."

Kady set her purse on the counter, her voice softening.

"You were at the treatment center," she said. "Are you like, an outpatient or something?"

Dion reached for his computer keyboard as he answered.

"I was next door," he said. "Helping a couple of friends break into a house."

He didn't watch for her reaction, staying focused on the display screen in front of him. When she spoke again, he couldn't tell if she believed him or not.

"And the house on Randolph Avenue?" Kady asked. "You break into that too?"

Dion shook his head. "Didn't need to. That's where I live. You could have come in while I was getting ready for work, instead of hiding in your car, or wherever you were."

"To hang out with your roommate who's a challenge?"

Now he frowned hard so she could see it, his eyes serious in meeting hers, the outside speakers harmonizing his breaths with a low static he could feel in his teeth.

"Challenging people are the only kind I seem to attract," he said.

She turned her gaze defensively to the window, and after a few seconds her eyebrows suddenly tightened.

"That's where they found him," she said, nodding beyond the impound lot fence, toward the high slope with Cesar Chavez Street at the top. "I remember from the file."

"Along the railroad track," Dion said. "At the bottom of the embankment."

He watched her as she thought that over, the corners of her mouth twitching slightly with the churn of each apparent calculation, until her lips finally parted in a quiet gasp of logic.

"It's why you're here," she said.

Dion gathered the papers on his desk.

"I'm here," he said, dividing the stack, "to get things done and get paid."

He processed towing reports for the next half hour while she left him to it, the two of them keeping to themselves in a way that, he realized, was not so different from the nights Shiner came to sit with him while he worked. They had an easy but edgy quiet that felt like a connection and an imposition at the same time.

When he heard Kady's breathing fall into a methodical rhythm, Dion looked over to see her dozing on the high stool, hugging herself with her arms crossed over her lap in a sweetly inviting slouch that left him fighting an urge to get up and join in.

He was nearly finished with his paperwork and close to nodding off himself when he shot bolt upright at the first of six shrill shrieks that erupted from Kady's suddenly gaping mouth.

Her eyes had opened by the time he turned, and he held out his arms as though he might corral the outburst before anyone from the neighboring overnight industrial sites came running to see if someone had been stabbed.

"Breathe," he directed, voice rising, the only thing he could think to say.

She did breathe then, heavy purging huffs that seemed practiced, like she had done it before, hands flat over her breastbone as she calmed herself, her eyes at first relieved behind her askew eyeglasses, and then quickly embarrassed.

"Sorry," she wheezed. "Sometimes I have night terrors."

Dion fell back onto his chair. "More like you are a night terror," he declared after a few loud seconds, one palm on his chest. "Jeez."

"I think it's from my new meds," she said, taking off her glasses and rubbing her eyes.

"New meds?" Dion asked, giving it a thought. "Does that mean there were old meds?"

- 28 -

In the hour before last call, what remained of the lounge crowd at Aplikowski's Matterhorn seemed indifferent to the return of Kady L'Orient. Easy Andrews was still on stage, skittering his piano through an energetic gypsy rhapsody that did not match the mood of either the room or Lauda Aplikowski, whose fleshy chin rested on one fist while his track suit overflowed a stool at the end of the bar. Lauda swirled ice in his glass, watching Kady as she cleared a space between two stools beside him so she could stand without getting too close. He spoke before she did, but not to her.

"Evan," he called out toward the opposite end of the bar. "We've got a customer."

Evan Arcade looked up from the sink as she washed champagne flutes.

"I'd say that you do," she said. "That's the cop who was here the other day. I told you she wouldn't give up."

Lauda took a sip of his charged water as he eyed Kady.

"It's kind of late," he observed. "I'm not sure what you want from me, but can't it wait until tomorrow?"

"According to my phone, it's almost tomorrow now," Kady said. "And what I want from you is about twenty years of your time on rewind."

Water splashed in the sink. The piano splashed an arpeggio.

"Speaking of wanting things," Evan said to Kady, "did you catch up with your pen pal tonight?"

Kady nodded slowly. "Twice."

Evan tilted her head, as though wondering what that meant. "And?" she asked.

Kady set her purse on the bar. "And now I'm ready for that glass of wine you offered me before I left."

"Ouch," Evan said. "Things didn't go so smooth?"

"I'm more interested in why you were being smooth," Kady said. "You were talking to him and his roommate when I came in. You could have pointed him out to me when you gave me his note, but you didn't."

"She sure sounds like a cop," Lauda said to Evan.

Evan wiped her hands on a towel and brought over a bottle and a glass that she placed in front of Kady.

"That's my fault for getting talked into helping him set you up," Evan told her. "I apologize if you had a bad time. Assuming it was a bad time?"

Kady watched as Evan poured. "Oh, it was a scream," Kady said.

She picked up her glass as Lauda raised his.

"Cheers," he said.

Kady swallowed and wiped her bottom lip with the back of her hand. She spoke while looking at the bottle's label. "So tell me about her last show."

She saw Evan's face faintly blanch.

"I've only heard the stories," Evan said.

Lauda sounded forcibly perplexed when he joined in. "Whose last show?"

"Don't play dumb, boss," Evan told him. "It just pisses people off."

The old man scratched his ear. "Well, it's been a long time since anyone has asked, and I'm not big on rehashing the past, but all I can say is that Ellie Andrews was a talented person," he said to Kady. "Good on the stage, great with a song. A big draw on Friday and Saturday nights. Could have made a living in Las Vegas or Lake Tahoe, but her life was here. She seemed okay with it, the small-potatoes gig with Easy. They had fun, and they had a lot of fans from the neighborhood."

He took another sip from his glass.

"I explained to the cops back then that I last saw her on a weekend," Lauda went on. "Easy was around all the next week doing his solo piano-bar thing as usual. Come that Friday, I've got Easy but no Ellie. We couldn't track her down, and eventually her husband is a story in the morning newspaper, a shooting victim found down along the city outskirts."

He shifted his tufted body on the stool.

"At the time, the police weren't sure if they should consider her a suspect or a victim," Lauda said.

"Still aren't," Kady said. "That's what I'm working on figuring out. If we can narrow down what happened to her, it might go a long way toward solving the who and why of his killing. And then we can close that book."

"Meaning justice is served?" Lauda asked, sounding like he wouldn't think so.

"Meaning a book is closed," Kady answered.

Evan refilled the wine glass. Lauda rubbed a finger against his forehead. A single coarse hair an inch long hooked out from the bridge of his nose, white in the light from above the bar. Kady shivered at the sight and took another drink.

"Listen," the old man said. "I went over a lot of this stuff with the cops back then. Cullen Arcade was not a good guy. He got himself into some bad business, is my theory, and made some enemies that finally got sick of him. Maybe Ellie knew some things about certain people, so the feds or someone got her into witness protection and gave her a new life. Today she's here, tomorrow she's gone and she's somebody else, no time for goodbyes, but that's tough shit. That's what I've always kind of thought."

"Gone underground and left her two kids behind?" Evan said flatly. "I don't think so."

Kady cocked her head toward Lauda. "The file notes did mention children," she recalled. "Do you know what happened to them?"

The old man looked down at his feet. Easy Andrews at the piano shuffled into a slow blues track that sounded like the prelude to an early hangover.

"You know, I still hear Ellie singing sometimes." Lauda said, the quiet words misting his chest. "Once in a while, when Easy is playing, I'll swear she's up there too."

Kady was about to repeat the question when Evan answered it for him.

"We went to live with our uncle," Evan said, nodding toward the stage.

Kady turned around to look at Easy, and when she did, her mind opened to a biography sheet deep within the Cullen Arcade papers.

"Evangeline," she said.

"Only to the family," Evan said. "To everyone else, I'm Evan."

Kady swiveled back toward the bar. "And there's a

brother," she added coldly, like an accusation, about to sound out the syllables before being silenced by the soft landing of Evan's finger upon her lips.

"Now you're getting the picture," Evan said.

Lauda was still gazing at the floor. When he finally raised his eyes toward the stage, his throat squeezed out a thin gargle, like an ice cube going down wrong.

- 29 -

Arno St. Albans was up early the following morning, taking time to stop at Brillo Ziemer's place before reporting to work. He checked the garage to confirm that no one had entered after he had locked the door the day before. Then he went into the house. The living room smelled dustier to him. He parted the curtains to let in more daylight and cracked open a window before heading for the stairs.

In the upstairs hallway, he encountered an acrid fume that crinkled his sinuses. He reached the main bedroom, remembering that he had left a lamp burning overnight as a deterrent to trespassers, and at first, he attributed the odor to the heat of the bulb in the musty room. He switched the lamp off and moved to the photo albums splayed over the bed, intending to grab the book that held a print he had marked the previous afternoon and forgotten to take when he left, a snapshot of a youthful Brillo Ziemer with Cullen Arcade and another young man.

The album was there, but the photograph was not.

He took a step backward. A dull funk curdled the air in the hallway, stronger than the lamp could have caused, and he followed it to the closed door of the bathroom. He opened the door and reached around to the wall switch. When the light came on, his left eye blinked. Glaring darkly at him from within the toilet bowl was a stiff missile of human excrement, defying both logic and flushing in its length and girth, jutting several spectacular inches into the open air above the rim and rising artfully tapered and fibrous at its apex, like a rhinoceros horn.

A thought that came into his mind came out of his mouth.

"What the fuck?"

- 30 -

Dion Drury drove out the gate of the impound lot at the end of his overnight shift and pulled over to the wrong side of the barge channel road at the entrance to Von Hanson's Auto Salvage and Parts. He rolled his window down. Hefty Von Hanson looked up while pushing a large broom over the driveway. Hefty stopped and rested the bristles against his toes, crossing his hands over the end of the broom handle while he cradled his chin on his knuckles. Dion reached across the car seat and picked up the old snapshot from Brillo Ziemer's photo album. He held it out the open window for Hefty to grab.

"I know I've seen this building somewhere, but I can't pin it down," Dion said. "Any ideas?"

Hefty squinted at the image in the early daylight. A towboat horn bawled on the river. The engine in Dion's car idled with a slow metallic heartbeat that sounded like someone sharpening a knife. Hefty leaned his hip against the car fender.

"Old picture, huh?" he said. "Who were the painters?"

"Tico's dad and Brillo," Dion said. "With my dad, back in the day."

Hefty was facing the lines of vehicles beyond the police fence, but after a minute of peering at the photograph, he turned the opposite way. He held the snapshot out at arm's length, aiming it toward the parcel that abutted the salvage yard on the other side. Before the big kid could speak, Dion could see what he was going to say. The small building in the photograph was now the refurbished streetside tier of a larger complex of terraced rooftops on the industrial structure next door.

"The chemical plant," Dion said.

"Before it got big, you know?" Hefty agreed.

He handed the picture back, then swung the broom over his shoulder.

"That do it for you?" Hefty asked.

Dion nodded slowly as he looked from the photograph to the actual building, and then back toward the Cesar Chavez Street embankment above the railroad track beyond the impound lot.

"Yeah, thanks," Dion said. "I knew I'd seen it someplace."

Hefty walked toward the corner of the driveway and kicked disgustedly at the remnants of a decrepit riding lawnmower, an apparent overnight anonymous deposit that was blocking the company mailbox.

"Everybody thinks we're some kind of dump down here," he said, bending over to pull it away. "Like, where's a cop when you need one?"

Dion was still looking at the embankment. "Where," he echoed quietly.

Then he asked if Hefty had eaten yet.

- 31 -

Corinne Nasseff did not appear to be present for the breakfast hour at the Amor Abrasadora cantina on Cesar Chavez Street. Dion Drury passed her office door twice, knocking once. When nothing happened, he reached into his jacket for his lock picks. A glow from the ceiling panels washed the small room in fluorescent white light when he got the door open and found the switch inside. He went in and closed the door, the muted clatter of the morning food service filtering through the wall. He reset the deadbolt and looked around.

A green leather love seat against one wall was half obscured by unfolded piles of workout attire, the tiled floor littered with several pairs of sneakers. Scattered over the desk in the corner were papers and stacks of menus under a half-empty plastic bottle of water. A nylon gym bag rested on the chair. Beside the desk stood a metal rack holding a dozen hangers draped with street clothes, matching sandals, and dress shoes arrayed on the floor beneath them.

A pocket door in the back wall opened to a tiny bathroom and shower that smelled like bleach. A thick towel hung from a hook over the toilet. Dion saw that the mirror over the sink was smudged with pink lipstick, as though someone had written a message and then wiped it away with bare fingers. He smoothed back his hair as he tried to decipher the obliterated letters.

He moved again to the office and was reaching for a desk drawer when he heard a jangle from the hallway. He turned that way just as Corinne opened the door, pulling her key from the lock at the same instant she looked up and saw him. Behind pale amber sunglasses, her eyes burned as dark as her hair, her face suddenly aflush with a murderous intensity. Before she could open her mouth, he opened his.

"I am the egg man," he said.

Corinne inhaled deeply through her nose, held it for a second, and then visibly deflated as she came in and closed the door.

"Just what I need," she said. "A visitor from walrus world."

"Sorry if I scared you," Dion said. "I didn't mean to."

He stepped aside as Corinne moved toward the desk. She dropped her keys, sunglasses, and visor atop the gym bag on the chair and unzipped her hooded sweatshirt. Beneath it she wore a sweaty tank top over athletic shorts and sneakers. Her shins were shiny against her low white socks. He had a hard time keeping his eyes off her bare legs.

"I'll let you know when it's time to be sorry," Corinne said.

Dion reached past her for the water bottle, uncapped it, and then offered it to her.

"How far did you go?" he asked.

"Three miles," she answered. "What I do most mornings."

She took the bottle from him and downed a long slug, her gaze slowly falling from his face to his feet and then back up again.

"Do you run?" she asked.

"Depends on who's chasing me."

She handed back the bottle and pushed aside some of the clothes on the love seat. "A wise guy, I see," she said as she sat down.

"I know you are," Dion said. "But what am I?"

Corinne bent over and began to untie her shoes. "I suppose I should wonder how you got in here."

The cushions sighed beneath her as she shifted her hips. Dion could hear himself swallow.

"I'm from West Seventh Street," he said.

Corinne sighed wearily. "Riddles and jokesters and code words from old songs and dumb movies," she said. "Life with Honest Mike Walerius is like some stupid cartoon that never stops."

Her sneakers rolled off, bumping together on the floor.

"Did he send you to scold me for biting on his new office playmate?" she said. "Tell him that if he's going to be a clueless twit, he should fight his battles in person."

Dion shook his head. "Your husband didn't send me."

"Then, kiddo, why are you here?"

He swiveled, looking around as he answered. "I'm trying to figure out where in this room I would be if I were a handgun that peppered a city car. I was just starting with the desk when you showed up."

Now the fire in her eyes returned. "He knows it was me?"

"I don't know if he knows," Dion said. "I only know that I know. And now you know I know."

Corinne sat with her hands on her knees, blinking at him. "So, we both know what we know," she said. "So what?"

Dion puffed his cheeks and let out a breath. "So that gives me something up my sleeve, I guess," he said. "Which is as good as having the gun, now that I think about it."

Corinne reached up and took the bottle from him again, tapping it against her tongue as she mused.

"So, the office girl got the drift of what I was telling her, and told you," she surmised aloud. "Why didn't she tell him?"

"Because she didn't get your drift," he explained. "She didn't know what you were talking about. She's not the office girl you thought she was. I think I might know who is, though."

Corinne took a drink and then made a point. "But she was there, in his office," she argued.

"She's in with me, sort of," Dion said. "She was only there because she was looking for something."

"His gun, like you?"

"You shot up his car with his own gun?" Dion asked, twirling the bottlecap between his fingers. "That's a nice touch."

Her expression softened, as though pleased by the compliment. Through the wall he could hear people shouting in the kitchen, and the rattle of dishes and pans.

"It was his spare," Corinne said. "What were you planning to do with it if you found it in here?"

"Use it for leverage, if it came to that."

"Against me?" she asked.

"If it would help, yeah," Dion said.

"Help with what?"

"With whatever," he told her.

The mouth of the bottle was at her tongue again, and

she circled the rim with a long, lazy lick as her eyes found his. Then she closed her lips over it and took a slow swig that felt to him like blood rushing to his kneecaps.

"I've seen you before, haven't I?" she said after swallowing. "Out in the bar?"

Before he could reply, they both turned toward the sound of two furtive raps against the hallway door. Dion laughed softly when he heard the shrouded voice of Hefty Von Hanson calling from the other side.

"D-man," Hefty stage-whispered. "You still okay in there?"

"Demon?" said Corinne.

Dion looked at her. "Huh?"

"D-man," repeated Hefty through the door. "You good?"

"Yeah," Dion called out. "Go back to your huevos."

He shrugged toward Corinne. "My lookout," he said. "I guess you snuck past him."

"But not past you, or your cute little gal pal snooping around the council office," she observed. "You said she's not my worry, but you might know who is?"

Dion nodded.

"Then let's see if maybe you can help me put something up my sleeve too," said Corinne. "Here, kiddo, hold this for me again."

She passed the bottle to him.

"Now, turn around and face the desk."

He turned around.

"And put your hands up," she said. "Don't worry, there's no gun here. I put it back in his closet at home."

Dion raised his arms toward the ceiling. His jacket and

shirt rose past his waist, prickling his body hair. As he wondered what she was up to, she clued him in.

"Very impressive," she said.

"My ass?" he said toward the wall.

"Your ears," Corinne told him. "I see a lot of value in a guy who can follow directions."

He heard a quiet slap on the leather love seat.

"Come on over here," she directed. "We'll talk about what we might be able to do for each other, and then it's shower time."

Dion lowered his hands and turned around. He brought her water bottle to his lips and took a sip while she watched him, her eyes deep and even. Diamond in-lays on her wedding ring glimmered as she drummed the cushion slowly with her fingers.

"If you insist," Dion said. "But I've just seen your shower, and I don't think we'll both fit."

- 32 -

As a lieutenant assigned to the staff of the chief of police, Honest Mike Walerius had the use of a small office on the main floor of the public safety building. A single window overlooked the parking lot outside. Arno St. Albans opened the vertical blinds to let in the morning light, throwing reflections on the glassed surfaces of framed professional certificates and photographs that dotted the walls.

Honest Mike sat behind the narrow desk, dressed in a suit and looking to St. Albans much as he did in most of the pictures, images which showed the city council representative trading handshakes and forced smiles with local political and business dignitaries.

"How large, you say?" Honest Mike asked dubiously.

St. Albans spread his hands open, about two feet apart.

"Oh, come now," the councilman said. "In truth?"

"No shit," said St. Albans. "Except that it was shit."

He leaned back and sat against the windowsill, saying that there was more shit to the story.

"Somebody being in the house, and all the stuff in the garage showing up out of nowhere, is only part of what's bugging me," the sergeant said. "While I was going through the dead painter's papers, trying to get a line on who we should notify, I came across some photo albums. I found an old picture of him with a couple other guys out on a job."

Honest Mike blinked absently behind the blue-tinted lenses of his eyeglasses as he reached for a pencil on the desk. A car alarm began a steady distant blaring outside in the parking lot.

"I suspect that you intend to share with me what you perceive to be the significance of this vintage photograph?" the councilman asked.

"It made me think of your missing file," St. Albans said.

"How so?"

"Because I figured out that one of the guys in the picture was Cullen Arcade," the sergeant told him. "And whoever was in the house last night left with that picture in their pocket."

Honest Mike sat forward on his chair and looked thoughtfully toward the ceiling for a few seconds.

"The plot of this narrative, then, would seem thus to be growing incrementally more thick," he observed.

"As shit," said St. Albans.

The councilman rolled his eyes and went on.

"I must say that the emergence of an investigation two decades dormant as a sudden daily thread of our conversations is highly mystifying," he said. "And your testimony of this most recent discovery would seem to defy a hypothesis of coincidence between what might arguably be unrelated events."

"That's what I'm thinking," St. Albans said. "If I'm understanding whatever you just said."

The councilman adjusted the knot of his necktie as he voiced his musings out loud.

"So, in revitalizing an inquiry into the untimely dispatching of Cullen Arcade some years ago, an active young officer has set into dramatic turmoil energies that may be increasing in intensity and, possibly, given your report this morning, participants," he said. "While I, due to my loss of the file, am relegated to a role on the margins."

The car alarm outside finally quieted. St. Albans turned his shoulder to look out the window, squinting into the morning sunlight.

"And you're not about to stand for that," the sergeant said. "Are you?"

"I am not above acting upon my pridefulness," Honest Mike agreed. "Although it will be a challenge to assert myself from a position of relative ignorance regarding the elements at play in this affair."

St. Albans rubbed a dry fingertip over his unblinking eye.

"Something occurs to me, boss," he said, rising from the windowsill. "You don't know where the Cullen Arcade file is, and you don't know who took it, or why. You also don't know how he fits in with my dead painter, or who might want to steal a picture of the two of them. So I'd have to say that right now, it sounds like you don't know—"

"Enough, if you please," Honest Mike interrupted, holding up a silencing palm. "It is far too early in the day to be indulging in such infantile amusements. I forbid you to say it."

St. Albans paused, his half smile percolating the tease for a moment, and then he said it.

- 33 -

Kady L'Orient steered her car out of the early traffic on Randolph Avenue and parked across the street from the small house where Dion Drury lived. She saw other cars along the curb, but not his, and she had not seen it in the driveway beside his garage off the alley in back. She thought about heading downtown to work.

The sight of the house in the daylight, though, triggered observations that unspooled in her mind and held her attention, much like an official report. The tidy yard, with shaped shrubs and a young tree just leafing out from careful trimming, decorative shutters bordering the windows, sheer curtains behind the glass panes allowing for privacy but also sunlight. It was the handiwork of a deliberate, engaged sensibility, someone seemingly unencumbered by an orphanhood of the worst possible circumstances.

She could imagine him studying the Cullen Arcade records over the past days in the same way she had been in the days before, but not at all in the same way either, since to her the facts of the case presented themselves as an unresolved equation, while to him they would have related a horrific testament to the sundering of his childhood.

Gazing out from her car, she wondered about his life now and about her own. She wondered how long a person could expect to mentally suppress their past and sustain the composure to stabilize themselves simply through a determined approach to daily survival.

She reached over to grab a facial tissue from a box on the seat beside her. Taking off her glasses, she cleaned the lenses and then wiped her moistening eyes. When she put her glasses back on, she looked over to see a figure coming from the back yard, striding quickly along narrow pavers beside the house.

Kady remembered Shiner O'Shea from the Matterhorn, and watched as Shiner pulled a jacket on over a uniform smock while hurrying out to the main sidewalk before turning to move up the street. Shiner's blond ponytail began to bounce when, three houses down, her stride elongated into a breezy, unselfconscious skip, the joyful image blurring slowly behind a more insistent welling within Kady's eyes.

New meds, old meds, old ghosts.

More tissues.

- 34 -

A little while later, Arno St. Albans needed a tissue himself as he stood on the sidewalk along West Seventh Street across from Aplikowski's Matterhorn, waiting for a break in the traffic.

"I don't see how Lauda Aplikowski is going to give a shit about a house trespass and some stolen building materials," said the sergeant, his bum eye stinging from the wind generated by a passing truck.

Honest Mike Walerius was standing at the rear corner of his city car, hands in the pockets of his overcoat as he edged out from the parking lane to get a view of oncoming vehicles.

"His reputation as one of my more unsavory constituents may be largely exaggerated," the councilman said. "But his establishment here is frequented by the locals as a Tenth Ward institution, and it is more than possible that he will have gathered from his clientele some hearsay knowledge of your dead decorator of houses."

"The sewer crew foreman did say that everyone in the neighborhood knew the painter," St. Albans admitted.

"Which we shall soon confirm or disprove," Honest Mike said. "I should enlighten you, however, that our endeavor this morning is faceted in multiples."

"Meaning?"

"Meaning that prior to your visit to my office this

morning, I had been made aware from a most reliable source that my removal of the Cullen Arcade papers from the possession of our young investigator has not deterred her from continued inquiries."

St. Albans looked over toward the Matterhorn building. "Here?" he asked.

"So it would seem," Honest Mike said.

The sergeant scowled. "But what would Lauda Aplikowski have to do with the Cullen Arcade case?" he wondered.

The councilman held up one hand to shield his face from the dusty backdraft of a passing transit bus.

"A pertinent question that we will hold in the recesses of our minds," he said. "You must recall, however, that the wife of the murder victim enjoyed a longtime presence here as a performer upon the stage. Since she has not been heard from since the killing, our intrepid officer would appear to be making this fact a focus of the current review of the event."

St. Albans rubbed at his eye. "We didn't get anywhere with that approach at the time, as I remember things," he said.

"We had precious little to work with," Honest Mike reminded him. "That was my primary motivation for advocating to leave the corpse in place and monitoring the site for a possible return by the perpetrator to the scene of the crime. We were grasping then upon the only straw at our disposal."

Nodding toward the building, St. Albans realized that Lauda Aplikowski was behind the councilman's seizure of the file in the first place, and asked if the suspicion was correct.

"You are astute," Honest Mike responded. "My intervention served as a quid pro quo in consideration of his earlier support, as a ranking member of the Restaurant and Tavern Association, for licensing the cantina of my sweet wife Corinne."

"But you haven't actually stopped anything for him," the sergeant noted. "And he's pissed off about it?"

Now it was Honest Mike's turn to nod. "This junior officer would seem to be a determined young woman," he said. "And not averse to working in an ambiguous environment, since she has made no report or complaint of the file going missing and would undoubtedly understand that its disappearance held some greater meaning in the grand scheme of things. She has instead pressed onward, a fearless persistence that I find most admirable."

He scraped at the pavement with his shoe.

"A fresh perspective on the case after twenty years of fermentation might prove advantageous to her efforts, as well as to my own," he continued. "Lauda Aplikowski is a businessman whose actions occasionally waver beyond the definitions of propriety, leaving him sometimes vulnerable to judicious application of targeted influence from outside sources. His increasing agitation over her reexamination of the killing leads me to suspect that he believes himself to be in some position of legal or personal disadvantage, which affords to me a desirable posture for negotiation, whether I possess the file or not."

St. Albans stared across the street at the Matterhorn entrance.

"What negotiation?"

"To perhaps enhance the interests of my deserving

Corinne," said Honest Mike. "And by association, the interests of myself. Upping the ante, as it were."

The sergeant drew a slow breath. Another transit bus roared past, heading away from downtown toward the airport.

"That's something out of your standard playbook, for sure," he said. "What's your idea?"

"I imagine that my dear wife might appreciate a role as a minor silent partner to the Matterhorn operations for some unspecified period of time," said the councilman. "In awarding her a financial equity, he would by extension receive my enhanced assistance toward suppressing any potential discoveries that, if disseminated, could blemish the Aplikowski mystique and profitability. He should likely see the value in that."

St. Albans came off the sidewalk and joined Honest Mike in the parking lane. He could see a clear interval in the approaching traffic and got ready to cross.

"How do you plan to get him agreeable to you muscling in?" the sergeant asked.

Honest Mike looked over at him and smiled. "I propose to utilize the timeless strategy championed throughout history by central European powers in exhorting their armed forces toward recurring invasions of sovereign Poland."

"Which would be?"

"Walk in backwards, and say you are leaving."

- 35 -

Dion Drury yawned as he watched the city sewer crew lowering materials down the manhole in the street outside of Brillo Ziemer's house. Tico Tocopilla gave directions to one of the workers on the surface, and then walked back to his pickup truck, where Dion leaned against the closed tailgate, one raised foot resting on the bumper. Beyond the long, open lot in front of the house, traffic on the river parkway whistled while crows in the trees chorused a raucous call-and-response of low shrieks. A service truck marked with advertising for a locksmith sat parked beside Brillo's van in his driveway.

"As if changing the locks is going to keep us out," Tico said, looking toward the house. "You good for another run at it later?"

"I've got something else going on," Dion said. "And I'm not certain that whatever might be inside that closet wall is worth getting caught over. I'd let things die down for a while. It's obvious that the cops have their radar up because of us already."

Tico reached into the bed of the pickup for his coffee and took a sip from the disposable cup.

"If you say so," he answered. "But like I said last night, there's only one way to find out what's in there, and I'd hate to hear that somebody else got to it first and scored big. From what my dad told me about the painting and drywall business, these outlaw guys like Brillo didn't go to the trouble of hiding things just for fun."

Dion gazed out toward the far side of the river valley, his mind uneasily considering dead painters and the things that they hid.

"When your dad remembers the old times," he said to Tico. "Does he ever say anything about Brillo being anything like my dad?"

Tico thought a minute before answering.

"See, here's the deal on that," he said. "He makes it sound like they were both crooks, if that's what you mean. Sorry to have to say so."

Dion told him no, that wasn't exactly what he meant, and described something more specific.

"He ever say anything about Brillo being maybe, like, violent?"

Tico took another sip of coffee and looked at him.

They both turned at the sound of a vehicle approaching from behind them on the street, a small truck from a local plumbing service that slowed to get around the sewer crew and their equipment, the driver waving a casual greeting as she passed before easing to a gentle stop at Brillo Ziemer's driveway.

- 36 -

The door to his bedroom was open the first time Dion Drury awoke that afternoon. Daylight from the hallway spilled through to cast a gray wedge across the textured ceiling. He heard something moving near the shaded window along the street-side wall.

"Everything okay?" he asked, rising on one elbow to see Shiner sitting on the upholstered chair in the corner, still wearing her outside jacket.

She looked up from her puzzle book and nodded, her hand guiding a pencil across the splayed page.

"I'm finding circle words," she said.

"I see that," Dion said through a long slow breath. "Any extra lemon bars today?"

"Pizza," Shiner said. "I already ate it."

He fumbled himself onto his side while straightening his pillow. He noticed a film of dust speckling the face of his clock radio atop the bedside table. He could taste the time on his tongue.

"Up for a car ride tonight?" he asked her. "I need to look at something for somebody before I go to work."

He didn't hear an answer, just the lazy scratch of the pencil on the paper as he closed his eyes, the sound looping through the quiet to corral the pulse of his heartbeats as he drifted back to sleep.

- 37 -

Half an hour into the late shift at the impound lot, Hefty Von Hanson wrinkled his nose at a small open bag of licorice bits, saying that he didn't want them. Dion Drury told him to throw them in the trash.

"I don't want them, either."

"Why'd you buy them then, huh?" Hefty asked logically as he shuffled a deck of playing cards on the service counter. At the corner desk, Dion adjusted the speaker volume for the outdoor security monitors and listened to the rising whine of a vehicle on the barge channel road, its headlights approaching.

"Shiner made me get them for her when we were at the gas station after dinner," he said. "Then she forgot the bag in my car when we got home. I was smelling licorice all the way here."

Hefty looked toward the kitchen, asking if there was any microwave popcorn instead. Dion told him it was on the shopping list, peering down out the window toward the gate as the driver stopped and parked along the fence. Hefty asked him if they needed to ditch the game.

"No," Dion decided, the desk speaker crackling with the dying of the engine and then light footsteps after the car door heaved closed. "It's somebody who won't care."

After the metal door at the bottom of the staircase creaked open, Dion saw Kady L'Orient's dark bristled haircut bobbing up the steps. She looked around as she reached the landing, light from the kitchen doorway yellowing her glasses. She focused on Hefty, who looked puffy in his official Von Hanson's Auto Salvage and Parts coveralls as he sat on a tall stool behind the counter.

"I don't work here, right?" he said.

"Nobody said you did," she responded, adjusting the long strap of her purse over her shoulder. The cuffs of her blue denim jacket were rolled back one rotation over her wrists. A nubby white sweater was untucked over khaki leggings and neon-orange sneakers.

"That's a good look on you," Dion told her, threading his hands into the pockets of his work pants. "I didn't know you were coming, or I'd have dressed up too."

She looked down at herself, and when her gaze came up her eyes were serious. She regarded Hefty for a moment, and then spoke to Dion.

"I know who you are now," she said.

A couple of seconds passed. Dion could sense Hefty turning to study him. "You knew last night at the cantina," Dion reminded her. "You ran my license plate."

"I only knew your name last night at the cantina," Kady said. "When I went back to the Matterhorn, I found out what your name meant."

Dion saw Hefty looking back and forth between the two of them.

"Your name means something, D-man?" Hefty asked him.

"To certain people," Dion said, his eyes steady on Kady.

"Like his sister, for one," Kady said, as she walked over and set her purse on the counter.

"I got the feeling that you guys took turns playing me last night, and I didn't like it," she said to Dion. "So, I stopped at Aplikowski's on my way home to chew on her a little. While we were going at it, she tossed out something for me to chew on. About who was who."

The desk speaker began amplifying the grumble of a freight train somewhere down the track beyond the fence. Dion looked out the window, past the lighted lot to the dark hillside that rose to Cesar Chavez Street.

"Who," he echoed as he nodded slowly.

Hefty began to shuffle the deck again, saying he could understand this woman inspiring Evan Arcade to make a play for her.

"What?" Kady said.

"You're her type," Dion offered as the cards fluttered between Hefty's thick fingers. "Small, smart, and cute."

She threw Dion a frown. "Now you're doing it again," she said flatly.

Dion shook his head. "I'm not playing you," he said. "I'm playing cribbage. You want to take on the winner?"

"I'm ahead, you know?" Hefty said.

"What I want is to talk about my file," she told Dion, edging slowly closer along the counter. "Maybe keep you from getting yourself into more trouble than you're already in."

"Right now, it's my file," Dion said. "My name isn't on it, but my name is in it, and those records show that I've already seen more trouble than maybe I understood. I didn't plan on this, and I guess you didn't plan on me, but here we are. Whatever way this thing turns out for anybody, I'm going to be there when it ends, like it or not."

She gave him a look that he was not expecting, a soft, misty grimace that suggested she was either biting back an observation he wouldn't care to hear, or feeling even more regretful about his history than he generally did himself—a surprise he found swelling his throat when Hefty tapped a handful of cards loudly against the countertop to align them.

"I've got files in my truck," Hefty told Kady. "Out in the toolbox. Are we talking about working on metal or wood?"

He pointed outside to his flatbed, shadowed under one of the overhead lights in the yard, then leaned closer to Dion and lowered his voice.

"Who is this chick, anyway?"

- 38 -

When Arno St. Albans got to the impound lot, he pulled his car to a stop behind another that was parked along the fence near the gate. Beside the empty car idled a taxi, the driver cradling a cell phone to one ear, the rear seat vacant. As the sergeant walked through the gate and into the yard, he spied near a light pole the flatbed truck he had seen ferrying the city sedan assigned to Honest Mike Walerius back to the street of Marnette Sims a couple of days before.

He heard the door to the office open and then foot-steps scuffling on the gravel. He turned to see someone come out from the building, a man in a bloodied shirt and pants, his nose and forehead latticed with white bandages as he sorted crumpled papers between his hands. The man headed toward a mangled pickup truck at the end of an aisle ahead.

St. Albans watched the fellow pass and rubbed his own brow in empathy, finding in the stars overhead a lonesome insistence that everyone and no one truly gets what they deserve. The endless night sealed him in damp and briny river air, its whisper broken only by the intermittent heavy growl of a truck crane lumbering across the grounds of a barge terminal along the channel.

The sergeant took a few steps toward the building, the stiff soles of his shoes amplifying the sharp pressure of pebbles underfoot, as he reached for the door to climb the stairs and face a demon.

- 39 -

Dion stood at the window, fingering a tow report and watching the sergeant and the injured man cross paths in the yard below. He sat down at the desk when he heard the downstairs door creak open. Arno St. Albans's shuffling footfalls on the steps ended when he reached the landing. Kady L'Orient shifted toward the far corner of the room, away from the arc of the sergeant's gaze, which slowly measured her in the dim light of the kitchen doorway, then settled upon Hefty Von Hanson, who sat behind the service counter.

"I still don't work here, you know?" Hefty told him.

St. Albans turned toward Dion, who set the tow report on the desk while smoothing back his hair with the other hand.

"I know you are," Dion said to the sergeant. "But what am I?"

"You guys have good memories," St. Albans said. He looked again at Kady and then back at Dion. "If you're in the middle of something, I can wait," he said.

Dion tilted his head toward Kady as though to question if she thought they were in the middle of something. She answered with a curt, irritated wave of her hand before he could ask. Dion regarded the sergeant again.

"What does your boss want now?"

St. Albans came away from the landing toward the

center of the floor, giving Kady another long scan as he passed. She deflected it with a sudden search into the contents of her shoulder bag.

"Nothing more than before," the sergeant said. "He admired the way you handled his automotive issue the other day. I did too, but my take later was that you and your friend Tico may have gotten yourselves onto some thin ice over this dead house painter I've been dealing with. Someone is trying to give me the impression that the guy's house is haunted or something. Stuff there has been appearing and disappearing like in a bad movie. I'm getting the idea that I'm being played."

Dion saw Kady's eyes dart upward.

"I want to make sure that certain people know I'm not enjoying the game," St. Albans said evenly.

Dion saw that the sergeant was looking out the window, so he looked too and caught sight of the battered motorist under the lights, scuttling across the yard toward the taxi waiting at the road, his arms loaded with items retrieved from his truck.

"He looks like an escapee from a slasher film," Dion said.

"Reminds me a little of my old neighborhood when I was a kid," St. Albans responded. "Before they robbed a liquor store or gas station, hooligans would take surgical tape or bandages and plaster them all over their faces. Victims and witnesses couldn't give a useful description of suspects. They would only remember the bandages."

"Smart, huh?" Hefty said.

"A clever diversion for its time," St. Albans agreed. "Criminals with some panache, not like the mental cases out there these days."

His expression settled into a confusing mixture of weary and stern that Dion could not quite grasp until the older man's eyes, one narrow and one wide, seemed to find a disjointed focus on the floor tiles.

"Hefty," Dion said, "you still hungry for some microwave popcorn?"

The big kid slid from his stool. "Store run, huh?" He sounded happy to have a task. "On my way, D-man."

Kady spoke up then, surprising Dion by saying that she would go along.

"Cool?" Hefty asked Dion.

Dion handed him some cash and regarded Kady curiously, sensing the sergeant studying the three of them.

"Cool," Hefty answered himself when no one else did, heading out of sight into the kitchen. When he reappeared in the other doorway at the top of the staircase, the sergeant pointed at him.

"You broke the toilet plunger the other day," St. Albans slowly recalled.

Hefty did not break stride as his bootsteps rang out, descending the risers. "What plunger?" he asked.

Kady seemed confused, her sneakers trailing soft raindrop patters on the steps as she followed him.

"I'll be back," she told Dion, her face saying that she was not all that sure.

St. Albans watched them go down the stairs. When they got outside, he turned to Dion.

"Interesting pals," he said.

"I'll let them know you think so."

"So, what's the word on this Brillo Ziemer character?" the sergeant asked.

Dion shrugged in response. "Tico told me that Brillo is dead," Dion said. "And that you were both there, in the storm sewer tunnel."

"Tico told me that most everyone on West Seventh Street knew the dead guy," St. Albans said.

"He's probably right."

"I can include you in that?" the sergeant probed.

"Sounds like you already have."

"Tell me then," St. Albans went on. "Does everyone on West Seventh Street also have keys to his place?"

Dion reached up and smoothed his hair back again. "I wouldn't know," he said. "If it makes you feel better, I can tell you that I've never had any keys to his place. Tico could probably say the same thing."

Hefty's flatbed fired to life outside with a low roar while the sergeant gave Dion a long silent stare.

"That's the story you're sticking to?" St. Albans finally asked. "One egg man to another?"

"That's the story I'm stuck with," Dion said with half a grin. "So, I guess it's stuck to you too." Then he grinned wider.

- 40 -

As the flatbed accelerated up the barge channel road, Kady fastened her seat belt while stray papers and loose metallic objects drifted around on the floor. She raised her heels up, hoping to keep her shoes clean. Hefty Von Hanson drove with his window halfway open, steering with one meaty hand as watery breezes from the river overlayed an interior odor that Kady deciphered as something like onion rings deep fried in automatic transmission fluid.

"Does your truck always smell like this?" she asked.

"What truck?"

"Okay," Kady said as they passed the salvage yard. "Forget that. Tell me, who is Tico?"

"He's a guy my older sister used to date," Hefty said, huffing a breath as he adjusted himself behind the wheel. "They still hang out. The D-man and him are buddies from high school, you know? They're my friends through her."

"And the dead painter the sergeant was talking about back there?"

The big kid scratched a fingernail against the short hairs over his ear. "Sergeant?" he said. "That guy's a cop?"

"Yes," she told him. "Like me."

She lurched forward against the shoulder restraint as the truck suddenly lost power. Hefty raised his broad thigh up against the bottom of the steering wheel, backing off on the gas.

"I better slow down then, huh?"

"The dead painter," Kady repeated, the truck rolling past the chemical plant.

The big kid didn't answer at first, and when he did, he sounded defensive. "Brillo Ziemer was an old guy from West Seventh Street that Tico and the D-man knew," he said. "I didn't really have anything to do with him, right?"

"Why was the sergeant asking about him?"

"Maybe because he's dead?" Hefty said. "He fell down some kind of shaft by his house the other day into a storm sewer tunnel. Tico and his city crew found him, you know?"

"Tico works for the city?"

Hefty tugged his cap from his head and then jammed it back on.

"You ask a lot of questions," he said.

"I just like to know things," Kady replied. "Especially when the subjects sound a little goofy. Why was the sergeant talking about a toilet plunger?"

Hefty went brusquely quiet, reaching over to switch on the radio. The truck bounced stiffly over bumps along the winding pavement to the fevered Spanish of a Mexican disc jockey. Kady clutched her shoulder bag against her belly.

"Nobody's under arrest," Hefty said, staring ahead through the windshield, talking, she thought, as much to himself as to her. "I'm not stupid, and the guys trust me."

He readjusted his cap again when they hit a bump. Something on the floor brushed her ankle. She pulled one leg up and locked her fingers over her knee.

"I didn't mean to be bugging you," Kady said.

Then she got an idea. "How about a peace offering? I'll pay for extra snacks at the store if you can help me with one thing that I'm curious about, and not as a cop."

He turned halfway and gave her a skeptical glance before looking away.

"It's the roommate," Kady said. "The challenged blond girl. What's going on there?"

Hefty rubbed a wrist against his chin and perked up.

"Shiner?" he said. "She's a sweetheart, huh? I don't know the whole story, but Tico told me something happened to her as a kid. Some accident. The D-man was her neighbor, and he's been looking out for her ever since."

He turned again and regarded her seriously, his voice less amiable.

"We all do now, right?"

Kady nodded. "I'll keep that in mind," she said.

Hefty lowered his gaze to the speedometer and appeared to lapse into a slow analysis.

"She bothers you?" he asked. "Like competition?"

"No," Kady answered, worried at once that her reply came too swiftly and would ring like a false denial, even to a stranger, and worried further that she already could not be certain for herself whether any denial might be false or not.

"No," she repeated more evenly. "It's really nothing at all like that."

"Oh," Hefty said. "I thought, maybe, you know?"

She wondered if she did know.

Coming out of the industrial park, the road made a tight curve to meet Cesar Chavez Street. As they rounded the bend, Kady saw the flatbed's headlights brighten the crossbuck signs and the reflectorized raised gate arms of the railroad crossing just before the intersection. Hefty leaned toward her suddenly and switched off the radio.

"Knock, knock," he said.

"What?"

"Knock, knock," he repeated. "You know?"

Kady shrugged an okay and answered. "Who's there?"

"Ya," Hefty said.

"Ya, who?"

With that, she felt herself slammed against the seat back as the big kid jumped on the accelerator, the flatbed hurtling forward to jounce hysterically over the uneven panels of the rail crossing, her body lifted weightless within the seatbelt for an instant before splaying itself sideways as the truck settled back to earth upon the pavement on the opposite side, her eyeglasses half off, her purse sailing from her grasp onto the floor amid the trash, and her ears assaulted by a furious caterwauling from across the cab.

"Ride 'em, cowgirl!"

- 41 -

Arno St. Albans stopped at the Amor Abrasadora cantina after he left the impound lot, thinking that Corinne
Nasseff might like to hear about the meeting that morning
at the Matterhorn, maybe favor his shoulder again with an
innocently illicit touch for the road. She was about to enter her office when he got there. The few people slumped
upon stools along the bar turned mutely to witness his
approach, a marimba song on the jukebox at the rear of
the long room blustering everyone with a bleak conceit of
weary mirth. She motioned for him to follow her.

Once inside the office, the door closed behind them,
he squinted uncomfortably toward the fluorescent ceiling
light. Corinne reached over to her desk and picked up her
sunglasses.

"Here," she said, stretching upward onto her toes to put
them on him. "Try these."

She raised a judging eyebrow as she stepped back.

"What?" he said.

"That's better," she decided. "Your face isn't so noticeable."

She grabbed a water bottle from the desk and opened
it. St. Albans went into the small bathroom. While he was
checking out his image in the mirror, pleased to discover
that she had a point, that the tinted amber lens filtered the
visual impact of his frozen eye, he heard her admit that she
had not expected to see him so soon.

"I thought maybe I scared you off yesterday," she called through the doorway. "I was only teasing, you know."

"Maybe that's why it shook me up," the sergeant said. "Because you were only teasing. The way this thing with my face is going, teasing might be all I can expect from women anymore, if even that. It hadn't really hit me until you got all flirty, even if you were joking with me."

She was on her chair behind the desk when he came out. She looked up at him over an invoice sheet as she took a sip from the water bottle and then set it down.

"I'm sorry I toyed with you," she said. "I was being naughty."

"You're not alone in that," St. Albans told her.

He then relayed to her an account of the exchange that morning between Honest Mike Walerius and Lauda Aplikowski. He recalled details while dodging sneakers and discarded gym socks on the narrow floor as he paced near the desk. Corinne watched him with an expression that made him feel as though she were teasing him again.

"How did Lauda take it?" she asked when he had finished the story. "This idea of pushing me off on him as an uninvited silent partner to keep everyone quiet about whatever it is you guys think you're holding over him?"

St. Albans frowned as best he could with half his mouth. "Not how I would have expected," he said. "And I think the boss was surprised too, by the sound of his description in the car afterward."

"What did my devoted husband say?"

"That Aplikowski was uncannily calmly amused," the sergeant replied. "Which was pretty much spot on." His voice grew suspicious as he finished the thought. "Not all that different from the vibe I'm getting from you right now," he noticed.

When she smiled at him, he leaned forward with his palms flat upon the desktop and his face close to hers.

"Suppose you let me in on the joke and tell me what it is that I'm not seeing here," he said.

Corinne twirled a finger through a shaped wisp of hair at her right ear as she answered. He could see the ceiling light reflected as a white line across the wide dark pupils of her eyes.

"Back when I was putting the deal together for the cantina, the bank financing came up short," she said. "I never told Honest Mike because I didn't want him to think I couldn't handle things myself. Lauda offered to make up the difference for me if I signed an agreement, which I did, so he probably thought it was funny to threaten him with me as his silent partner when he's already my silent partner."

She brought her hand away from her ear and rapped the desk. The sharp sound of her wedding ring striking the hard surface made his good eye blink.

"Not a word of this to the walrus," she said. "Is that clear?"

St. Albans didn't move for a few seconds. When he did, it was to reach for her water bottle. He took a long swallow and saw her expression change as he set the bottle down. She seemed suddenly flustered.

"Why did you do that?" she wondered.

"I was thirsty and didn't think you'd care."

She teetered forward on the chair. "I don't, but something happened this morning," she told him. "There was an interesting kid in here for some personal business. We were talking, and he did what you just did with my water."

"A little too familiar for you?"

"It just surprised me," Corinne said, her voice going low. "Put me off balance."

She crawled her hand across the desk to rest atop his. He looked down at her manicured nails and then up at her face. She curled her lips inward, as though working through a serious thought.

"It gave me ideas," she went on. "Tingly ones."

Her palm was warm. Her fingerprints began to trace a tentative scan of his knuckle hairs, while his skin went rigid. He cleared his throat.

"Please," he said.

"Please, don't?" she asked, lowering her eyelids suggestively. "Or please don't stop?"

"Please," he said again, with greater urgency as he pointed to the sunglasses on his face. "Can I keep these?"

She was still laughing a minute later as he went out the door wearing them, leaving the water with her.

- 42 -

Kady L'Orient did not go straight home after leaving the impound lot either. She ended up at the bar in the Matterhorn lounge, where Evan Arcade tried to explain the rules of cribbage using a flaccid deck of vintage playing cards where the numbered sides were enhanced by suggestive photographs of unclothed human females. Turning the seven of spades in her hand, Kady held it up for Evan to see.

"Would you say this one is a fifteen-two, or a fifteen-four?" Kady asked.

Evan peered at the picture while refilling their wine glasses. "More like a pair," she said.

She set the bottle aside and used the back of her hand to scratch her cheek, then hiked up the sleeves of her sweatshirt to expose her forearms while Kady watched.

"Bartending gives you muscle tone like that?" Kady asked.

Evan looked down, studying her arms quizzically, as though thinking about it for the first time.

"Hockey in the winter, then parks-and-recreation league softball when the weather warms up," she said. "Both a good excuse to get drunk on a weeknight."

Kady sipped her wine as she considered the bleary customers that dotted the room.

"Last summer must have gone into extra innings," she said.

Up on the small stage, Easy Andrews was at the piano, bullying his way through a tarantella that sounded to Kady like a cartoon car chase. She turned on her stool to watch. Evan asked if she wanted to order something from the kitchen. Kady said no.

"Your brother made popcorn in the microwave, after the goofball friend with the flatbed truck took me on Mister Toad's wild ride."

"Knock, knock," Evan said with a chuckle. "Hefty is a sweetheart."

Kady swiveled on the stool to face her.

"That's what you said about Shiner, the roommate," she recalled. "And so did he. He couldn't tell me much more, except that she was your neighbor as a kid."

Evan moved down the bar halfway, talking as she poured a beer for a customer on a far stool.

"Shiner lived down the street," said Evan. "She was just a normal kid. A bunch from our block were riding their bikes in the alley one day with her and my brother after school. I wasn't home. I was thirteen. They were both eight. That was a couple of years before everything else happened with my folks."

She dried her hands on a bar towel as she came back.

"My father had a motorcycle," she went on. "He wasn't like in a biker gang or anything, but he was a tough, rowdy kind of guy. He owned a handgun. Don't know why he thought he needed one. Anyway, he was out with his painting truck that day and his motorcycle was parked next to our garage. Shiner must have been playing with the saddlebags because she found his gun in there and somehow it went off, got her up around the eye, where her scar is now. Her bike helmet took some of it, otherwise she probably would have died. My brother started looking out for her in school, I guess. Not sure I'd have the patience, but she's hard to get mad at."

She wiped the bar with the towel and then picked up her glass, seeming to grasp at a thought. Kady took a stab at reading the other woman's mind.

"He feels responsible," Kady said. "For your dad being irresponsible."

Evan sipped her wine and frowned, suddenly glum. "You sound like my therapist," she said.

Kady looked down at the seven of spades and the less-than-tasteful portrait that decorated the center. She tapped it with her fingernail.

"My therapist would have an opinion about these cards," she said.

"My therapist gave me these cards," Evan replied.

Kady turned again to watch Easy at the piano. "Why is your brother's last name not the same as yours or your folks'?" she asked Evan after a minute.

Evan scratched her cheek again as she explained.

"Drury is my mother's family name. Easy's real last name too. When Easy took us in, he changed ours to make us more anonymous. I changed mine back later."

"You resented him for changing it?" Kady said.

Evan gave an answer that wasn't quite an answer. "I moved in with some girlfriends when I turned eighteen. I was only at his place for three years."

"You weren't happy there?"

Evan thought about it. "It was just kind of awkward," she said.

"Working together doesn't bother you, though?"

The piano went quiet before Evan could respond. Easy got up from his bench, shuffled some sheet music in a stack atop the piano, then came down off the stage and made his way through the tables while greeting people. When he got to the bar, Evan poured a glass of ice water for him and dropped a straw into it. Rings on the old man's fingers clinked against the tumbler as he picked it up. He nodded at Kady and sucked on the straw while pulling his other hand backward over his scalp, smoothing his hair. The bump on his jawline and the facial contusions made her think of the bandaged man at the impound lot.

"Car accident?" she asked him.

"Car," he confirmed, the words hissed through closed teeth as he set his glass down. "But no accident."

"Patrol cops pulled him over for driving under the influence," Evan told her. "He put up a fight, and he didn't win."

"For which the city will pay dearly," Easy said.

Evan picked up a paring knife and sliced a wedge of lemon that she dropped into his glass. He jabbed at it with his straw.

"You're filing a claim with the city attorney?" Kady asked.

"For the pain and humiliation of my wired jaw," he nodded. "The papers are already in, and I have a witness who's an insider. The case is over before it starts, and I win."

Then he eyed her suspiciously.

"You sound like you know something about how that stuff works," he said.

Evan reminded him that a police investigator had been looking for, and finally caught up with, Lauda for some questions.

"Yeah," Easy said. "So?"

Evan gestured toward Kady.

Easy looked back and forth between the two women. He began to speak as though Kady weren't there.

"If she already caught up with the boss, why is she back?" he wanted to know.

Evan flashed Kady a slightly defeated grin, while telling Easy that an unanticipated complication had arisen in the inquiry. "Dionysius."

Easy regarded Kady as he picked up his glass again and aimed his lips toward the straw. "Ahh," he said. "That would make sense."

Kady felt her own jaw tighten as she asked Evan what the old man meant. Easy spoke up instead as he stepped away from the bar and ambled past her toward the tables and his scattered audience.

"You're his type."

Kady looked at Evan, who did not return the gaze but slowly began to gather up the playing cards.

"So, I guess we're finished here," Evan said.

Kady sensed a quickening flatness in the other woman's breathing that caused her own lungs to stiffen, recognizing a sadly familiar feeling of somehow failing to meet an unexpected expectation. A topic for her next therapy session.

She pushed a few cards timidly toward Evan, trying to help. She wasn't sure if she should get up. Evan folded those cards into the rest of the deck, not saying anything.

Nervous now, with a sense of being irresponsible herself without understanding exactly why, Kady took another swallow of wine. It tasted, when she thought about it, like dead leaves.

- 43 -

By lunchtime the next day, the change of seasons seemed more insistent. A warm sun climbed in a clear sky above downtown Saint Paul, and a squadron of mobile restaurant trucks arrayed themselves along the street outside the public library. People wandered the sidewalks of the adjacent park in light jackets or shirtsleeves. Dion Drury and Tico Tocopilla watched from a bench near a dormant fountain under budding trees near the center of the plaza.

"Tight skirt at the barbecue truck?" Tico said, unzipping his work jacket. "Or the stiletto heels and cleavage by the taco stand?"

"You go," Dion said. "I'm not ready to decide."

"About chatting up the ladies or about the food?"

Dion yawned as he gazed toward the crowd, but then he suddenly was on his feet and moving fast over the pavers, leaving Tico to call after him.

"What the hell?"

Kady L'Orient was studying a chalkboard sign on the side of a sandwich truck as Dion approached from her left. He tapped her lightly on the shoulder and kept going, but she didn't look left. She turned instead toward her right shoulder and smirked at him as he stopped beside her.

"That's an interesting reflex," he said. "I've never seen anyone do that."

"Maybe I'm magic," she replied.

She was wearing a sleeved sweaterdress beneath a crocheted poncho shawl. Her short suede boots were adorned with silver ankle chains. Her knees were round and smooth. Her eyeglasses shanked slivers of sunlight that he had to dodge to look at her.

He told her she appeared to be dressed for court, and she grinned a little and said that maybe he was a bit magic himself.

"I'm testifying in a felony case at the courthouse," she said. "I have to be back there in an hour."

Someone was shouting orders inside the sandwich truck. A generator mounted to the rear bumper deck revved out a slow groaning pulse. Sparrows flapped and darted along the gutter, mining for seeds and scraps.

"At least now I know that you're not a vampire," Kady observed. "You can actually come out in the daylight."

"The city attorney scheduled me for a deposition that she's probably going to regret," Dion said.

"Your uncle's broken jaw?" she interrupted, stopping him short for a second.

"Good guess," he said. "I decided that as long as I was awake anyway, I'd meet a buddy for lunch."

"And here I am?" she said.

This time he stopped for more than a second. Her grin was back, and she held it as she turned to the fountain. Dion looked that direction and saw Tico walking toward them.

"Okay, then this would be the friend?" Kady asked. "Tico?"

Dion heard quick surprise in his voice. "You're on top of everything, aren't you?"

"Magic," Kady whispered as Tico neared. "Don't forget it."

Then she tacked on a quietly emphatic coda that Dion found vaguely suggestive. "Ever."

Dion introduced her to Tico as someone from work. He noticed that she didn't confirm or deny it, letting him take the lead. Tico looked mildly confused.

"I didn't know that we were meeting up with somebody, D-man," he told Dion.

Dion said that he hadn't known it himself. Kady gestured toward the line of food trucks.

"He told me that lunch was on you," she said to Tico.

Tico snorted out a laugh. "See, here's the deal on that," he said. "There's an old rule on West Seventh Street. New kid buys."

Kady pointed out that they were nowhere near West Seventh Street.

"If you're with us, you are," Tico said.

Dion pulled his wallet from his pocket.

"Your treat again?" Kady asked. "No more microwave popcorn, thanks."

Tico looked at the two of them. "Sounds like the D-man has been keeping secrets from his pals," he said.

"She was down at the lot last night," Dion told him. "Hefty showed up too. They went on a store run for me that sounded like it got a little shaky."

Kady folded her arms across her chest. "My first ride in a flatbed tow truck," she said. "And my first flight that wasn't on an airplane."

Tico raised an eyebrow.

"Railroad crossing," Dion explained.

Tico considered that for a time, and then his mouth spread into a smile.

"Cowgirl?" he said.

"Ya, who?" replied Kady.

Dion moved closer to the truck to read the specials. A young woman in a tank top was working the window. When she turned around to speak to someone behind her in the tiny kitchen, he noticed an odd pattern of small, discolored skin contusions exposed on the back of her arm just above her elbow, four on the inside and one opposite.

He tilted his head toward Kady and lowered his voice.

"How do you suppose somebody gets bruised up like that?" he wondered.

Kady looked, and after a moment her answer came, not in words, but as a startling shy touch from behind, her hand on his triceps, softly electrifying with bashful promise until the slow tightening of the grip between her fingers and thumb became a knowing, painful squeeze of domination and impunity; a physical melding that steadily darkened in his mind from a playful first fantasy of possibility into an unspoken confession, one heart revealing itself to another with hopeful trust couched in embarrassment and shame.

When her fingers relaxed after a few seconds, he wasn't sure how many breaths he had skipped.

"Are we eating here, or what?" Tico said.

Kady stepped back from the truck, her movements jangling the ankle bracelets on her boots. Tico stared down at her feet as though formulating a theory on what the chains implied. Dion looked at her arm, imagining bruises that heal but don't go away. He brought his eyes to hers when she sniffed, but she wasn't upset or fighting back tears. She was facing the direction of the barbecue vendor, testing the air. He turned that way too.

"What are you craving?" Dion asked, his wallet still in his hand.

She sniffed again and settled upon a decision.

"I'm craving me some hot pulled pork."

"Well, yeah," Tico said, "but what do you want for lunch?"

- 44 -

Arno St. Albans, ensnared by paperwork he had been neglecting, did not get to his lunch until long past the noon hour. He ate at his desk and then went for a stroll along the corridors of the public safety building, carrying a notebook to make it look like he was doing something. On the third floor he entered a large room of desks and offices and found his way to the nameplate of Kady L'Orient on a cubicle near a window. He could hear the clack of typing and peered over her wall. She was hunched at her computer keyboard and did not look up but seemed to sense him there.

"Give me a second," she said.

The sergeant told her that there was no hurry, and at the sound of his voice her fingers stalled over the keys. She sat back on her chair and turned, looking up at him as he stood in the door opening, his hands holding the notebook over his belt buckle.

"Nice sunglasses," she said.

He touched the bridge of the glasses to reset them on his nose.

"Thanks," he answered. "A friend gave them to me, to help."

Kady nodded. "I heard about your face," she said. "Sounds like a drag."

"The doctors are still saying I'll recover."

He looked down at the folders on her desk, telling her that if it made any difference to how she might feel about talking to him, he wasn't the one who had removed the Cullen Arcade file from her stack.

She waited for him to continue.

"When I saw you last night at the impound lot, I knew I'd seen you someplace before. Then I checked the records for who had signed out the file and figured out who you were and how deep you must be getting into this thing if you're digging around down there."

"Well, that's where the body ended up," Kady reminded him. "Along the railroad track, where you guys left it."

The sergeant pulled off the sunglasses and examined the lenses for smudges in the sunlight from the window.

"That was Honest Mike," he said. "I think he got the idea from some crime show he saw on television. Sit tight on the body and see if the perpetrator returns to the scene of the crime when nothing hits the local news outlets. We didn't have much evidence or useful information to work with, so we set up some surveillance and saw one car slow down on Cesar Chavez Street in the middle of the night a couple of weeks later, but it didn't stop, and we couldn't trace it."

Kady swiveled on her chair and crossed her right leg over her left. She smoothed the hem of her sweaterdress and clasped her fingers together over her bare knee.

"Kind of like the case file?" she asked him.

St. Albans felt his good eye blink. He put the sunglasses back on. Across the room a printer wheezed as it burped out papers. A telephone bleated nearby.

"You know where it is?" he asked.

"I know the lieutenant doesn't know where it is," Kady said. "Which serves him right, from where I'm sitting. I'm just trying to do my job here, and I'm getting sidetracked by my own superiors."

The sergeant took a deep breath and told her there were reasons for the interference, though he didn't admit they weren't necessarily good ones. Then he began to wonder how she had managed to connect Honest Mike Walerius to the file.

"That clerk at the impound lot," St. Albans said. "He knows about the lieutenant and the Arcade file, and he told you?"

Kady wrinkled her nose. "I'm not going to say," she decided. "You told him last night that you don't like being played and that you weren't enjoying his game. Well, right now I'm not enjoying yours. I don't like being leaned on."

The sergeant gripped the top of the cubicle wall with one hand, finding in his voice a rising sympathy for her and an abashed regret for needing to defend himself.

"I'm not leaning on you," he said. "I only came to warn you that I feel like the kid is up to something and doesn't tell everything he knows. It sounds like maybe you're doing better with him than I am, though."

Kady let go of her knee and brought both feet to the floor. She made a thoughtful face as she peered for a moment into her computer screen, her fingers bridged together like a steeple at the tip of her nose.

"What I'm doing with him," she said, "is feeling that he doesn't know everything he tells."

Before he could ask her what she meant, she tossed him a question of her own.

"Am I seriously being told, without being told, that I'm not supposed to solve this case, even if maybe I can?"

He took a long look out the window, watching traffic passing on the nearby freeway, the sun heating his face.

"Officially, you're getting paid to solve every case that comes your way," he said finally. "Whether you can or not."

He knocked his knuckles against the cubicle wall a couple of times softly, remembering something.

"Superficially," he added, "so am I."

He nodded at her before turning around. As he crossed the room, he could hear her tapping on the keyboard, picking up where she had left off.

- 45 -

Later that evening, Shiner O'Shea said out loud what Dion Drury was thinking as he steered them in his car along University Avenue and turned a corner onto a familiar street of townhomes.

"It's here this time."

Parked beneath a glowing streetlight up the block was the city sedan assigned to Honest Mike Walerius, near the address that his wife had given to Dion.

Shiner reached for a small carton on the seat between them, saying, "Now?"

"Not now," Dion answered. "Soon, maybe. We'll see."

He pulled to the curb a few car lengths back, headlights off as he considered where he should park to allow himself a quick escape. As he was reviewing his options, two people descended the steps of a house just ahead and moved away along the sidewalk toward the city vehicle. Dion recognized Marnette Sims from the council office walking beside her boss. He aimed his phone and captured a shadowed image as the pair climbed into the sedan.

"Is that what we wanted?" Shiner asked.

Dion wasn't sure he could explain the concept of a compromising photograph, but she seemed to understand when he told her he didn't think it was enough. As the taillights on the sedan burst redly to life, Shiner pointed.

"It's leaving," she said.

Dion put the car into gear and switched on the head-lights. "We'll go along," he told her. "To see what happens."

Honest Mike at the wheel led them around the block and back onto University Avenue. Both cars kept pace with a light-rail train heading west in the median. Shin-er mimicked the warning chime and horn when the train crossed intersection traffic signals.

After passing through several cross streets, Dion saw the sedan brake to enter a small parking lot beside a low brick-storefront building. He slowed but kept going, Mar-nette and the councilman just getting out of the car as he and Shiner passed the lot entrance. He then slowed fur-ther, silently reading the signs over the darkened windows of the businesses along the street.

Dion turned the car around at the next opportunity and backtracked. Passing in the opposite direction, he saw lights suddenly glowing in the window of Capital City Coiffures. He picked up the carton on the seat beside Shin-er and handed it to her.

"Now," he said.

Shiner emptied the box onto her lap as she made a clanging bell sound again, her blustery attempt at repli-cating the train horn enhanced by a giggle and the audible scritch of paper wrappers being torn open.

- 46 -

A transit bus ablaze with lights passed on University Avenue later as Arno St. Albans watched from inside Capital City Coiffures. Water whistled from a faucet at one of the shampoo sinks along the back wall as Marnette Sims rinsed brushes and combs, the sound washing over strains of mellow jazz that drifted from two ceiling speakers.

"What makes you think this has something to do with Lauda Aplikowski?" the sergeant asked Honest Mike Walerius.

The councilman replied while gently smoothing his silver curls in front of a big wall mirror at one of the styling stations, his voice impatient and his neck slightly red against his shirt collar.

"Consider the timing," he suggested. "After our unexpectedly tepid confrontation yesterday and his dismissive response to my unsupportable threat of leverage over him, we can imagine that he might have calculated the future defensive advantage available to him if he could possess some counterbalancing leverage over me."

St. Albans thought of Corinne Nasseff and her revelation of the secret Aplikowski investment in her cantina, which sounded like leverage enough, but he wasn't going to get himself into the middle of that. When he turned from the front windows and shrugged, Honest Mike's reflection in the mirror went still, looking at him for a second before he spoke.

"Have I seen that eyewear before?"

The sergeant reached as though to scratch his forehead, partially obscuring the amber sunglasses, and nodded toward the window to change the subject.

"You said he had a camera?"

"Some type of device," Honest Mike said. "Perhaps a cellular phone. In any case, he was likely stationed there on the sidewalk for some time before we noticed him."

St. Albans glanced toward Marnette at the back of the room, and then at the councilman in the mirror.

"What were the two of you doing?"

Marnette responded with a laugh as melodic as the background music, which became more audible when she turned off the water. Honest Mike puffed himself up indignantly.

"Nothing, I assure you, that merited inclusion into any visual record," he said.

The sergeant shifted his focus again to the street outside. He could see himself in the window's reflection.

"And you're both pretty convinced that it was a guy?" he asked.

He listened as the others agreed, and then he asked them if they could tell him anything else related to the man's age or appearance. The councilman stepped from the mirror and came to stand beside him at the window.

"That is a most curious thing regarding the encounter," Honest Mike said, peering out toward the street. "The circumstances make it difficult in my memory to be more specific with details."

"How so?"

Honest Mike touched his finger to his face, drawing invisible lines that started on his forehead and crisscrossed over his cheekbones and nose to end on his chin.

"Bandages," he said. "Small ones, such as those purchased in a packet from a pharmacy. Very much in the fashion favored for holdups by the petty hoodlums of our youth."

He was stroking his upper lip, his voice softening with apparent wonder.

"Do you remember?" he asked.

St. Albans frowned into the passing traffic outside, his limbs stiffened by a puffy indignation of their own.

He remembered.

- 47 -

People walking through the lounge at the Matterhorn slowed when they passed the bar, taking long glances at Shiner O'Shea as she leisurely twirled back and forth on a stool, her cheeks crosshatched with bandages. Evan Arcade poured her a glass of soda, giving a look to Dion Drury, who was standing off to one side and fumbling with his phone.

"Here, let me do it," Evan said, holding out a hand.

She took the phone and stared down at the images on the display.

"Who are these people, anyway?" she asked.

Dion climbed onto a stool beside Shiner.

"One is our Tenth Ward representative on the city council," he said.

"The guy who got you your job?"

"That's the man," Dion said. "The woman is his newest legislative aide. Kind of a dish."

Shiner blew thin bubbles through a straw into her soda and hummed like a kazoo, the tune something Dion recalled singing during fourth-grade music class. "Fifteen Miles on the Erie Canal."

Evan asked him where he wanted the images sent, and he pointed to a number scrolled onto the screen.

"His wife," he answered.

Evan raised an eyebrow. "What have you gotten yourself into?" she wanted to know.

He touched his tongue against the corner of his mouth for a second and then answered. "The Cullen Arcade case file."

Evan finished with his phone and set it on the bar in front of him. She grabbed a towel and wiped her hands, looking thoughtful.

"Kady," she said, like an answer to a question she had just asked herself.

"Nice ring," said Shiner.

"Your new connection with her," Evan asked Dion. "It's all about the murder?"

Dion picked up his phone and fingered the screen. The list of recent contacts included Kady, so he supposed that qualified as being connected, even if he couldn't say exactly what that meant or if it was all about anything. The only thing he knew for certain was that his discovery of the file had become something like stepping through a doorway that opened to a chute, his past hurtling down first and pulling him with it. There was nothing to be done but ride out the fall to whatever landing awaited. He spoke without looking up.

"Everything has been about the murder since we were kids," he said. "If you haven't figured that out by now, those therapy sessions you're always talking about have been a waste of your time and money."

When he raised his gaze, Evan was regarding him with surprise.

"Wow," she said. "I've never heard you say anything like that before. Our cute lady cop must have touched a nerve."

Dion realized he was breathing heavily, surprised by

the sudden surge of heat to his throat. He swallowed it down and waited for a minute before opening his mouth again.

"You said the other day Brillo Ziemer would tell you things you didn't want to know when he was hanging out down here," Dion said to his sister. "Did he ever give you a sense of how things were between him and our dad?"

Evan settled into thought as she rubbed her left ear, the line of diamond studs that rimmed it bright against her painted fingernails.

Dion continued. "The reason I'm asking is that I figured out Brillo was familiar with the place where the body was found. The cops could tell he was dumped there, that the killing happened someplace else. It makes me wonder if maybe Brillo had something to do with it."

Evan shook her head. "Brillo usually talked about our mom," she said. "I think he had a bit of a thing for her that kind of carried over to me, like I was supposed to understand him because of how he felt about her, and I'd say he was frustrated that she probably never felt the same about him. I know he thought that Ellie deserved better than what she had going on at home with her husband."

"And us," added Dion, feeling the dry pressure in his throat returning.

Evan poured more soda for Shiner. "You're remembering how much fun it wasn't," Evan said to him, as his mind generated resentful images of their father and the regrettably frequent shockwaves of his flattened palm crashing upon the kitchen table to declare an imperious end to any dinner discussion or opinion his judgmental nature could not abide, instilling a silence of confused, humiliated suffering and an unforgivable legacy of intolerance that had diminished everyone in the family, especially himself.

"He was so mad and jumpy," Dion recalled. "I could never figure it out as a kid, all the tension in the house, what was wrong with everybody all the time."

"Don't forget the fear and shame," Evan reminded him. "My therapist says our folks had high school sweetheart syndrome, where a couple gets together too young. One grows emotionally and the other doesn't, or they grow in different directions, or not at all, and they end up angry and resenting each other for what they think they're missing, but neither knows how to live without the other. Totally screws them up. And their kids, by association."

She picked up Shiner's soda and took a sip. Shiner grabbed the straw and buzzed air at her.

"Maybe he just knew inside that he was going to die young," Dion mused. "Made him mad at the world and us too."

"Maybe he knew that he deserved to die young." Evan wiped a glass against her shirt. "We could ask my therapist. Come along to my next appointment."

"No thanks," he said. "I'm afraid I might like it."

Evan offered him Shiner's soda. Dion took a swallow.

"Tag along with Kady then," Evan suggested. "For one of her sessions."

Dion looked at her. "Your new connection with her?" he said. "It's all about therapists?"

"The three of us could go see one together," Evan said. "Share a couch."

"Wouldn't that be interesting."

She set down the glass, eyeing him with a suddenly playful smile. "Wouldn't it, though?"

Shiner had the straw in the soda again, blowing musical bubbles. Dion smoothed back his hair, entertaining a thought he felt slightly guilty to share.

"What Brillo told you about Ellie deserving better than what she was getting at home," he said. "You think she ever went looking?"

"I would have," Evan said, not needing to think.

He knew he didn't need to say that he would have too.

- 48 -

Arno St. Albans was pleased to find the kitchen at the Amor Abrasadora still open when he got there. He scanned the room, searching unsuccessfully for Corinne Nasseff. He was hungry, but first things first. He headed toward her office in the back and saw her in the hallway, coming out. As he passed the pool table, he heard a familiar voice beneath the blaring of the big televisions over the bar. He turned and saw the sewer crew foreman and the Von Hanson kid paused in a game, picking at a plate of potato-skin appetizers that rested on a shelf above a stand of cue sticks along the wall.

"Sergeant," Tico Tocopilla greeted cheerily, holding up a skin as though making a ceremonial toast. "Hefty and me are in a serious battle here. You want to take on the winner?"

St. Albans reached for a cube of blue chalk on the table's siderail, then set it back down.

"No thanks," he said, blowing chalk dust from his fingers. "If I wanted to take on the two of you, it'd be over at the Ziemer place, where the big guy here would probably be taking a huge Frankenstein shit."

He pointed at Hefty before going on.

"And you," he said, turning his focus to Tico, "would be taking a picture."

In the bright light above the pool table, the pair appeared to blanch, but only for a moment, their faces going defensively stupid.

Hefty said, "What place?"

"What picture?" Tico added.

The sergeant shook his head in irritation. "Goddamn jokers," he muttered, just as Corinne came nearer.

"No, seriously," Tico said, biting into the skin. "Why would I want to take a picture of Brillo's house?"

St. Albans brought his hands to his face as though aiming a camera. "Not of," he said, and then mimed picking up one of the numbered billiard balls. "From."

From the expressions of confusion they exchanged, he wondered for a moment if maybe they really didn't know what he was talking about, but then Hefty's eyebrows went into a slow rise. The big kid adjusted the bill of his baseball cap and spoke to Tico quietly, but loud enough for the sergeant to hear.

"The D-man."

Corinne stepped over in time to hear too. She looked up from the cell phone in her hand and stopped beside St. Albans, her eyes fixed on Hefty in dawning recognition.

"That's a whisper I've heard before, kiddo," she said. "You're the lookout, aren't you?"

Tico and the sergeant both turned.

"Lookout?" St. Albans said. "For what?"

Corinne chuckled and held up the phone for him to see. On the screen looped a short video of Marnette Sims in a brightly colored smock sweeping the floor of Capital City Coiffures, while at her elbow Honest Mike Walerius, wrapped to his chin in a protective floral-print cape that billowed over his chair, appeared to doze beneath the hooded bonnet of a commercial hair dryer that encapsulated most of his head, looking like Whistler's mother's sister.

"For the demon," Corinne said, before smiling wider with an afterthought and repeating herself. "My demon, I mean."

- 49 -

After the desk officer at the public safety building confirmed that Dion Drury was a certified civilian employee of the police, she gave him the interoffice mail envelope he had requested. Dion used her pen to scrawl the destination on an open line and then stuffed the envelope full. After he handed the envelope and pen back to her, he watched her place the mailer into a basket filled with others. Then, apparently deciding she needed more room, she gathered all of them into her arms and carried them out of sight into an adjoining office. When she left, he shouldered his way out the main door to the parking lot.

Back in his car and driving toward the river, he found himself contemplating the late evening and the way that downtown thrummed in two octaves once the sun went down. The boisterous islands of nightlife around restaurants, hotels, and the sports and arts complexes rang with the beat of chorused voices on crowded bright sidewalks, while the numerous dim, desolate blocks between vibrated with menace along the cold facades of office towers in overnight mode.

Secured residential buildings implied the contradiction of apartment dwellers surrendering to the desire, and sequestered fear, of a dense urban lifestyle. They had coveted social entertainment within walking distance, but the treks beyond their barricaded enclaves were likely to prove more darkly exhilarating than the destinations, their routes nervously enlivened by the disquieting presence of a furtive pedestrian populace drawn to the camouflage of the city core and exercising the right to be visible and inconvenient.

Waiting at a traffic signal, Dion was forced to keep his foot on the brake pedal when a disheveled couple, sharing the handle of an ancient aluminum picnic cooler that swung between them, ambled into the crosswalk just as the light went green. They stopped to adjust their grip, holding up their free hands to keep him at bay, a headlight tableau of overstressed life hanging on by its fingernails— bleeding-out, disregarded, and downtrodden souls whose one claim to power rested in a regrettably unmarketable capacity to annoy.

When their hands rose to ward off his car, his hands went to his eyes. He could still remember the pressure on his arm where Kady had squeezed him that morning and the tumble of thoughts her touch had generated for the rest of his day.

He brought his palms down to the steering wheel and watched the walkers move slowly past. He wondered where they were headed, and where he was headed himself, and why he was so suddenly bothered with wondering.

As the signal went yellow, he put his foot to the accelerator and drove on through, his mind too unsettled to have any tolerance for caution.

- 50 -

Arno St. Albans vigorously stabbed a fork into a tamale while listening to Corinne Nasseff across the table. She was grinning at the video on her phone, still looking pleased with herself. Tico Tocopilla and Hefty Von Hanson had quietly resumed their pool game nearby, glancing over every few minutes like they expected something to happen.

"Bandages?" Corinne said to the sergeant. "That's pretty clever."

"He got the idea from me," St. Albans said. "That's how I knew it was him. The way you've been talking lately, it occurred to me that unless the kid had his own agenda, you and Lauda Aplikowski were the most likely to want to put the screws to Honest Mike. So, I thought I'd dance with you first."

Corinne sipped at a bottle of flavored water. When she saw that he was waiting for her to tell him more of her story, she spoke again. "I can see now that it was stupid to go off on the kid's little gal pal in the council office like I did," she said. "I assumed the chick was the hot new aide I'd been hearing about, and I'd been angry over it for a few days. Once I got started, I got a little bit mean."

"I think she can take care of herself," the sergeant said. "She's a cop."

Corinne blinked. "Christ," she cried. "I threatened to shoot up her car like I'd done to the walrus."

St. Albans stopped chewing. "The attack on his car?" he said. "That was you?"

She took a breath and shrugged, saying it had seemed like a good idea at the time, and that she was surprised no one had suspected her.

"We figured it might have been a random thing for that neighborhood," the sergeant said. "When the boss heard that the file was gone from the front seat, though, he had an idea that there was more to it. I didn't think of you going ballistic over his new aide. If he thought of it, he didn't tell me."

Corinne wanted to know what file he was talking about, and he told her that it was the record of an old criminal case.

"You didn't take it?" he asked.

"No," she answered. "I just looked in the windows to make sure there wasn't anybody in the car before I opened fire."

St. Albans tapped his fork against his tongue, thinking. Corinne resumed her tale of the encounter in Honest Mike's office.

"Like I was saying, I came down pretty hard on the cute girl, and when her friend heard from her what I'd done to the car, he came to see me," she said. "He was thinking that maybe he could use the information as leverage with me."

"Leverage for what?"

"For whatever," she answered, laughing a little at the memory. "That's what he said, and I knew what he meant. It gave me the idea for this."

She held up the phone with the video still playing. "Well, not quite this, exactly," she admitted with a louder snicker. "I was thinking more of something like the two of them holding hands at a restaurant. This is even better, in a way. The walrus looks like a walrus. He'd hate having anyone see him looking this ridiculous, so now I've got something to threaten him with."

"You plan to send him the video, so he knows?"

Corinne nodded. St. Albans took another bite of his tamale, watching her think and hoping she was close to finishing with him, but she wasn't. She leaned closer, elbows resting on the table.

"You've got leverage too, in a way," she pointed out. "Knowledge is power, and you know some things he doesn't."

He reached for the glass of beer beside his plate and leaned farther back. "You realize that you're making me your accomplice against my will by telling me all this," the sergeant said.

Corinne brought her voice to a murmur. In the light from the pool table her face was soft with shadows. The easy smack of rolling balls slowly striking each other made him think of the sound of her teeth coming together when she smiled.

"We both know how long that will last," she said. "You'll clear your conscience by reporting everything to my husband, and the only effect on me is that I won't have to bother telling him myself. I'll still have the upper hand on him because now he'll have to wonder what else I might be up to that he doesn't know about."

St. Albans took a slurp of beer and licked his lip, telling her that at the moment, she appeared to have the upper hand on everyone.

"You and your demon, both," he added.

Her mouth puckered thoughtfully. "You know, I hadn't factored him in," she said. "I suppose he knows enough to cause a few of us trouble if he gets ambitious. Especially with that pretty cop as a wingman. He's probably worth keeping an eye on."

"An eye," the sergeant agreed. "Not hands, though, if that's what you've got in mind. It wouldn't sit well with the boss."

"Oh, please," Corinne said. "You wouldn't cover for me now that you're my unwilling accomplice? Or are you thinking more about how it would sit with you?"

St. Albans peered at her over the rim of his glass.

"I am the egg man," he said.

"I know you are," she responded with a weary sigh, shaking her head as though she'd been hearing it all her life. "But what am I?"

A scuffing of boots on the floor tiles announced that Hefty had wandered over, big fingers clutching a cue stick as he stood fidgeting beside an empty chair while Tico reset a rack of balls on the pool table.

"I'm sorry," Hefty said to the sergeant, taking several seconds to get it all out. "About the thing at the house, you know?"

St. Albans saw on the big kid's face an expression of such abject chagrin that the sergeant immediately grasped the pained meaning behind the apology and felt his own cheeks flaring hot, reliving every recent memory of seeing reflections of himself in mirrors and windows and imagining that others saw him as some deformed mutant. His vision began to cloud, and he quickly reached for a napkin as he set aside his beer.

"I'm sorry for what I said, kid," he mumbled as he rubbed his frozen eyelid. "It wasn't very nice of me."

The sergeant got up from his chair then, telling the others that he'd be back, and hurried toward the restrooms. As he stepped away, he could hear Hefty with forced cheer gamely struggling to relieve the awkward silence left behind.

"So," the big kid was saying to Corinne, "how long have you been Lebanese?"

- 51 -

Headlights on the barge channel road caused Dion Drury to turn toward the impound lot office windows a few minutes into his work shift. As the approaching car slowed and came into the reach of the outside lights, he recognized it and pushed the gate button to let the driver through. Dion positioned himself behind the service counter as Arno St. Albans parked and came inside, the sergeant climbing each stair to a rhythm of one pronounced breath, finally resting for a few seconds when he reached the top of the landing, one hand on the steel railing. Light coming through the kitchen doorway illuminated the softly tinted sunglasses on his face. With the other hand, he held out a small white paper sack.

"French fries from Corinne's place, if you're interested," he said. "Your buddies, Tico and the Von Hanson kid, were there. They told me you like onion rings, but I like fries."

"I like free," Dion said.

St. Albans took a gaze around the office and toward the kitchen door to peek through the window there.

"I'm alone," Dion told him.

The sergeant made clear that he wasn't looking for people. "I thought I might spot an old photograph of Brillo Ziemer," he said. "And maybe a face bandage or two."

Dion puffed out a long breath. The police radio on the desk in the corner frizzled static in the background. After half a minute, he found his voice.

"I guess it didn't take long for that news to break," he observed.

"Welcome to walrus world," St. Albans replied with an expression that Dion interpreted as a smirk. "Where secrets don't like to stay secret."

Dion pushed the button to unlock the kitchen entry.

"Come on around," he invited the sergeant. "There's coffee next to the sink if you want some."

St. Albans took a seat on one of the tall stools behind the counter and stared out the big windows at the expanse of vehicles under the overhead lights outside. Dion asked if Honest Mike Walerius tended to hold a grudge.

"The boss knows his wife can be persuasive, so you should be okay," St. Albans reasoned, chewing a french fry and holding out the sack for Dion to share. "He'll appreciate that you were just trying to get an edge for yourself. His mind works the same way."

Dion dug out a couple of fries and gave a thought to his visit in Corinne's office and the dull charge he'd felt coursing through the hairs on his lower back as he stood with his arms in the air while she ogled him from behind.

"She was playing me," he said.

"There's a lot of that going around," the sergeant pointed out. "Like with your two pals. I know damn well that at least one of them was inside the Ziemer place the other day, and maybe you were too, not that I'm likely to get anybody to admit it."

Dion didn't say anything. St. Albans answered the silence with an irritated sniff.

"You told me that you didn't have a key," he reminded Dion.

Dion chewed quietly as he weighed the possible consequences of what he decided to say next.

"We didn't need one."

This time the sergeant burbled out a laugh. "Sounds like welcome to West Seventh Street," he said.

Dion then related the recent details behind the stolen building materials and their sudden appearance in Brillo Ziemer's garage. The sergeant listened without comment until Dion finished.

"You can swear that Tico wasn't involved in the original thefts?" St. Albans asked.

"He came in later," Dion said. "Got caught in the middle of doing a favor for a friend. Not exactly on the up-and-up, but not the crime of the century, either."

The sergeant ate another french fry and nodded.

"Okay," he said. "I suppose we can live with that."

The room went quiet then, calm with the low buzz of distant industrial sounds carried in from the outside speakers and the intermittent chirping of the police radio, Dion suddenly aware of a sensation rising within himself, an illogical and uncomfortable anxiety about the presence of the older man that stirred memories of both the hair-trigger tension that had radiated from his father and the martyred indifference of his uncle as guardian later on, the frustrating relationships of misconnection and unease that had left him always wondering how he could have been so persistently unlikable to them both.

The room seemed to shrink around him then, and Dion felt a need to move, but St. Albans blocked the path to the kitchen. Just as Dion turned to shuffle toward the nearest corner to make more space between them, the sergeant pointed to something out beyond the big windows and spoke.

"Your gal pal investigator working her cold case," he was saying. "She told you that the body was found out there along the railroad, and that I was one of the original officers assigned to the incident?"

"I think I'm up to speed, yeah."

"More than she is, maybe," St. Albans said, "if you've been holding on to that case file from the city car like I'm starting to suspect. Does she think that you have it? Is that what brought her down here?"

Dion clasped his arms around himself.

"She knows that I had it," he said. "Where it is now and what brought her down here would be hard for me to say because I'm not certain about either one right this minute."

The sergeant looked confused. "I've made myself pretty clear that the walrus wants that file, right?"

"I used to think a lot of things were pretty clear," Dion said. "Lately, I'm not so sure."

"That sounds like something I'd say," St. Albans replied. "Maybe you can tell me this, anyway. In the old photograph from Ziemer's album, I figured out that one of the guys was him, and another was our cold-case homicide victim that we found out here in the snow." He pointed again toward the railroad track out beyond the fence. "Assuming that you've seen the picture, do you have an idea who the third guy was?" he asked.

Dion blew out a breath, pressure in his chest easing as he replied. "Tico's dad."

The sergeant pushed his sunglasses up over his forehead, one eye wide, the other eerily wider.

"Tico's dad?" he said. "Any significance to that?"

"Not to me."

"How about to your investigator sidekick?"

Dion told him that she didn't know about the photograph, and that he wasn't sure that she needed to.

St. Albans rubbed the back of his hand against his nose for a minute.

"I suppose you know what you're doing with her, but if it was me, I'd be careful," he said. "Don't let yourself be fooled by the pixie look."

Dion felt himself tense up again and asked what the other man was trying to say.

"Only that she has some history," the sergeant answered.

Dion said he didn't want to hear.

St. Albans said he wasn't surprised.

- 52 -

When Kady got to her cubicle at the public safety building in the morning, the tray on her desk for incoming material was stacked high. She set her shoulder bag on the floor and adjusted her slacks and the brocaded vest over her satin blouse before settling onto her chair. She began sorting through the papers, discovering that the height of the stack was caused mostly by one overstuffed interoffice mail envelope with no listed sender. She braced herself for what she feared might be an unwelcome surprise as she brought the envelope onto her lap and opened the flap. Peering inside, though, her lips soon stretched into a smile.

"Ha," she said out loud.

She reached in and began pulling out folders, methodically reassembling the Cullen Arcade case file in its spot on her desk. The last piece to emerge made her chuckle to herself as she placed it beside the folders and the mail envelope. She recognized it as a flat pouch of unfired microwave popcorn.

Swiveling on her chair, she leaned back as she looked out the window to the sky over downtown and the traffic moving on the nearby freeway. She stayed that way for a while, hands clasped over her belly as her mind drifted into ruminations on speed and motion, of time and intention, of yearning and fear.

After a few minutes she began stroking two fingertips

over the front placket of her blouse, finally sliding them into a gap between buttons to absently probe along her ribcage, where they closed around a wispy copper chain, easing into a slow rhythm of gentle but insistent tugs.

- 53 -

Honest Mike Walerius stared into his cell-phone screen, elbows on the desk in his office suite on the fourth floor of the city hall and county courthouse building downtown. Marnette Sims stood behind his chair, peering over his shoulder as the video he was watching played out. She held one fist against her nose, struggling, it seemed to Arno St. Albans, to suppress a snicker. The sergeant sat himself halfway onto the windowsill nearest the desk and folded his arms, pondering her outfit. One of her sandaled feet was visibly poking from the hem of a flowing floral skirt, a silver toe ring matching the sheen of the councilman's curls. Honest Mike closed the screen and put the phone into the pocket of his suit jacket, grumbling.

"That horrid depiction is in no way representative of my actual appearance."

"You mean that was you in the video?" Marnette teased as she slipped around the side of the desk, a motion in tune with the rustle of fabric sweeping against her legs.

As she moved in a slow glide toward the door, she turned to St. Albans.

"'Horrid' sounds harsh, but that clip got me thinking that your hair could use a little help," she said. "Let me know if you want to meet some evening at the shop."

The gazes of both men followed her out of the room, then met one another.

"This demon of Corinne's," Honest Mike said as he crinkled his eyes vexedly behind the blue lenses of his eyeglasses. "Was he not supposed to be a demon of ours?"

"He still is," said St. Albans. "But like you put it the other day, the kid has an expansive mind. He's playing a couple of hands at the same time while seeing how the cards fall. I told him you'd be able to relate to that."

The councilman's expression softened.

"I would acknowledge a grudging respect for his resourcefulness," he said. "With the caveat that he should understand I will countenance no further friendly fire ridicule on his part."

St. Albans told him not to worry about it. "The kid knows better than to stick his neck out twice," the sergeant said as he looked through the doorway to the outer office where Marnette was feeding papers into the copier.

"Does your shampoo-and-set buddy out there have any idea what this business with the video and the bullet wounds in your car are all about?" he asked.

Honest Mike shook his head emphatically. "She does not, nor shall you apprise her. For the moment, my trusted legislative aide has attributed the unflattering footage to the histrionic contentiousness of local politics, and the targeting of my car to the vagaries of violence endemic to her neighborhood. I am content to not disabuse her of those convenient misconceptions."

St. Albans reached into his pocket for his eye drops. He removed his sunglasses and set them on the windowsill, then uncapped the drops. He spoke as he raised his face toward the ceiling and aimed the bottle.

"Speaking of misconceptions," he began as he used a finger to wink his frozen eye.

"Yes?"

"There's another thing that Corinne told me about," the sergeant said. "Besides setting up the video and putting air holes in your car. One that I'm not supposed to tell you."

"All the more reason I should hear it then."

St. Albans nodded and pocketed the eye drops as he summarized her revelation of Lauda Aplikowski's financial involvement in the cantina.

"That's why your threat to push her into his business went nowhere with him," he said. "He's already knee deep in hers. With documentation to protect his investment."

Honest Mike sat back on his chair, nodding thoughtfully toward the door for some time. St. Albans could see Marnette looking back from the outer office with a subtle smile that hinted she assumed the men were talking about her. When the councilman spoke again, he sounded menacingly unperturbed, his thought wheels turning.

"Your information regarding this labyrinthian congress between my wife and the Aplikowski operation is most enlightening," he said. "It suggests that there may yet exist some opportunity to impose myself upon the situation."

St. Albans put his sunglasses back on, saying, "You do have something on each of them now, for whatever that's worth. Lauda Aplikowski might think you still owe him for greasing Corinne's license approval, but he also went behind your back to get his fingers into the pie as part of his deal with her, and she kept you in the dark about it."

The councilman jabbed a finger toward the ceiling as he worked his way mentally around the idea.

"His discomfort with the inquiries into the Cullen Arcade killing and ire for my lack of intervention so far remain the most valuable factors within my knowledge," he said. "He would not be fearful without reason. If our young investigator remains unwavering in her resolve to ferret out some actionable information, she may create an environment in which his defenses falter."

St. Albans turned toward the window and looked out at the river, watching as a towboat in the channel churned hard upstream against the current, loaded barges clustered before it, gliding low on the water.

"If we stay out of her way, she might just dig up something useful, which is more than you or I were ever able to do," he said.

"It appears, then, that she has gained your esteem."

"Any headway she makes on this thing could be big for her career," he reflected. "Take her a long way from where she started out."

"You evoke a surprisingly paternal perspective," Honest Mike said. "I am very nearly moved to tears."

St. Albans touched a finger softly to the glass, saying that sometimes in life a person meets another who brings out a protective impulse.

"Like your wife with you," he said, then made a show of stroking his chin in mock thought. "Or maybe not so much like that, you think?"

The councilman coughed out a sound like a drain clearing.

"Corinne," he said, "will discover that your briefing this morning has neutralized any fear of her weaponizing the demeaning video she commissioned. She overestimates both my vanity and her advantage."

"She'll be disappointed."

Honest Mike declared himself unsympathetic as he sat forward and unfolded a newspaper on his desk, spreading open the sports pages.

"She should necessarily attribute any ill feelings to her own misguided decisions," he said. "Rather like you, I should say, in keeping with the uncharitable but accurate spirit of Marnette's evaluation of your personal grooming."

The sergeant, frowning, ran a hand slowly over his hair.

- 54 -

Dion Drury woke up early in the afternoon to voices. By the time he convinced himself that he needed to tell Shiner to turn down the volume on the living-room television, he heard footsteps in the hallway outside his bedroom and a squeak as the doorknob turned, Shiner pushing the door open to make an announcement.

"She brought popcorn."

He rolled against his blankets to squint at her in the half light. "What?"

Shiner raised an arm and pointed toward the kitchen.

Dion watched her walk away, then got out of the bed and pulled on pants and a shirt from the chair in the corner. He padded barefoot into the hall, smoothing back his hair with one hand. In the kitchen, he found Kady standing near the back door, looking embarrassed. Shiner, still in her white work smock, stood at the microwave oven reading the directions on the popcorn packet.

"Sorry about this," Kady said to him. "I wasn't sure about your sleeping schedule."

Dion blinked a couple times and went over to the sink. "Some days there isn't one," he said as he filled a glass with water and took a drink. "Like today."

The microwave awakened in a series of beeps as Shiner worked the keypad. Dion gestured toward the square table in the center of the room and pulled out a chair for himself. Kady took the chair across from him, lowering her shoulder bag onto the floor as she sat down. Threads woven into her dark vest sparkled beneath the ceiling light.

"I like your outfit," Dion said, scratching whisker stubble on his neck. "Sorry about mine."

"She's Kady," Shiner told him. "The name from your papers."

"Thanks for introducing me," Dion replied. "Do you remember from the papers what kind of name we decided it was?"

Shiner paused as she opened the microwave door.

"A nice name," she recalled.

"That's right," Dion said. "A very nice name."

He looked at Kady, and she looked back. Shiner clunked the microwave door closed and stood peering through the glass as the machine hummed. When the popping of kernels began, Shiner mimicked the sound, making a song out of it.

"We should go outside," Dion suggested, gazing out through the window above the sink. "I could stand some sun."

When the popcorn was ready, they poured it into a big bowl and carried it out the back door. Dion sat down on the top step of the small porch outside, his toes resting two risers below. Kady settled next to him with their hips not quite touching, but close enough for him to feel like they were. Shiner stood on the narrow sidewalk at the base of the stairs, holding the bowl toward them.

"Thanks," Kady said to her, scooping a handful.

Dion plucked a kernel from Kady's palm and let it soften between his teeth. He could hear passing traffic on

Randolph Avenue out front, and the jangling collar tags of the neighbor's dog as it roamed the backyard next door. Shiner took the bowl to the fence and called the dog over.

"Your sister told me a little about what happened to your roommate," Kady said through a chew. "When you were eight."

"I didn't see it," Dion said, swallowing. "I was in the yard. I heard it, though. The gunshot."

"Must have been scary."

He nodded as he thought back to the day.

"Crazy scary. Blood, cops, the ambulance. Kids screaming and crying, my mother screaming, her mother screaming, all the neighbors coming out." He picked another kernel from her hand. "My father had to go down to the police station later," he remembered. "But I guess they didn't do much to him."

Kady nodded toward Shiner. "Does she have a memory of it?"

"Nothing she's ever shown," he said. "I don't think she knows that she was different before. She's just happy as she is, working with the lunch ladies at our old elementary school and doing her puzzle books."

"How'd she end up living with you?"

Dion sucked in a breath. "She doesn't exactly," he replied. "Not all the time, anyway. She's with her folks quite a bit. My place is sort of like a getaway when they all need a break from each other."

"They must be very forgiving people," Kady said. "Given your shared history."

Dion extended his arms in a broad, groaning wake-up stretch that made her duck slightly forward out of his way.

It brought on a yawn as he brought his elbows back to his thighs and resumed talking.

"One thing she always did remember was that I was her friend," he said. "They didn't want to take that away from her."

At the fence, Shiner tossed popcorn. The dog danced after it.

"In high school, I'd drive her to games and stuff if she needed a ride," Dion went on. "Her parents were glad to have her out socializing, and most of our classmates were good about having her around. When I got out on my own, she started asking for sleepovers, so we tried it and things worked out. They're on some European river cruise right now. When they get back, she'll go live with them again until she wants to come back here."

"When she misses you."

He shook his head, smiling toward Shiner and the dog. "When she misses my friends and what passes for my social life," he said. He wrapped his hands around his knees and talked toward his toes. "Lunch with you downtown yesterday was a definite improvement, by the way."

He turned his face toward Kady just as she stuck out her tongue to stab a kernel in her mouth, her eyes meeting his as he watched her draw it back slowly through her lips.

"We should go on a date some night," he told her.

"You work nights."

"Not every night."

She looked down at her shoes and grew quiet. Dion leaned over until their shoulders touched.

"I can hear you thinking about it," he said.

She slid her arm his way, offering more popcorn. "I'm

thinking somebody could get hurt," she responded.

He spooned a few kernels from her cupped hand, his fingertips pressing across her palm with a slow, purposeful optimism.

"That's why you came over today and woke me up?"

She didn't say anything, just scooted sideways on the step, moving a couple of inches away from him, but then turning and tucking her feet onto the riser behind his legs so that her ankles rested tight and friendly against his calves. He didn't say anything either for a while, trying to enjoy the feeling for as long as possible, knowing from experience that it would last only for those brief moments of hope just before grateful surprise succumbs, sadly and most always, to a suspicion that it can't be real. After a minute, he said, "Maybe you should tell me what's going on."

She finished the rest of her popcorn and folded her hands in her lap.

"You know what the cop culture is like," she began. "It's a very macho working environment. When you're my size and you look like me, you can't really pull that off, so at the training academy and my first few years on patrol, I went the mascot route instead. Class clown, everybody's buddy and all that." She paused for a rueful breath. "I kind of let it get away from me," she said.

Dion could feel her feet rocking almost imperceptibly against his legs, working on his mind, softening his heart to the blow she was obviously building toward.

"I was just trying to be one of the guys," she said. "Trying to fit in, you know?"

Shiner was giggling at the fence, the dog bouncing in loopy circles on the other side, snatching tossed popcorn out of the air. Dion watched and thought of the sergeant at the impound lot the night before, of the older man's observation about being careful. He cleared his throat quietly, the persistent slow motion of her feet against him pumping heat up into his jaw when he found the words he wanted.

"How many of these guys did you manage to fit in?"

He heard her take a long inhale before she answered. "They weren't all guys."

An old pickup truck from down the block rattled up the alley, the neighbor extending a slow wave to them as she passed the yard. Dion watched the truck go out of sight behind his garage and tapped his teeth together lightly in thought.

"I guess Hefty and I were right," he said. "About my sister and you. You really are her type."

"Your uncle told me and her that I'm your type."

Dion looked at her. "Just how much time have you been spending at the Matterhorn?" he wondered.

Kady raised her clasped fingers and hung them gently over his shoulder, leaning on him.

"Enough to disappoint your sister and make us both feel bad about it," she answered. "I got a sense from the way she was reading me that this kind of thing between the two of you has happened before."

"Maybe once or twice," Dion said. "Nothing too tragic. Nothing that was going anywhere for either of us."

The dog barked. Shiner barked back and threw more popcorn its way. Dion felt Kady's breath closing in on his neck.

"Are you sure you want to try going somewhere with me, knowing where I've been?" she asked him.

His eyes on the happy pair at the fence, he reached up to his shoulder and covered her hands with one of his own. When she hooked a pinky finger into his, it made his mouth move.

"Haven't you always been here?"

Then her chin was on his hand, her knees tight under his, her body growing itself into him there on the top step.

"That is the most romantic thing anyone has ever said to me, guy or girl," she said seriously.

"Don't count my sister out yet," Dion said.

"What do you mean?"

"Evangeline is competitive," he told her. "She's not going to give up on you after only a couple of tries, no matter how she thinks I'm doing. So be prepared."

He could feel her slip a finger free, and then a nail streaking the skin behind his ear.

"You think she'll hit on me again?"

"I would," he said. "I am right now."

"If she does, will you be jealous?"

"I will," he said. "But that's only fair. She'll say she saw you first, and that will give her some incentive to push back."

Dion sensed a pressure above his collarbone as she moved her chin, her eyeglasses brushing his cheek, and he realized that she was looking past him toward Shiner.

"What about your old schoolmate there?" Kady said.

"What about her?"

"She can go with the flow, whatever happens?"

The dog was turning circles again in the adjacent yard, yapping. Shiner was holding the popcorn bowl above her head and twirling circles of her own.

"You can see for yourself," Dion said. "She lives in the flow."

"She's never gotten clingy with you?"

"Not really."

"Never made your girlfriends jealous?"

Dion had to think about that for half a minute before saying, "More like inhibited, sometimes."

Kady raised an eyebrow. "Why inhibited?"

His thumb stretched to lightly toggle one tapered lock of her spiky sideburns as he explained.

"She likes to watch."

- 55 -

The evening rush hour traffic on University Avenue was just beginning to ease as Arno St. Albans let his head loll back over the shampoo sink at Capital City Coiffures. A waterproof apron over his chest made crinkling sounds when he moved on the reclining chair. Marnette Sims leaned close against him as she reached to adjust the faucet, the spray of warm water loud over the indistinct conversation between another stylist and client across the room. When Marnette slowed the flow and turned the jets toward his head, he became aware of her fingers furrowing across his scalp as she wetted him down. He brought his hands together over his belly and relaxed.

After she cut the water off, she squirted soap from a bottle into one palm and worked both hands into a lather that she began kneading into his hair. The gentle pressure of her fingertips meandered in lazy waves that curled and expanded on him for several slow minutes in a sensory conversation between her knuckles and his brain, his thoughts drifting off with a slackness that matched his tongue, every sultry tug behind his ears or pinch against the back of his neck quickening the pace of his lungs and feeling like the metaphysical definition of perpetual bliss.

As she worked, he could sense her body brushing his shoulder and imagined for a moment that her breathing had joined into a conspiratorial rhythm with his. When he glanced up in his sleepy euphoria, her hands singing to him through his hair, he was disheartened to discover that her face was turned toward the window, eyes focused upon the street outside. He realized from her vapid expression that she was working on him by rote, her lips thin with the same stoic resignation of hapless souls at a light-rail station defenselessly awaiting the arrival of an overdue train in bad weather.

He instantly regretted looking at her and seeing the disinterest on her face. He tried to hide the dim humiliation of his fantasy by willing himself invisible with a tight squeeze of his eyelids.

One of them refused to take the hint.

- 56 -

Dion Drury unloaded the dishwasher as Kady L'Orient hunched forward on a chair beside his kitchen table and studied the old photograph from Brillo Ziemer's house. The murmur of an advertising jingle played on the television in the living room came, while Shiner O'Shea sang along.

"This Ziemer guy," Kady said. "Did I see his name in the case file, from one of the interviews?"

Dion piled warm dinner plates onto the counter, saying Brillo had given a routine statement to investigators after being identified as the business partner of Cullen Arcade. He relayed to her what Tico Tocopilla had revealed about the early days of the three painters in the photograph, of the thievery that had continued after Tico's father had walked away, and of the cache of looted building materials that had recently moved between Tico's garage and Brillo's.

"I told the sergeant about Tico moving the stuff around," he said. "But that was all I told him."

"He still doesn't know who you are?"

Dion shrugged, saying, "I guess he's not the detective you are."

Kady looked up and gave him half a smile.

"Do you think their illegal side business had something to do with what happened to your dad?"

"I'm not sure what to think," Dion answered. "But it bugs me that the picture shows Brillo worked on the chemical plant on the barge channel road, and that the body ended up close to there."

He grabbed a handful of flatware and clattered the pieces into an organizer in an open drawer.

"It also bugs me that Evangeline told me yesterday that she thought Brillo maybe had a thing for our mother," he said. "Makes me wonder what he might have been willing to do about it."

Kady rose from the chair and smoothed the creases in her slacks.

"She disappeared, though," she said. "So, it's not like they ran away together after your dad died."

She came over to the sink and pulled a towel from a hook beside the window, then picked up a saucepan from the bottom rack of the dishwasher.

"It wouldn't hurt to know more about Ziemer," she said. "It doesn't sound like he was a boy scout."

"Talk to my sister," Dion said. "She saw him a lot more than I did. The Matterhorn was his hangout."

As Kady buffed water droplets off the pan, sunlight from the window shone on the metal and cast rippling beams over the cabinets. Dion pointed to a low drawer, and she stashed the pan inside, then picked up a plastic pitcher from the center of the rack.

"That goes up there," he said, pointing to a high cupboard in front of her.

Before his last word was out, she had slipped off her shoes and boosted one knee and both hands onto the counter, clambering up like a praying mantis until she was standing on top of it, her chin level with the center of the high cabinets, hair not quite touching the ceiling.

"Whoa," he said, laughing as he looked up at her. "That's totally weird."

Kady opened the cabinet door.

"Not to me," she said. "It's what I do at home."

He came in close behind her as she put the pitcher away, his hand reaching up to subtly touch her ankle, his voice lowered by a sudden burst of imagination.

"What else do you do at home?"

Her flesh beneath his fingertips seemed to ripple in his mind, as though he could feel waves on her skin that undulated to the current of his intentions.

"I could tell you what I'd do if I was home with you," he purred.

Kady looked at the ceiling, hands curling into soft claws. "Interesting," she said, sounding suddenly distant. "You're a talker when things take a steamy turn. Are you hearing what you're saying, though?"

While he was trying to understand what she meant, muted footsteps from the living room became shuffles in the kitchen. Dion slipped his hand from Kady's ankle. Shiner stopped in the doorway and stared up at Kady standing on the counter.

"I want to do that," Shiner said, pointing.

"You're probably too tall," Dion said. "I know I am."

Kady climbed down and had Shiner stand still while tucking in behind her until their backs were touching. Shiner began to giggle so hard she couldn't stand straight. Dion sized them together and told Shiner he was right, that she would need to keep her feet on the floor.

"One flying squirrel in the house is enough."

Still giggling, Shiner went to the refrigerator and pulled out a juice box, opened it, and took a drink, then handed it to Kady before going back to the living room.

"Did I want this?" Kady asked.

"Welcome to life with Shiner," Dion said. "You learn to roll with things."

Kady leaned back against the counter. She took a sip from the juice box, then offered him some.

"What you said about her liking to watch," Kady said. "I can't believe her parents wouldn't throw a fit if they found out."

"I was worried the first time I caught her," he admitted. "But they've never mentioned it, so I guess she's never told them, and I'm sure not going to."

He reached into the dishwasher, frowning as he slowly stacked two clean cereal bowls together. Kady asked what was wrong.

"I was thinking about Shiner's folks not saying any-thing," he answered. "You suppose she likes to watch them, too?"

Kady made a face like she didn't want the juice any-more.

- 57 -

Arno St. Albans put his sunglasses back on and rubbed a fleck of hair from his cheek, admiring his fresh styling in a mirror near the exit. He watched a reflection of Marnette Sims disinfecting some combs and thought about asking her to dinner, until she turned to him with a distracted gaze that seemed to show she had forgotten he was still there. He made a quick feint of checking his cell phone for messages and excused himself.

Twenty minutes later, he got to the front door of the Amor Abrasadora still remembering Marnette's vacant look and replaying the feel of her fingers on his scalp, embarrassed by how far he had let himself fall into a reverie under her electrifying but dispassionate touch, and thinking that having no better place to go than the cantina two nights in a row might be a damning commentary on his life.

The first voice he heard didn't help. Tico Tocopilla was standing at the bar between a quartet of large men in motorcycle leathers and a group of workers from a light-rail maintenance crew, who, in their bright safety vests, all turned to look when the front door opened.

"Sergeant," Tico Tocopilla called out over the voices around him. "Didn't figure you for a repeat offender."

St. Albans spotted Hefty Von Hanson farther down the room, cue stick in hand beside the pool table.

"Takes one to know one," the sergeant answered. "I see that you guys are back from yesterday too."

"Who says we ever left?"

Tico was waving some cash in his hand, trying to get the attention of a bartender while talking to St. Albans at the same time.

"We're going to order a pizza," Tico said. "You want in?"

St. Albans caught a breath, surprised by the surge of gratitude he felt for being invited. He pulled out his wallet for a couple of bills.

"My treat," he said. "For being kind of a pain last night about your shenanigans around Ziemer's house."

"No problem," Tico said. "We had it coming."

"That's what your compadre from the impound lot told me."

Tico's eyes went a little wide as he turned sideways, talking over noise from the kitchen and the large televisions over the bar.

"See, here's the deal on that," Tico said. "Anything we did was my idea, so if you're pissed off, put it on me and not the D-man or Hefty. They were just covering my back."

"I'm willing to call things square this time," St. Albans told him. "But you'll have to buy the first round."

Tico put the order in for a pizza and bought a bottle of beer that he handed to St. Albans, who followed him to a table where Hefty was sitting, a pool cue leaning against his thigh.

"Your shot," Hefty said to Tico, pointing toward the pool table.

"Haircut?" Hefty observed, addressing St. Albans from under the bill of his baseball cap.

The sergeant saluted with his bottle.

As St. Albans watched the others take turns at the game, he reflected about life at their age, years alive with friendships and the collective group energy of chasing excitement while waiting for the future to happen, unable to foresee or forestall the eventual settling in of a tedious, perpetual present where it would forever seem like the future had already passed.

In the form of muffled voices in the back hallway, the present reasserted itself before the pizza arrived. St. Albans saw Honest Mike Walerius halfway through the open door to the office, coming out under protest at the insistence of a slim hand pushing on his shoulder, the animated face of Corinne Nasseff behind it. They stood chirping at one another testily for a few seconds, flushed in the bright light from within the office before Corinne withdrew inside and slammed the door closed to leave her husband in the shadows.

St. Albans watched him stand there for a while, then waved a hand when the councilman appeared to gaze toward the bar. Honest Mike trudged slowly out from the hall and came over to the table, his suit and face both distressed.

"You should've told me you'd be down here fighting with Corinne," the sergeant told him. "I'd have brought a first aid kit."

The councilman straightened his necktie glumly. "Contrary to my appearance, I have steadfastly weathered the scouring gales of spousal fury," the councilman said, standing between chairs as St. Albans peered up at him, Tico and Hefty watching from the pool table. St. Albans asked what had set off the storm.

"The revelation of my discovery of her silent partner, whose existence negates one avenue for coercion on my part, yet inversely provides a second," Honest Mike answered. "I illustrated to her that having been denied an opportunity to willfully annex a percentage of his operation on her behalf, a gain of reciprocal magnitude might be achieved by orchestrating the forcible withdrawal of his ongoing interest in her receipts."

"Which segment of your presentation did she appreciate the least?"

The councilman rubbed his chin in thought. "In retrospect," he said, "I am uncertain as to whether any position I advanced completely registered within the scope of her comprehension. Her participation in the discussion wavered little from a decidedly vocal displeasure with the presence of my face in her field of vision."

St. Albans took a sip of beer. "I suppose if you're on her shit-list tonight, then I probably am too. I should get out of here before she sees me."

Honest Mike smoothed the lapels of his suit jacket, his silver curls and blue glasses coolly ablaze from the light over the pool table as he took a deep breath.

"A most judicious appraisal of the situation," he said. "Though your departure would interrupt what I perceive must only be some strategically calculated social interaction with these young scamps."

Tico and Hefty, studying a pool shot, looked up.

"They're friends of the demon," St. Albans said quietly to the councilman.

The others began talking to one another then, not so quietly.

"I didn't hear the sergeant, but I think his fancy friend just called either me or you a skank, you know?" Hefty said to Tico.

Tico replied that he thought so too, unless the fancy friend was speaking of his own wife, which was no insult to them but still wasn't very friendly. St. Albans assured them that they had misheard but told Honest Mike that an apology to the boys might be a good idea anyway.

"Offer to buy a round."

"I beg your pardon?" the councilman argued. "For what supposed transgression am I to be absolved? My indifference to their stunted vocabulary?"

The sergeant said to think of it as an early campaign exercise. Hefty, listening, asked what campaign they were talking about. Honest Mike lit up with a rehearsed smile.

"The Tenth Ward council seat," he answered. "Which I currently occupy and aspire to vigorously defend at the conclusion of my term."

He held out his right palm. "Walerius is the name to remember on the ballot," he said. "And you are?"

Hefty looked a little puzzled at needing to explain, and said, "Playing pool?"

Honest Mike laughed as he shook Tico's hand next.

"Gentlemen, I sincerely regret if our dialogue to this point has in any fashion been interpreted as an affront on my part. I suggest that a replenishment of your beverages with my compliments might allow us to begin afresh. If you will excuse me, I shall repair to the bar."

As he turned, the councilman took a longer gaze at St. Albans.

"You were eager to quickly accept the offer of my legislative aide to triage your hair, I see," Honest Mike said. "I trust you found the encounter transformative?"

"Do I really need to tell you?"

"No," the councilman answered, shaking his head as though guiltily reliving a memory. "Indeed, you do not."

The others sat down at the table with St. Albans when Honest Mike walked away, their eyes following him. As he got to the bar, voices there rose in greeting, faces gathering around.

"He's popular, huh?" Hefty said.

"My boss, the lieutenant, has a knack for the political glad hand," St. Albans responded. "At heart he's a salesman, on a first name basis with a lot of people he doesn't know."

The sergeant took a drink, hoping that he didn't sound as irritated as he was beginning to feel. His bad eye burned.

"What's with the bullshit each time he opens his mouth?" Tico wondered. "When the guy talks, it sounds like we're all stuck in some old black-and-white movie."

St. Albans pushed his sunglasses up to the top of his head and pulled his eyedrops from his pocket.

"He believes it makes him sound sophisticated and worldly," he said, tilting his head back as he aimed the dropper. "An affectation he picked up as he climbed the ranks with the department. Now it's kind of his signature, but not always in the way he thinks it is. People in the office mimic him when he's not around. I can do a few sentences after a couple of beers if I'm annoyed enough."

Hefty fingered a cube of chalk on the table. "Can we hear some?" he asked.

"Maybe later," the sergeant answered, putting the eyedrops away. He brought his sunglasses back to his nose and picked up his beer, swirling the bottle and watching the foam. "We'll see how the night goes."

Honest Mike came back after a few minutes carrying two trays, one with drinks and one with their pizza, sounding slightly annoyed himself.

"I have been conscripted into temporary servitude by the kitchen staff," he complained as he set the pizza on the table. "Deputized to render for your enjoyment this dreary excuse for an entree which is apparently vital to the plebeian entertainments of the evening, and for which I might advise my wife to scrutinize the credentials of her chef."

Tico and Hefty each gave him a look, then looked at one another, as he passed the drinks around,

"So, first we're skanks, and now we're lesbians?" Hefty said.

"That's what I heard, I think," Tico nodded. "With his wife thrown in this time for certain."

The councilman huffed, saying that he had uttered no such thing. St. Albans opened his mouth to intervene again but picked up on a glance between the two younger men and dimly realized that they were joking, and had been from the start, amusing themselves at the befuddled expense of the condescending blowhard who had blundered uninvited into their night of pizza and pool.

"Councilman Hilarious here isn't being fair to his missus, right?" Hefty said, adjusting his cap as he looked at Tico. "She didn't sound lesbian, if you ask me."

"When she was leaving, you mean?" Tico said, seeming to grasp from habit the call-and-response of a recycled conversation easily tailored to fit the audience at hand.

"Yeah," Hefty answered, his gaze drifting toward the front door. "With those bikers."

Honest Mike turned toward the hallway and Corinne's office, looking confused.

St. Albans looked the other way, following Hefty's eyes. The men in motorcycle leathers were still there beside the light-rail workers at the end of the bar, watching a hockey game on one of the large televisions, and the sergeant felt a smile tug at the corner of his mouth.

"My wife?" Honest Mike said as he stared down the hallway toward Corinne's office, clearly confounded. "And bikers?"

"From the railroad," explained Hefty, adding the maintenance workers to his setup. "At least it sounded like they were from the railroad, you know?"

Tico picked up the clue to where Hefty was looking and delivered the punchline while reaching for a slice of pizza.

"It sure did," he agreed, nodding dramatically. "They were talking about taking her back to their place and having her pull a train."

- 58 -

Kady L'Orient was still fighting off the aftertaste of boxed juice when she got to the Matterhorn, so she declined the wine suggested by Evan Arcade and asked, instead, for ice water. Evan filled a glass and set it on the bar, then picked up a paring knife.

"You don't need to do that," Kady said, draping her shoulder bag onto a stool.

Evan sliced into a lemon and hung a sliver on the rim of the glass.

"I want to," she said. "So, there."

Kady climbed onto the stool as she scanned the sparse clusters of faces in the lounge, the stage lights up but Easy Andrews not yet at his piano. She watched as Evan, boyish-ly cute in a hockey jersey and cycling shorts, drifted busily back and forth behind the bar, the two of them catching one another now and then in surreptitious glances that made them each look away.

"Have you ever noticed," Kady said when Evan passed close by, "that you and your brother look a lot alike?"

"We practice that when we're alone," Evan said, asking if Kady really wanted to be talking about him. Kady slid the lemon slice aside to take a sip from the glass and wondered aloud why not.

"You might have to admit that you're still on the fence," Evan responded, wiping a towel in a brisk circle over the bar.

Kady pouted her lips. "I'm okay with where things stand so far," she said. "Coming straight here from his place got me disoriented for a second, that's all."

Evan reached for the glass and took a sip herself, saying, "Coming straight and disoriented from him to me? Somebody's having an attack of Freudian slippage, I think. If you're looking for a sympathetic perspective, though, I have some experience with orientation, if you know what I mean."

Kady reached to take the glass back, talking across it. "Hands-on experience?"

Evan grunted out a laugh as she moved down the bar to retrieve an empty brandy snifter.

"Careful with the wisecracks," she said. "They might get you a tongue-lashing."

"Who's slipping Freudian now?"

Kady felt someone passing behind her, and then Easy Andrews was at her shoulder, natty in a pressed shirt and cravat, and a blazer with a nautical crest beneath the pocket square. He pointed at her glass, rings at his knuckles shining and his fingernails clear.

"Is that plain water?" he asked Evan through his clenched teeth, the swelling along his wired jaw still obvious. "If it is, do me the same."

The women looked at one another.

"Do me?" Kady said to Evan. "Freud strikes again."

She expected a laugh, but what came back from the other woman was something more like an exaggerated wince that made Kady sorry for the innuendo. Evan grabbed a clean glass, keeping her eyes down. Easy spoke toward her.

"Does Lauda know his policewoman friend is back?"

"I'm not after your boss tonight," Kady said.

Easy watched Evan pour his drink, and after a second, he breathed out a knowing exhale. "You won't find out much about Dionysius from us. He's never been big on sharing the details of his life."

Kady took a slow swallow from her glass while shaking her head.

"Him I've got covered," she said. "The person I'm interested in talking about was an old fan of your sister back in her duet days with you, and I'm trying to place him in the context of her disappearance."

She saw the others both pause over the glass on the bar between them, Easy looking stiffly thoughtful, Evan more like surprised. Easy spoke first.

"Elysia left an impression on lots of people in the neighborhood," he said.

"Brillo Ziemer included, I hear," Kady said.

Easy made a sound behind his teeth.

"My sister and Brillo knew each other a long time through her husband's painting business," he said. "He probably felt as bad as anyone when she went missing."

"Not everyone," Evan said as she handed him the glass.

"I'm sorry, you're right," Easy said. "Anyway, I heard a few days ago that he crashed himself down some hole, so I'm not sure how he's going to help you now."

Kady told him it was true that Brillo was gone. Easy raised his glass.

"I'll offer a toast to the old barfly, then," he said.

Kady took another sip, joining in. Evan shrugged and said she just hoped that somebody would be paying off the dead man's bar tab.

"He left a debt?" Kady asked.

"He must have," Evan replied. "Brillo never paid for any food or drinks he got from me, and he was here a lot. He told me his credit was part of a deal with the boss for some work on the building after a fire that happened back before I was around."

She looked at her uncle and asked if he remembered anything about a fire. Easy didn't reply, merely pointed toward the stage.

"I'm on," he said.

Kady told him to break a leg.

"That's very showbiz of you," he praised cheerily, but then darkened his tone. "If we don't meet again, it's been great fun knowing you."

She watched him thread his way through the tables, the gray in his hair brilliant in the lights as he stepped up onto the stage and settled himself at the piano.

"What did he mean about meeting me again?" she asked Evan. "It sounded like a sneer."

"It was," Evan answered. "He's teasing you about Dionysius. Anytime you see my brother with a girl, you always feel a little bad for her because there's a pretty good chance it will be the last time you see her. He's always trying to find a woman to give him what he thinks he's missing and fix whatever is wrong with him, which my therapist and yours would tell him can't be done, so he goes through quite a few partners. He doesn't understand that no relationship is going to work for him until he fixes himself."

Kady ran her tongue across her bottom lip, thinking. "Or finds someone who can show him how," she said.

Evan sliced more lemon that she draped on the glass.

"By setting an example with a close family member?" she asked, sucking her finger clean.

"Your uncle isn't my type," Kady said.

"That narrows down the competition then."

At the piano, Easy warmed up by feathering out a series of bass runs and folded chords. Kady asked Evan about living with him after the killing.

"He was our only option," Evan told her. "My folks were both from small families, and all the grandparents were dead by then. I don't think he was thrilled to take us in, but he probably felt like he owed it to my mother."

She wiped her hand on her thigh, saying that she hated to sound like everyone always did when talking about growing up, but that she supposed he had done the best that he could.

"When my mom went missing, he went a little off course mentally, I think," she said. "They were best friends."

The room fell into a dull hush as the piano went silent, the gathered drinkers seemingly conditioned to a predictable moment of polite anticipation for a distraction they could probably have done without, before Easy started in on a jazzy ballad and the voices around the tables and booths began talking over him again.

Kady watched him play and tried to imagine being shuffled into the custody of an unprepared and grieving relative, the household chosen out of necessity or survival. She considered how many ill social behaviors such a past might reasonably justify and excuse. She drank some more water, feeling herself melting into the barstool.

"My parents didn't just go off course," she said. "They drove into a ditch and stayed there."

Evan looked at her and said, "At least they're alive?"

"Depends on your perspective," Kady told her. "One is a hoarder in a house with a yard full of junk cars, and the other is so depressed it takes all her energy to go down the hall at her apartment to pick up the mail every day."

"Divorced?"

"After I finished high school and my older brother moved out." Kady nodded, then chuckled bitterly. "They must have worried that doing it sooner might mess us up."

She pulled a lemon slice from the glass and squeezed it dead onto the bar, saying, "I'd divorce all of them if there was a way to do it."

Evan reached into a sink behind the bar to rinse the knife blade.

"Has my brother heard this?" she asked. "I'm trying to picture how he deals with actual feelings when someone shoves them in his face."

Kady answered that she hadn't told him any of it yet, but had a sense that in a strange, subliminal way, he already knew.

"My therapist says that damaged people find each other," she said. "And your brother found me. On a sticky note."

"You're forgetting that I saw you first."

Kady straightened a bit on the stool and smiled slightly. "He told me you'd say so," she said.

"Game on, then," Evan said.

Kady watched as Evan went down the bar to refill a vodka-highball combination for an elderly man slouched on his elbows who looked both like he didn't need another cocktail and like he could use another five.

"Brillo Ziemer," Kady called after her. "What was his game?"

Evan shrugged as she made her way back and said he was just around a lot.

"Like I said to my brother, I think Brillo might have had a thing for our mom, but I don't know if it was mutual."

"He always ate and drank for free?"

"Everything went onto his account," Evan said. "He tipped with cash, though."

Kady stared into her water glass. Easy's playing had moved on to a staccato classical piece with ringing arpeggios that contrasted the deflated boozy pall of the room and made her think of memorizing multiplication tables while at a picnic with bad food.

"Does your boss keep the books himself?" she asked.

"Lauda uses an accounting service," Evan responded. "They do my taxes too. I can give you their name."

She picked up her cell phone from the back bar. "What's your number?"

Kady recited the digits and within seconds, heard a buzzing from her shoulder bag. She pulled out her phone to find a text message from an unfamiliar source.

"Did it go through?" Evan said.

Kady opened the message expecting to find the business information, but instead saw only an image of a pulsing romantic heart, then looked up to see Evan beaming a victorious grin.

"Gotcha."

Pointing toward a cooler behind the bar, Kady said that now she was ready for some wine.

- 59 -

Working on her own glass of wine in the Amor Abrasadora office, Corinne Nasseff paused between swallows to process papers on her desk as Arno St. Albans watched from the sofa and mutely absorbed her irritated glowering.

"Pulling a train," she grumbled, shaking her head while initialing a purchase order. "I'm sorry, but that's just plain nasty."

The sergeant tipped his beer bottle and drank as he oozed himself wider across the leather cushions, his tongue feeling thick when he came up for air. From a pile of disheveled clothes beside him, he picked up one of her workout hats.

"The kids thought it was funny," he said, not letting on that he thought so too. "You have to give them credit, it's not often that you see the boss speechless."

"He wasn't exactly saying much when he was in here with me yelling at him," said Corinne.

"Well, he wasn't saying anything at all when he left."

"If those boys pissed him off, it serves him right," Corinne declared. "Serves both of you right."

He balanced the hat over his eyes, hiding behind it while he defended himself, saying that he'd reported her deal with Lauda Aplikowski to her husband because he had to.

He heard Corinne ask why, telling him testily that she'd

half expected him to rat her out over the video and shoot-ing up the city car, but believed he would at least keep her business arrangement secret. As he considered how to respond, he stared through the fabric of the hat toward the ceiling light, the entwined fibers sharply defined in the filtered bright fluorescence, and he slowly began to appre-ciate with remorse what it meant to her to share a confi-dence that was then thrown back in her face.

"Because he's my best friend," he answered, knowing that it wasn't reason enough.

"I could say that too," Corinne pointed out, angrily rus-tling papers. "You think he'd say that about either of us?"

St. Albans lifted the hat to down a couple more swigs from his bottle. When the words finally came to him, he warbled them out in an officious timbre reminiscent of Honest Mike Walerius.

"One would do well to concede the obvious, that re-sponsibility for distress over unrequited esteem in a rela-tionship must be borne by the party who believes them-selves aggrieved, with the recognition that their aspira-tions for some idealized confederation cannot be success-fully projected in force upon a partner who is devoid of similar expectations."

He dropped the hat back over his face. Corinne's move-ments went into a suspended silence.

"Goddamn, kiddo," she said, almost whistling in admi-ration. "That sounds exactly like something he would say."

"That's because it's exactly something that he did say," the sergeant sighed as he held his beer in one hand and raised the hat from his nose with the other.

"About one of his lovelorn staffers at the office?"

St. Albans took another chug from the bottle, sad with the memory and with his fudged reply.

"Close enough."

His elbow was resting on one of her sweatshirts that had been tossed akimbo atop a tangled pair of yoga pants. When he took his next breath, he was almost sadder to realize that her dirty laundry smelled better than he did.

- 60 -

The telephone at the police impound lot rang a few times in the hour after Dion Drury reported for the start of his overnight shift, disrupting the plodding momentum of the cribbage game that Kady had initiated. With each call, as he spoke into the receiver and scratched out notes on a paper pad, he also kept a sideways eye on her at the service counter, where she hunched over the board while analyzing her cards, her gaze fiercely serious behind her glasses. He could imagine her as a feared rival in a school classroom, envied and resented, distorting the grading curve for everyone else.

When the phone finally fell quiet, he retook his seat on a stool beside hers at the counter, the cribbage board between them, a darkened fluorescent ceiling fixture overhead. Light from the kitchen doorway threw a suggestive dimness over the pegs and lines of holes on the board, and the stacked folders of the Cullen Arcade case file farther down the countertop.

"So, why is it you think that Brillo Ziemer's tab at the Matterhorn might be important?" he asked her.

"I don't know that it's important," she answered, not looking up from her cards. "But I think it's interesting, partly because your uncle didn't seem to want anything to do with talking about him, or about a fire and restoration work in the building some years back that your sister said she heard about from Ziemer as the reason Lauda Apli-kowski allowed him a line of credit."

Dion thought back to the day Brillo's body had been found in the storm-sewer tunnel.

"Evangeline said that Easy and Lauda both got kind of weird when they heard Brillo was dead," he recalled.

"That's interesting too."

Kady swiveled from side to side on her stool as she re-arranged her cards. He thought he heard her faintly count-ing to herself, and then she spoke up.

"Your sister told me what you said she would, that she saw me first," she informed him. "I told her you warned me to expect it."

"How'd she take that?"

The police radio on the desk hissed. Kady turned her ear toward it while she replied.

"Like a challenge that she was going to enjoy," she said. "I'm getting a sense that there's a freaky energy between the two of you. Maybe a love-hate type of thing?"

Dion twisted on his stool to look out the window, tell-ing her that he knew what she meant, but that he didn't really understand it himself. The lines of vehicles beneath the dome of desolate light over the yard and the dark sky beyond got him thinking of history as a physical dimen-sion with time as its border and memory as its atmosphere, a space within the mind where life competed with itself in endless rewind.

"Some odd things happened," he said. "One time, I came home from school when she was in the eighth grade. My folks were gone someplace, and she was already there with two boys and a girl from her class, down in the basement kissing and making out, boy to girl. Clothes on, nothing too intense. She told me that if I didn't tell on them, I could watch."

Kady set her cards down. She reached into her shoulder bag on the counter and pulled out a tiny jar of lip gloss.

"Did you want to watch?" she said as she unscrewed the lid.

"Not until she told me I could."

His eyes followed as the tip of her pinky finger smeared a thin sheen over her lips.

"Did it do anything for you?" she asked.

"Not as much as watching you do that," he said. "I got bored and went outside to play."

He shook his head thinking about it, saying, "I was in the third grade. Why would she think I'd want to watch?"

Kady stashed the jar back inside her bag.

"It probably says more about her than you," she reasoned. "She was a kid herself, remember, but a little older than you. Things were waking up inside her, and that can show itself in different ways."

Dion took a minute to ponder that, and then Kady made him ponder something else, pointing out that he had said some odd things happened, which implied more than one. It took him another minute to wonder if what he was thinking of telling her said more about himself than his sister. He met her gaze, soft and patient upon him, and gave in.

"Later on," he began, "when we went to live with my uncle, I'd wake up sometimes in the middle of the night and Evangeline would be in my bed, hanging onto me."

He smoothed back his hair. He could hear himself breathing.

"She was a teenager, and she obviously knew about boys, and maybe even girls by then," he went on. "I didn't know a lot about sex yet, but I had a feeling that what she was doing wasn't about that. It was more like she was keeping me covered, like a protection kind of thing, wrapping me up with an arm or an ankle. It didn't happen a lot, but after she moved out, I missed it."

Kady didn't say anything, but he could see her eyebrows slowly clinching in thought.

"You're thinking that I'm a really messed-up person," he said.

She turned her face toward the floor, frowning while she drummed two fingers on her knee for several seconds.

"I'm thinking that it might not have been you that she was trying to protect," she said.

He felt a slow whir building in his brain as he weighed the possibilities of what she meant, and then a vibration erupted from her shoulder bag to drown it out.

"There's your sister now," Kady said, retrieving her cell phone and studying the screen. "With contact information for the Matterhorn accountants so I can find out what they can tell me about Brillo Ziemer's credit situation. Hand me a pen."

Dion gave her a pen from the desk. She opened a folder from the Arcade case file on the counter and copied the numbers from her phone.

"I'm also going to follow up with the fire records office and the building permit folks to see if there's any truth to what he told her."

He waited until she finished writing, then asked if she had been carrying the case file around all day.

"I didn't want to leave it on my desk again," she said. "I had it in the car when I was at your place, but now I think I've got a better plan for keeping it safe."

"Don't tell me what it is."

"I wasn't going to."

The phone buzzed again in Kady's hand. She grinned.

"Your sister again," she said. "Must be a slow night at the bar."

"What does she want?"

"She's sending a photo this time and demanding one back," Kady said. "Quid pro quo."

"Is that like tit for tat?" Dion asked.

Kady held up the phone to aim its camera at him.

"In this case it's more like tit for tit," she said. "Lift up your shirt."

"What?"

"Your shirt," she repeated. "I'm assuming that nipples run in your family. If your sister wants to share hers, we'll share yours."

He hesitated.

"Don't tell me you don't have nipples," she said, beginning to bubble up with giggles. Then she abruptly stopped.

"Or don't you believe that your sister does?"

She moved her hand as though about to turn the phone around to let him see. He felt the sudden rise of his tongue against his molars while her voice dropped low, matching the motion of his hands as he reached past his belly for the bottom of his shirt.

"Now you're thinking that I'm a really messed-up person too?" she said, staring intently as his shirt came up, the phone in her hand hovering near his chest.

"No," he told her. "I'm thinking that I've never kissed a girl on city time."

"I have," murmured Kady slowly, the words liquid with the suggestion of fond memory. "It's fun." She leaned in, with a warm whisper he could feel on his nose hairs. "Close your eyes," she said. "You'll see."

When he closed his eyes, he saw.

- 61 -

After midnight, Kady pushed a rolling staircase ladder along the concrete floor of a warehouse annex attached to the public safety building, the wheels offering a mild squeal against the classical music that wafted from a radio at the front desk. The lone civilian clerk stationed there yawned over a college textbook.

Kady maneuvered the ladder with both hands, the paperwork folders of the Cullen Arcade case file resting on a step at eye level. She steered it into an aisle flanked by industrial shelving that rose from the floor to the open latticework of steel beams that supported the corrugated ceiling fifteen feet above. The air smelled of metal and insects, suspended lights over the aisle brightly radiating a white electric hum.

Climbing to an upper shelf, she located the bin that held the physical evidence of the unsolved Arcade killing in various translucent bags tagged with notes and numbers, then reached in to rearrange things, making room for the folders. One small parcel contained the shoes found on the body. Folded clothes in a larger, heavier bag made her think of the dead man as having once been an actual person, which gave way to thoughts of his surviving children and the stimulating sheen of phone-screen skin, of the shared tingly taste of a sociable tongue.

Moving items around in the bin, she came upon a dusty plastic storage box with a conflicting case number. Suspecting that it had been misfiled from an adjacent receptacle, she turned it over and saw Cullen Arcade's name clearly marked on the outside in bold script, with a note dated years earlier explaining that an archivist maximizing space on the shelves had decided to consolidate evidence from two case files that seemed related according to the referenced name.

She pulled the box onto the ladder and opened it. Inside she found a child's shattered bicycle helmet adorned with images of cartoon rainbow stars and unicorns; some small old clothes, dark with dried blood; and an envelope that held copies of a police report and a slightly misshapen spent bullet.

- 62 -

Stashing away the cribbage board and playing cards, Dion Drury busied himself at his desk as the clock made its slow turn toward morning, the sunrise over the impound lot still hours away. Each blink of his eyes against the blue wash of his computer display revived in his mind the flash from Kady's cell phone camera. Each time he sniffed hard, he smelled her lip gloss at the base of his nostrils and his chest hair went wiry.

In the quiet between sporadic arrivals of tow trucks and incoming phone calls, the desk speaker for the security microphones outside filtered slow waves of sound like ocean surf, his head bobbing in sympathetic time, the distant voice of city life at half throttle subsuming him into the lazy smoldering energy of a night awake with waiting.

He was filling out a report when he got distracted by a series of headlights passing on Cesar Chavez Street, up the railroad embankment beyond the lot's farthest fence. He checked the clock and saw that bar-close time was near, which always corresponded to an increase in police activity from traffic mishaps and arrests, so he got up to get a snack from the refrigerator before things got busy.

He passed one of the big windows behind the service counter and peered out to see a single pair of headlights slowing on the far side of Cesar Chavez Street, a vehicle outbound from the city pulling over, then doubling back in a looping swerve to stop at the near curb above the embankment. It was overlooking the spot along the railroad track where the body of Cullen Arcade had been found twenty years earlier.

Dion stopped too, a surge of blood rising suddenly warm in his forehead as he wondered if, for the first time in his months of passive vigil, he was witnessing the return of someone to the scene of the crime.

He went over to the desk and picked up the office binoculars. He focused the lenses out the big windows into the distance, telescoping his sight into the patchy illumination misting from a streetlight. His breath caught short when he saw the definitive boxy outline of a classic old Chrysler convertible.

As he tried to get a view of the driver, Dion could see light growing over the car from the rear, slowly at first as though from approaching traffic, but then brighter and brighter until its intensity doubled in a flare of high beams pulling in close behind the rear bumper. In the headlights, the Chrysler became pasty as the pale head of its pilot, suddenly punctuated by the red-and-blue strobe of police flashers.

- 63 -

Hefty Von Hanson plodded heavily up the stairs to the impound lot office just as dawn was brightening the sky outside into a shade of dull chrome. Behind the service counter, Dion Drury heard a subtle crinkle of paper with each ascending step, then an exuberant cascade of crumpling when Hefty reached the top of the landing and noisily dug into the bakery sack in his hand.

"I should have bought more stuff, huh, D-man?" the big kid said as he looked around.

Evan Arcade, standing in the center of the room, impatiently zipped her hooded sweatshirt and raised a finger to her lips to shush him gently. She pointed toward the counter, where Lauda Aplikowski, resplendent in a plush burgundy loungewear ensemble of a velour jacket and pants with pearl piping, was not-so-subtly fuming.

"How can I be charged for a day of storage?" the old man complained. "The car has only been here a few goddamn hours."

Dion recited in his practiced bureaucratic monotone that the rates were based on the calendar day and not on the clock, adding a more personal disclaimer that it wasn't his fault, and he did not make the rules.

"So, keep your shirt on," he said.

When he saw his sister smirking at him, he remembered her earlier exchange of cell phone photos with Kady and knew that she was remembering too.

"That's easier said than done for some of us, in my experience," Evan said.

He felt himself blush.

She stepped over to Hefty and poked at the paper sack. "Any apple fritters in there?"

"Save one for me," Dion said.

Lauda pulled out his wallet and growled something about people wasting his time and not wanting to be around when the sworn police staff came on duty.

"I'll be damned if I'm going to let the bastards see me put money in their pockets," he said. "It's been enough of a pain with the cops who've been showing up at my place the past few days, trying to crawl up my ass for one thing or another. I'm not giving any of them the satisfaction of watching me pay."

Dion gathered release paperwork to be signed, saying that maybe Easy Andrews should not have been given the keys to the old Chrysler in the first place.

"The guy is in enough trouble already," he pointed out. "Adding violations for an improper turn that crossed a double yellow centerline and driving with a temporarily suspended license won't help him any."

"I didn't give him the keys," Lauda defended, rubbing a finger into one eye sleepily, his shiny forehead the color of undercooked turkey. "He must have grabbed them off my desk."

Dion looked out the window toward the railroad track.

"At least we've got a pretty good idea where Easy was going the other night when the cops picked him up the first time," he said.

Then he turned and fixed an accusing scowl toward the old man, saying, "Anybody besides me wondering why, and why now? Or why it seems to me like Brillo Ziemer being dead has something to do with it?"

Lauda dodged the look without comment and bent down to sign the release. Evan was behind him, burrowing a hand into the bakery sack, the paper crackling loudly and spasmodically like there was a squirrel inside.

"You said cops have been at our place," she said to Lauda. "Who else besides the cute little chick?"

Dion frowned at the paperwork on the counter, thinking of his uncle's first arrest and now Lauda's old convertible, but more so of the interest shown by the disfigured police sergeant regarding the sedan assigned to the Tenth Ward City Council representative that had arrived and departed without record of its detention, lighter upon its exit by the exact physical weight of the Cullen Arcade case file.

"Honest Mike Walerius," he guessed.

Lauda looked up at him uneasily. "Don't tell me you're in cahoots with the guy."

"Mostly with his wife."

"Same here," the old man responded, sounding a little mystified. At Dion's mention of Corinne Nasseff, Evan shot a knowing eye roll toward the ceiling. Lauda changed the subject quickly, calling over his shoulder to Hefty.

"Von Hanson, I want you as an impartial witness when I check my car for dings." He finished signing and appraised Dion uncertainly.

"Now, let's go bail out Easy," Evan said. "Again."

"You sure you want to?" Dion asked her, thinking about how Kady had reacted to his story of Evan protecting him as a boy by implying that his sister had perhaps been thinking of safety from a perspective that he had not entirely considered.

Evan gave him a puzzled look for a couple of seconds. She tore a fritter in half and came over to pass a piece to him.

"Maybe the fool will want me to punch him some more," she said with a shrug. "I could get into that."

"Because he still has it coming to him?"

Her eyes narrowed on his in a suggestion of sibling dominance that brought back to him memories of childhood, the gaze telling him that even though she didn't know what he meant, she was still senior to him, and he had best be careful with his words in case he didn't know what he meant either. Then, when she answered, he wondered with some apprehension if it was possible that they each knew exactly what they both weren't saying.

"We've all got things coming to us," she assured him flatly. "That's life in the big city."

Lauda stepped back from the counter, the old man looking at the two of them like he hadn't been listening. But he was inclined to agree with whatever had been said just to get out of there. He folded the papers and stuffed them into the pocket of his shimmering velour jacket. Hefty gestured at him with the bakery sack.

"So, what time do you hit the stage at your place, huh?" he wanted to know.

"Me?" asked Lauda, confused. "No, Easy works the stage alone."

"Oh," Hefty said with a shake of his head, his ball cap low over his ears and his eyes wrinkling into smile lines in the shadow of the bill. "It looked like maybe you guys were working up some weird new show."

Lauda stared blankly while Hefty scanned the bag slowly up and down over him, from floor to face like a floating X-ray.

"That's a costume you've got on, right?"

Dion smothered a chuckle as he picked up the Chrysler tow report.

"Excuse me?" Lauda choked, voice quickly rising.

"I'm wrong?" responded Hefty, beaming a slow grin toward Evan while saying it was a logical gaffe, given the nature of the old man's outfit.

"I thought he was a character from that old Christmas story, you know?" Hefty explained. "The Ghost of Cadillac Upholstery Past."

- 64 -

Telephones rang in the Tenth Ward suite, on the fourth floor of the city hall and county courthouse downtown, as the staff assigned to Honest Mike Walerius eased into the business day. The councilman confirmed with Marnette Sims his schedule for the morning and then sat down to review the local-features section of the daily newspaper on his desk.

Arno St. Albans stood looking out a window off to one side, watching traffic crawl along the Wabasha Street Bridge. He turned around as Honest Mike turned a page.

"Should I ask how breakfast with the wife went today?" the sergeant teased.

Honest Mike fingered an unruly silver curl above one ear and huffed an answer.

"I am as yet uncertain that I should acknowledge your presence given your complicity in my humiliation at the hands of those rascals last night at her cantina."

With a regal flourish, he flipped another page, giving the newsprint an ostentatious snap.

"As for the tenor of my conjugal entanglements at the moment," he went on, "suffice to say that I strategically roused myself well in advance of Corinne awakening and provided to both of us the buffer of my staying one step ahead in our preparations for the day. I am hopeful that her present antipathy toward me will, by this evening, have sufficiently waned to allow for negotiations toward an armistice."

Bending forward to read, he added a final scolding thought.

"The unwelcome gestation of enmity on your part may not be so readily resolved."

The sergeant reached inside his tinted sunglasses to wink his frozen eye, arguing that he had been unable to stop himself from laughing as the boys mocked the politician.

"They had your number," he said. "And you sort of walked right into it. You can't blame me if you set yourself up for a joke."

The councilman grunted a wordless indignant retort.

"I'm just saying," St. Albans persisted. "If you go around sounding like you swallowed a thesaurus, people will push back if they think that the way you talk is code for looking down your nose at them. Kids like those two don't take anybody's shit. You and I were no different at their age."

Honest Mike swiveled on his office chair. "You indicated that the young men are associates of the demon?"

"Tight pals as near as I can tell, which might explain the attitude."

"A common swagger, befitting a shared disdain for conventional authority," the councilman said. "Perhaps, then, a measure of clemency in my opinion would be courteous in consideration of the recent interventions on behalf of my city vehicle, though I shall retain my displeasure at the duplicitous production of my wife's impolitic video."

St. Albans turned back toward the window and stuffed his hands into the pockets of his trousers, his shoulders flexing.

"I'm sure the whole bunch would be overwhelmed by the depth of your graciousness," he said.

Honest Mike frowned sourly. "I detect an acerbic element in your tone specifically for my benefit."

St. Albans was ready to reply that not every waking moment had to be about the councilman, as difficult as it would have been for the other man to believe, when he realized that the immediate moment was as much about Honest Mike as it was about anything else. He remembered being happy the previous night sharing pizza and beer with the two younger men. He'd been accepted as an interesting and welcome guest in their uprising against his boss, and he was liberated from any sense of obligation or deeper meaning than just trying to have some fun at the end of a workday. Looking now at Honest Mike behind the desk, St. Albans felt himself welling with a slow burn of anger, upset partly over the grim unfairness of his unresponsive facial muscles, partly over the unrelenting entitled presumptions of his best friend, and partly over letting himself become an eternal afterthought to everyone around him.

"I'll talk to you later," he said curtly, moving toward the door as another page of newsprint snapped behind him.

In the outer office he passed Marnette Sims in her cubicle. She looked up blankly at him when he told her he was leaving to get some coffee. He smiled tightly and was proud for being strong, if only for that instant.

He didn't care that she didn't care.

- 65 -

The shadow of a cloud passed slowly over the Amor Abrasadora as Dion steered his car to a stop along the South Robert Street curb. Corinne Nasseff was on the sidewalk, her head down in a deep lean against the building as though shoring up the wall. She looked sporty in sneakers and shorts topped by a fleece pullover as she stretched her legs to warm up for her morning jog. She turned her head, peering up when he killed the engine.

"I'm glad I caught you," Dion said as he opened his door and climbed out.

She stepped away from the wall while resetting the elastic headband that held her hair back from her face.

"I didn't know I was being chased," she said. "Not that I'm complaining."

She twisted at the waist a few times, still limbering up as he came around the car and walked toward her. He had a thought that in her school days she could have likely been found in team colors scurrying around an athletic field or gymnasium.

"You look like you're in shape for a marathon," he told her.

She took the headband off, dissatisfied about something he couldn't decipher, then put it back on as he stopped in front of her.

"Thanks," she said. "I'd return the compliment, but you look like you've been up all night."

"I have."

A city bus rollicked past, eddying dust in its wake that skittered along the sidewalk and around their feet.

"Then what brings you to me, kiddo?" Corinne asked. "Again, not that I'm complaining."

Dion stuffed his hands into the pockets of his windbreaker.

"Lauda Aplikowski," he said. "I'm wondering why your husband would be leaning on him. I figured that if anyone could tell me, it'd be you or his number one egg man, and that you'd be more likely to tell me than the sergeant would."

Corinne's face twitched. "You know Aplikowski?" she exclaimed, startled.

She raised one hand to her forehead to shield her eyes from the early low sun. Dion moved so she could put the rays at her back.

"Family friend," he answered.

Now he was squinting into the glare, his distorted vision etching a fuzzy halo around her soft face.

"This about leverage again?"

"Maybe," he said.

Her gaze turned downward as she thought for a few moments, and then she told him about the assistance she'd gotten in obtaining her license for the cantina and her subsequent financial exposure from the final deal.

"I guess that Lauda wants a return of the favor over some kind of police thing that's going on, and the walrus was hoping to use that to wedge our way into the Matterhorn business," she said. "His new idea, now that the reality is clear to him, is to squeeze Lauda out from the cantina. I raised hell with Honest Mike last night for meddling, but I'm starting to think one fewer hand in the till here would be a pretty cool thing if he can pull it off."

She moved closer, tapping the toe of her left sneaker on the toe of his three times.

"Maybe he could make it happen with a little help from the right bandits," she said, her eyes coming up to find his. "Then I'd choose my associates on my own terms. I don't suppose you'd happen to know anything about working in hospitality?"

"Only what my sister tells me."

Corinne pulled her toe back. "Who's your sister?" she asked.

Dion stretched out his foot and tapped his toe on her sneaker just once.

"She works at the Matterhorn," he replied.

Corinne narrowed one eye and curled the tip of her tongue as she looked up at him for a few seconds. Then she reached up to remove her headband again, twisting it in her hands into a figure eight that she slowly slipped onto her wrists like a pair of handcuffs and then just as slowly slipped back off.

"What are you doing later, kiddo?" she asked him.

Dion took a breath that tasted like a solar flare. "Sleeping," he said.

- 66 -

The sleep didn't last long. Awakening in his bed to thin squares of sunlight that outlined the closed window shades, Dion heard Shiner pushing open the door to his room.

"She's here again," Shiner said.

Dion blinked a few times into the dimness.

"More popcorn?" he asked, then heard shuffling in the hallway.

"No popcorn," Kady called. "Just some notes to share."

He scratched a clawed hand over his bare belly beneath the blankets.

"They couldn't wait?" he called back through a yawn. Then Kady was at the door too, crisp in blue jeans and a rugby shirt in the maroon and gold of the university, the school emblem over her heart.

"I couldn't wait," she said.

Dion heard a zipper, and Shiner asked him if she needed to wear something warmer than just her work smock. Kady told her a jacket would be a good idea and asked if she wanted a ride to the school. Shiner said no.

"No, thank you," Dion reminded her.

"You're welcome," Shiner said as she shouldered past Kady and stepped quickly down the hall.

"We go through some job stress at times," he told Kady when she seemed confused, then said that he would meet her in the kitchen in a few minutes, after he woke up a little.

"Just slide over," she directed, bending to untie her shoes. "I won't stay long."

He scooched to the far side of the bed and slouched back against the headboard while tucking the bedding around his waist. Kady climbed onto the mattress and sat near his feet, legs crossed atop the covers with one knee resting on his blanketed shin. She nodded toward his exposed chest.

"Why am I thinking of your sister right now?"

From the kitchen came the rustle of Shiner pulling on a coat, and then the whump of the back door as it opened and closed. A few seconds later Dion heard her footsteps outside on the sidewalk. He reached over to tug lightly on the toe of Kady's sock, telling her that if she wanted to send his sister an updated photo, they could probably provide an image more jointly provocative since they were both on his bed.

"There's the steamy talk again," she said with a sigh.

"You started it."

He raised one hand to rake his fingers through his hair, but she leaned forward and did it for him, her touch cool and surprising on his forehead.

"Before I give you my news, I want to hear about how things played out at home when you first learned about your folks," she said, her voice low and serious.

"What do you mean?" Dion said. "What's going on?"

"Just tell me what you remember about the last time you saw them and what happened next."

She stroked his hair once more and then sat back, her fingers clasped together between her knees. He pushed his hands under the blankets and tried to recall.

"I was at home with my dad after dinner," he began. "My uncle had picked up my mother to go sing. I don't know if they were working that night or rehearsing, but she was with Easy at the Matterhorn a lot, and I remember my dad complaining about that pretty often. When I went to bed, Evangeline was still out somewhere. I heard her come home just before I fell asleep. The two of them were talking."

Dion stopped to take a breath, squinting toward the darkened windows as he struggled to recreate the scene in his mind.

"I got up the next morning," he went on. "It must have been on a weekend because we didn't have school. My parents weren't there. I didn't think that much of it. My dad worked weird hours all the time with his painting business. After my sister got up and they hadn't come back by lunchtime, she called Easy. He came over and said we should go with him until he figured out what was going on."

"And that was it?"

"Pretty much," Dion said. "Easy reported them missing to the police. A couple of weeks later, they were still gone, and he told us that the police had found my dad, that somebody had killed him, but that no one knew where my mother was."

He turned his gaze toward Kady.

"The report in the file said my father was shot in the back of the head," he said, frowning. "Like an execution. That his body was moved, and after he was found, they left him there for a while to see if anyone came back to check the scene."

"You never knew that?"

"Not until this past week."

Kady told him that most details of the case would not have been made public since the investigation had never officially closed. She dropped a hand to his thigh and gave it a soft squeeze.

"Did your uncle say anything about your mom leaving the bar that night?" she said. "Why he didn't bring her home?"

"He said my dad came for her, the same thing the case file says he told the cops."

While he watched Kady thinking, Dion felt himself back in his boyhood, a memory of being bewildered and shunted to the fringes of questions that never quite got answered or asked, growing up with a sense that life was, more or less, a discouraging tension that echoed out loud, and that expecting any improvement only led to frustration.

"I'm telling you things," he said. "I thought you were here to tell me things."

She nodded as she adjusted her eyeglasses.

"The first is that whatever his reputation, Lauda Aplikowski apparently doesn't fudge his books," she said. "Without a court order to back me up, I couldn't push his accounting service too hard, but they confirmed that your Brillo Ziemer guy ran a tab that wasn't just forgiven, that Aplikowski paid the bill himself every month to keep things straight for taxes."

"For how long?" Dion asked.

"They wouldn't say," she answered. "But fire records show that an engine company was dispatched to the Matterhorn a week or two before your father was found. There was a report of flames in a circuit-breaker box in the music stage area of the lounge."

She fingered the open collar of her rugby shirt and continued.

"At the city's building permit office, I found an entry for the electrician who pulled the permit for the repair, with a certain painting and drywall company listed as a subcontractor for the restoration work."

"Brillo and my dad," Dion guessed. "But what do you think it means?"

Kady shook her head slowly, saying she wasn't sure.

"It confirms that Ziemer was telling your sister the truth," she decided. "I wonder, though, why Aplikowski would think that some minor work on his building would be worth giving Ziemer a free ride for twenty years, if that's really how long things went on."

Dion ran his tongue across the back of his teeth. "You're thinking there must be more to what he thought Brillo deserved," he said.

"Or demanded," Kady said.

Dion pulled at a willowy hair above his navel as he considered what she seemed to be implying, seeing her eyes turning toward the lazy motion of his fingers. Her hand squeezed his leg again, and she asked what he was thinking.

"About the timeline and coincidences," he told her. "The fire and my folks, you dusting off the investigation and people trying to put you off it, Brillo getting killed, and the old Matterhorn crew getting weird when they heard."

He looked at her. "You figure maybe Brillo Ziemer

knew something about what happened to my dad, and that Lauda and my uncle knew that he knew, and they're afraid you'll find out?"

Her palm was warm atop the blankets, her face warmer in his gaze. He saw her lips curl inward with a thought, and then part.

"No idea," she said. "But I do know something that you should hear."

She then recounted her discovery of the bicycle helmet and artifacts related to Shiner's wounding as a child mingled with the physical evidence of the Cullen Arcade murder, and of the ballistics test that she'd ordered for the bullet she had found. Dion allowed himself a low exhale, blinking toward the darkened windows when a tilt of her head and a widening of her eyes behind her glasses was her silent revelation of the result.

"Shot with his own gun?" he said. "Does that make any difference to how you look at things?"

Kady trilled her fingers on his knee as she brought her hand away, then shrugged.

"At this point, it's just one confirmed fact in a case that doesn't have many to work with, so I wouldn't commit myself to any particular theory."

She uncrossed her legs and moved to slide off the mattress. Dion reached over and gently gripped her ankle, stopping her.

"You need to sleep," she reminded him with a playful scold.

"After what you just told me, I don't think I can," he said. "Besides, I'm off work tonight. I'll sleep then."

He motioned with his eyes to the empty space beside

him on the bed. "So could you." He massaged her leg lazily. "Or we could see how many ways we can keep each other awake."

She brought her hand down over his, her face settling into a smile he thought withdrawn and slightly sad, and he had a sudden revelation of his own.

"I think I'm beginning to get it," he grasped aloud. "Steamy talk equals bad memories."

Her slow nod matched his, and he sensed himself sinking into the distantly alarming idea that he was about to be invited to a dance party with a higher cover charge for getting out than getting in. Traffic on the street outside the shaded windows swished past in hushes that sounded like breaths creasing the hairs on his chest.

"Heartache?" he said.

"Headache."

"Girl or boy?" he wondered.

He could feel his mind unsteadily navigating unfamiliar ground, his jaw clenched with an instinctive machismo at the thought of her being mistreated by some guy with him not there to intervene, but not so sure of what to think about a female pairing gone off the rails. When her eyes found his, he felt that she was afraid to hold them. She looked down quickly as she threaded her fingers tightly through his so he couldn't pull free.

"Brother," she said.

Her hand pressed harder. He nodded toward the door and told her he would see her in the kitchen.

He was getting up.

- 67 -

The coffee at the Matterhorn dining room was served in nondescript cups of white stoneware. Arno St. Albans rose from his table as people trickled in for the brunch seating. He carried his cup into the lounge and stood near the entryway, watching as a young woman behind the bar used a towel to polish the beer taps. Ceiling lights above her captured the glint of diamond studs that lined the curve of her left ear. He had an impression that he had seen her before but couldn't place the memory.

He took a sip of coffee and turned back toward his table to see Lauda Aplikowski coming out of the kitchen in a chef jacket and pants, looking like one of the kitchen staff. The sergeant raised his cup in greeting when the other man saw him, and Lauda came over.

"I knew you owned the place," St. Albans said. "I didn't know you were the cook too."

"I had to change from what I wore when I got up this morning," Lauda explained grumpily. "Does seeing you mean your pain-in-the-ass boss isn't far behind?"

The sergeant answered that Honest Mike Walerius was busy downtown, being important.

"I'm here for myself," he said. "To even things out some, if I can."

"How do you mean?"

"After I was here with the lieutenant the other day, his

wife told me about the business arrangement between you and her," St. Albans said. "I told him what she told me, and I shouldn't have done that."

Lauda dodged an employee who was hustling clean dishes to the buffet setup and pointed the sergeant to a table near the bar in the lounge. He asked if St. Albans knew the amount of money they were talking about.

"She didn't tell me that," St. Albans replied as they crossed the room. "And I don't want to know."

"Why did she tell you anything?"

The sergeant chose a chair, saying he thought that she enjoyed knowing something that her husband didn't and had wanted to share the secret with a friend.

"I let her down by passing it on," he said while Lauda took a seat across the table. "I figure the fair thing to do is let you in on what Honest Mike knows, since you and Corinne are partners. Maybe she'll believe I'm sorry if she hears it from you."

He took off his sunglasses and rubbed his wonky eye, then wondered if he appeared to be crying, because the other man grew suddenly earnest.

"You've got me convinced," Lauda assured him.

When St. Albans put the sunglasses back on, Lauda was regarding him warily.

"You sure it's smart to be that tight with someone else's wife, especially if you work with the guy?"

Before the sergeant could answer, a uniformed postal carrier came in from the dining room with a cluster of mail that she handed to Lauda. After she left, the question seemed forgotten and the subject of the conversation changed.

"Since it seems like you're trying to be straight with me, I'll let you in on what I see happening here," Lauda said as he spread the mail over the table. "After my asking him to repay a simple favor, our shady councilman got the idea to up the ante and take a run at muscling his wife into my affairs as his price for reciprocating. Now that he knows why his plan went nowhere, he needs to find a new angle, and once he does, he'll be coming back at me."

St. Albans lifted his coffee and took a swallow before saying that it sounded like the other man had a pretty clear perspective on the situation.

"The boss got a sense that the investigator who dug up the old Cullen Arcade case rattled you some," he said. "He thought he could take advantage."

"That's why he hasn't shut her down like I wanted?"

The sergeant turned the cup in his hand. "He did try," he answered. "Indirectly, so he wouldn't get caught publicly interfering on your behalf, which might cause a political scandal. But his plan hit an unexpected snag, so he recalibrated and realized that our officer working the file is an asset, because the reason for you to want her boxed out raises questions he didn't care about at first. With her refusing to back down, he's had time to consider how badly you're worried and why. Gives him a chance to see how tight he can squeeze you."

Lauda lifted a large envelope, studied it, then set it aside, arguing that he just didn't like having bad feelings stirred up for no good reason.

"She's picking at old scabs," he complained.

"The better to bleed you with, if it gets results," St. Albans said. "I can tell you that she's not going to stop just because you're bothered, and that I'm in her corner no matter what Honest Mike decides to do, because I'm wondering what we might have missed twenty years ago."

Lauda pawed through the jumble of papers while declaring, without sounding overly sincere or concerned, that he appreciated the information and the warning. St. Albans took it as an invitation to leave and finished his coffee.

A sink tap whistled behind the bar. The sergeant turned to see the young diamond-eared bartender rinsing glassware.

"Evan," Lauda suddenly called to her, hoisting an envelope. "You've got a letter here in care of the business, from some law office."

The bartender responded over the running water that she had given her apartment address to her uncle's lawyer and the city attorney, so she didn't know why anything would show up at the restaurant. Lauda looked perplexed as he slid a similar piece from the pile.

"There's one for the D-man too," he said.

St. Albans leaned forward to read the envelopes and then looked over to the bar, instantly energized by the coffee, the names he saw, the name he'd heard, and the surprise of understanding that he had been correct in thinking that the young woman seemed familiar to him. He had been talking with a vaguely parallel rendering of her for the past few days.

- 68 -

With a juice box for each of them in one hand, Dion closed the refrigerator and took a seat opposite Kady at the kitchen table. Then he changed his mind and moved to a spot to her side.

"Four years," she said. "Starting when I was seven."

Dion passed a box to her across the corner of the table and watched as she unwrapped the attached plastic drinking straw.

"What finally stopped it?"

"I think that when he turned eighteen, he figured out that he could go to jail," Kady said.

Dion stabbed his box open and sipped, staring silently at the strap of her shoulder bag, which hung from the back of the empty chair nearest the sink. Sunlight from the window behind it dusted the room with an ironic softness that made every word sound too loud.

"I told my mother early on," she recounted. "I guess she just couldn't process it because nothing changed. I told one of her sisters too, and that didn't help either. I asked that aunt about it when I got older, and she told me that sometimes when she was young and wearing a dress around the house, her dad would feel her up when she walked past, and that it was something that you just tolerated."

Kady made a face as she went on. "I mean, that's my grandpa being a creep, you know? And that must have been the family mindset. Men do what they do. Get over it."

She took a slow drink, her lips flat around the straw. Dion frowned, troubled by an image that had crept into his mind.

"With your brother," he began, but she cut him short.

"No, no," she said, shaking her head firmly. "No details. Too icky."

He nearly joked that it wasn't often that he heard such a girly word, stopping himself when he sensed that the description arose from the emotion of the child she had been at the time, the elements of violation naturally coalesced into an abiding curt summary of invisibility and helplessness that could never be outgrown or verbally refined. He fingered the sleeve of her rugby shirt.

"You're talking to a decorated veteran of the boy-girl wars," he confessed. "I've got some icky history of my own, with scars I try to not think about. Especially the ones I inflicted."

"On yourself?"

"Those too," he said thoughtfully, pausing for a moment before making an admission that he realized he had long been stifling. "I've done a lot of things I'm not proud of."

She eased her juice box across the tabletop like a boat traversing water to crash it slowly into his.

"That sounds like remorse," she said. "I'm impressed."

He pulled his juice box away, waxy in his hand, and then slid it back to bump hers softly, two children at play. He felt his chin quiver and tensed his teeth.

"I hurt," he told her. "I always have, and I don't know why."

He heard the dog next door barking in the yard. Kady looked toward the window.

"My therapist talks about how trauma is like a time stamp," she said. "The event alters how you process everything that comes afterward—physically because the chemistry of your brain changes, and emotionally because of how feelings get experienced out of context when your mind has gone into a defensive shutdown. Your brain is telling you that it's missing something, and you make bad decisions and impulsive choices trying to satisfy a need that you can't identify."

"That's what the meds are about?"

She nodded.

"They reestablish the chemical balance so you can work on recognizing the cognitive distortions that have been messing up how you see things," she answered. "Then the challenge is to understand your own situation and how to reconnect to yourself and get on with your life from a healthier footing. You can stop feeling so much like you don't fit in anywhere no matter how hard you try. That way, you don't respond to your frustration by behaving in ways that give people no reason to like you, and you don't judge everyone badly just because subconsciously, you believe something is wrong with you and you can't trust that anyone could really like you because you don't like yourself. Not doing that work leaves you angry because you know you're smart, but not smart enough to think yourself out of the box you're trapped in."

Dion felt a prickle low within his ears.

"Wow," he said. "That's really deep."

"Like the box that trapped me," she replied. "I've been learning that it has handholds, though, for climbing out."

She steered her elbow into his, the bone insistent.

"You lost your parents in about as rotten a way as anybody could think of," she said. "But that's not you, that's something that happened to you. There's a difference."

He lifted his juice box for a sip. The straw smelled sweet, and so did her shirt.

"In your mind then," he said, "the thing with your brother is just something that happened to you? That's what therapy does? To me, it sounds like pie-in-the-sky-when-you-die talk."

"There's a lot more to it," Kady agreed. "And I've got a long way to go. My brother is still my brother, and I can't change that, but I don't have to let what he did define me. Maybe I've been victimized, but I don't have to be a victim forever because of it."

Dion asked if her brother was still around. She gave her juice box a gentle shake and took a drink before nodding.

"He lives over in Minneapolis with his wife and two kids," she answered, "in a nice neighborhood by the lakes. He runs a warehouse for some big home-appliance distributor out in the western suburbs. I don't talk to him or see him much. If our parents weren't still around and needing help sometimes, the two of us probably wouldn't talk at all."

"His wife knows what he did to you?"

"I'm not really sure," she said. "When I was in high school, he typed out a letter on my old word processor in my bedroom and left it with my homework for me to find—him trying to make himself feel less guilty rather than apologize, is the way I remember it. He was more concerned about how he might be judged than about how I was doing. I don't know if he's ever shared anything with her. She's always kept her distance, though, and I have a sense that even if he didn't tell her, she suspects that there's something weird between us. She's never asked me. She probably doesn't want me in her head, hanging around on the fringe of her marriage as an inconvenient truth reminding her that her dream kitchen was delivered with some factory dents."

Dion had a thought and said, "Does she look like you?"

Kady wrinkled her nose, calculating.

"Not really," she decided. "My brother does, but not as much as your sister looks like you."

"Evangeline would say that I look like her," he pointed out. "She'd play the seniority card."

Kady replied that either way, the resemblance was oddly titillating.

"Like, exotic, with me in the middle." she said, stretching her arm along his.

"Who's talking steamy now?"

She smiled around the straw of her juice box.

"Maybe you're starting to rub off on me," she said. "I'm picking up on your kinky side. My sordid past isn't putting you off, it's turning you on. Like the competition between you and your sister is turning me on."

The dog outside barked again. Dion pushed aside his juice box.

"I kind of like the idea of rubbing off on you," he said, raising a hand toward a button at the neckline of her rugby shirt. "Maybe the two of us should try rubbing off on each other."

"I have to go back to work," Kady protested.

"Shiner is working," Dion argued. "If it's lunchtime for the kids at school, it's lunchtime for you too."

Then, slowly, he sensed the room around them become a moment and the soft daylight a sound he could see, like infinity distilled in desperate hope, their past and future to be forever defined in the close physical rhythms of moist concussions and melded heartbeats he could already hear in his mind. He brought his hands to either side of her eyeglasses.

"On or off?" he asked.

"On," she whispered, her eyes fast on his, breaths rising faster. "I want to see what you're doing to me."

His fingers drifted to her collar. Her gaze drifted sideways atop a frown. He turned to see what she saw, the empty chair where her shoulder bag hung from the backrest.

"What's wrong?" he asked.

"Your roommate," she told him. "I just figured out that she took my jacket."

- 69 -

Arno St. Albans stayed at the table in the Matterhorn lounge after Lauda Aplikowski had finished reviewing the rest of the business mail and gone back to the dining room to meet the brunch crowd. Behind the bar, Evan Arcade looked up from one of the letters Lauda had passed to her on his way out and asked the sergeant if he wanted more coffee. St. Albans rose and brought his cup over, saying that he wasn't sure, but that if she didn't mind a question, he was wondering something. Her eyes narrowed on him as he set the cup in front of her, and she began talking past him as though recycling a memory.

"An older guy who looked sort of grim, nosing around," she said. "You're the cop who's not Kady."

She surprised him enough that it took a second before he could ask her how she knew.

"And who said I looked grim?" he said defensively.

Evan replied by turning her gaze downward to the envelopes Lauda had fished from the mail for her, both lying flat on the bar, the one sent to her torn open, the other still sealed. His eyes followed, and then he understood.

"The names aren't the same," he observed, tapping a finger on the addresses. "But the faces are close."

Evan nodded absently, studying her letter. "Not just our faces," she said.

"Any relation to a name from an old case of mine?" asked St. Albans. "Cullen Arcade?"

"He was our dad."

The sergeant thought back to the vintage photograph of the three young painters that included the two dead men and Tico's father, the one that had gone missing from Brillo Ziemer's house.

"If the kid from this other letter is your brother, then that picture he took probably means something more than I thought," he said quietly, thinking out loud while testing her for a reaction.

"He took a picture of something?" Evan asked, sounding as though she didn't know what he was talking about.

"From somewhere," St. Albans corrected, feeling like he had carried on this conversation before. "He stole an old photo from a guy named Brillo Ziemer's house. A shot of your father with Ziemer and Tico's dad. You know Tico, your brother's friend?"

"I know Tico," Evan said. "I know about Brillo too, and if my brother took something from Brillo's house, he wasn't stealing. It was half his."

She showed him the letter. "This attorney here says that the other half is mine, as an equal beneficiary to the estate."

The sergeant reached for the paper.

"The three of you must have been close," he mused as he read.

"Seems like Brillo sure thought so," she agreed. "I'm sorry now that I wasn't nicer to him all the times he was in here. He really felt a connection, I guess."

"His perception was off the mark?"

"Let's call it chronically impaired," Evan said. "There's

usually a reason, you know, for somebody doing something stupid like falling down a hole. Like it says in the Bible, he who lives by the grape shall die by the grape."

"I don't think the Bible says that."

"Well, if it doesn't, it should."

St. Albans finished the letter and asked her if she thought her brother would share her assessment of the dead painter. Evan answered that she couldn't say, but that the two of them shared a lot of things. She pulled her cell phone from her pants pocket and scrolled the screen. When the sergeant looked up, she was holding the phone toward him, the display ablaze with the headless image of a bare male chest.

"That's my baby brother," she said, then swiped the screen to a headless shot of a bare chest that was strikingly not male. "And that's me. Like I told you, it's not just our faces that are close."

The saliva on his tongue thickening, St. Albans shook his head. The sounds of commotion from the dining room grew louder with new arrivals.

"My week just keeps getting weirder and weirder," he said, pointing at the phone. "What the hell was that all about?"

"Kady, of course," Evan said, grinning. "You ready for more coffee now?"

He looked at his empty cup, then pointed down the bar toward the beer taps.

- 70 -

Drifting just beneath the surface of sleep, Dion sensed a motion within his field of awareness, an erratic, tense movement that came with a sound like someone struggling to uncap a stubborn jar or shed an overtight sweater—and then came the scream. He awakened to Kady sitting upright and shaking beside him, the bedsheets clustered around her waist, and, as he had done their first night together at the impound lot, he told her to breathe—except this time he also touched her, moving his hand soothingly over the hot, damp skin between her shoulder blades.

"It's okay," he said, repeating it between her slowing exhales until she had calmed herself and settled onto the mattress again, his arm pinned beneath the small of her back.

He could see that strong sunlight was still straining the edges of the closed window shades. He had not been sleeping long, or long enough.

"I thought you said they were night terrors," he complained through a yawn.

Her spiky hair tickled his jaw as she nestled in closer to him, her breaths now coming steadier and slow.

"It's night for you, right?" she pointed out.

The tease in her voice suited the comfortable dimness of the room and the friendly contact of her thigh alongside his, and he let his eyes fall closed in a hopeful attempt to delay what he expected would, as always, come next: the fated letdown when euphoria dissipates amid the fading carnal spasms of conquest, and the pained lessons of experience see the prospect of a lengthy shared future going nowhere and gaining speed. As he felt himself slipping into that familiar misgiving, he also felt her back muscles tighten atop his arm at a sound coming from the edge of the room, the sedate flap of a book page being turned.

"She's in here, isn't she?" Kady whispered.

Dion didn't need to look, but he raised his head and looked anyway to regard Shiner ensconced in the shadows past the foot of the bed, sharing the corner chair with their discarded clothes, a puzzle book in her grip.

"What do you want me to do?" he whispered back as his hair found the pillow once more.

Her nose brushed his shoulder when she craned her neck toward him, all worry evaporating in the heat of her voice, her tongue a torch at his ear.

"Talk to me."

He stretched his trapped arm under her to curl it up and out along her waist, his palm cradling the soft, rounded knob of her opposite hip.

"Knock, knock," he mouthed quietly.

She answered with a gasp of consenting anticipation that fanned his eyelashes wide.

"Ooh," she exhaled hotly. "Who's there?"

With one motion his arm swept her up and she was astraddle, the hazy room alive with staccato triads of halting breaths and the fat slurp of devilish smiles.

"Ya," he said.

- 71 -

After the Amor Abrasadora lunch crowd thinned out, Arno St. Albans sat alone at a table near the back hallway, a beer in hand as he tried to follow a European automobile race on the big televisions over the bar, the broadcast audio too far across the room to be useful. Corinne Nasseff came out from the kitchen, untying her apron as she made her way toward him.

"Okay," she said, folding the apron onto the table and pulling out a chair. "Now I can talk."

She nodded toward his bottle as she sat down.

"You must be off today."

He tilted his head back and forth with the motion of the cars streaking across the television screens, leaning himself into the road-course turns.

"I am a little off today," he decided. "I think I've been a little off for a lot of days."

She fluffed her hair away from the collar of her pastel oxford blouse and gave him a look.

"If this thing with your face is getting to you, maybe you should be talking to somebody else," she suggested. "Like a therapist."

He took a drink and told her that he had been talking to somebody else, explaining that he had just come from the Matterhorn.

"I let Lauda Aplikowski in on everything I think Honest Mike knows, or thinks he knows," he said, then told her the reason and that he hoped she knew he was trying to make amends with her. "I didn't keep your secret, and that made me a bad friend."

"Could be worse," she said. "You could be a bad husband too."

"Well, you deserve better," he declared, head swiveling as a race car on the screens careered through a chicane. "On both fronts."

She reached across the table and gently wedged the bottle from his hand. She took a sip of his beer.

"How did Lauda react?"

The sergeant turned toward her, thinking.

"He didn't, really," he said. "Just kind of banking what I was saying for future use, I suppose. There was something interesting I found out while I was with him, though."

"I found out something interesting this morning too," Corinne interrupted. "The demon came to see me and wanted to know what the walrus was trying to do to Lauda. It surprised me that he knew as much as he did, so I told him, and it turns out that the kid has a sister who works at the Matterhorn."

"That's what I was about to say," said St. Albans. "She tends bar there. I actually ended up talking to her."

Corinne took another drink and passed the bottle back to him.

"You know, I was thinking that if this sister is anything like him, she could come in handy as a mole," she said.

St. Albans wormed a finger under his sunglasses and gave his frozen eye a wink.

"Oh, they're alike," he said. "Especially with their shirts

pulled up. She's the curvier of the two, though, which you'd expect."

"Their shirts pulled up?"

"She showed me a stark comparison of their pectoral topography," he said. "She had pictures on her phone. The one of her was more impressive than the one of him, if you were to judge by contours. More fun too."

"'Stark' meaning, like, naked with nipples and everything?"

"And everything."

"Why did she show you that?" cried Corinne.

The sergeant held up the bottle and studied the label for a long moment.

"I was hoping this second beer of the day would help me figure that out," he answered. "So far, I'm drawing a blank, but she did agree with an earlier report from her brother that I looked sort of grim, so maybe she was trying to boost my spirits. She seemed like the type of nice person who would do that."

"She sounds like the type of nice person who knows how to push someone's buttons," Corinne pointed out, then added a wistful complaint. "Like her brother."

She brought her hand across the table and took his beer away again.

"Go back to work," she scolded. "Before you get into trouble. We can talk later. And don't worry, we're still pals."

He watched her as she rose to leave, his bottle going with her, and nodded seriously, saying he was glad to be forgiven but that it was clear he was already in trouble in his head. That was why the beer wasn't helping.

"Jeez, what's with you?" she said. "It was only a picture, right?"

"Yeah, but you didn't see it."

Her short heels clicked over the floor as she headed down the back hallway toward her office, shaking her head as she walked away. He stayed for several minutes at the table, watching the race and thinking that there likely existed some profound parallel between the circular repetition of the cars and the mindless mosaic of his day, but had to admit that he was probably not the first person to ponder such a comparison and that meditating upon its relevance wasn't going to improve anything anyway, so he finally roused himself to his feet.

Outside on the way to his car, he felt a vibration from his coat pocket. He pulled out his cell phone to find a text message waiting. He stopped on the sidewalk to swipe the screen and laughed when it opened to a frontal snapshot of a headless female with her pastel oxford blouse unbuttoned past her navel, hints of dark areolae peeking above the ribboned limits of a demi-cup brassiere.

The beer was helping after all.

- 72 -

Evan poured herself a glass of water from her brother's kitchen sink and then sat back down at the table with him and the others. Dion reread the letter she had brought over, occasionally looking up as Shiner and Kady passed a pencil back and forth between themselves, playing a word game in an activity book. Waning sunlight from the window refracted itself in Evan's diamond ear studs.

"I'm just as surprised as you," Evan said to him.

"But at least you and Brillo had a connection from him hanging out at the Matterhorn," Dion said. "I hardly ever talked to him."

Kady spoke without looking up from the book, scratching her chin on the sleeve of her rugby shirt.

"This is about past connections, I think," she said. "He and your father were partners, and you said that Ziemer might have had a thing for your mother. Well, leaving everything to you two proves that there was definitely something on his mind."

Dion looked over at his sister, saying, "On his mind, or his conscience?"

She shrugged and took a drink at the same time Shiner raised a question related to their present connections.

"Are we moving?"

Dion set the letter down next to Evan. "Are we?" he asked her.

Kady suggested that perhaps they should talk to an attorney of their own before meeting with Brillo's.

"Whoever we talk to, I'm claiming dibs on the biggest bedroom," Evan said. "And Brillo's van."

Then she pointed at Shiner.

"I'll take the cute jacket she's wearing too."

"That's mine," Kady said. "It went along with her to school on an unauthorized field trip at lunchtime."

Evan made a thoughtful face, saying, "You've been here awhile."

"She screamed in bed," Shiner said.

Evan raised an eyebrow toward Dion. Kady rose from her chair quickly, asking Shiner if there were other books they could try, maybe some in the living room. As they left the kitchen, Dion felt an unexpected rush of pride.

"Fitting herself right in," Evan remarked. "Not exactly taking her time, is she?"

Dion answered that he just hoped it would last. She pointed out that he always seemed to hope for that. He reached over for her water glass, disagreeing.

"I always wish," he said between sips. "Hope is new."

"Well, if the pillow talk turns intense, just remember that a girl giving up her heart will tell you secrets she expects you to forget," Evan advised. "You'll be sorry if you don't."

Dion thought about Kady's confessions as he handed the glass back. Evan swirled one finger slowly over the rim, looking out toward the living room.

"She told me that her therapist says that damaged people find each other," she said.

"That would explain her finding us," Dion said.

"She thinks that you found her. On a sticky note."

In the dull whine of the basement furnace hurling itself into a heating cycle and the sober impact of her words, he could hear his mind forming a notion that both life and love might be less a question of timing and chance than pure preordained destiny, where the innocent action of taking a pen to paper can spawn cosmic runes that transcend logic to etch binding and irrepressible shared cryptograms upon two receptive hearts.

"She's right," he nodded. "That's exactly what happened."

From the living room came sounds of Shiner humming and book pages turning. Dion cocked one ear and listened as he picked up the bequest letter again.

"Easy used to hum around the house when I lived with him," he said. "Trying to force music into my brain, I guess. I don't think he ever forgave me for how bad I was at trying to learn the piano."

Evan stroked her thumb down the water glass. "Or me for leaving?" she asked him.

"He never said."

He could hear louder humming in the other room, a second voice joining in, and he recalled something Kady had indirectly implied.

"You and Easy," he said to Evan. "He mostly left me to myself, but with you was he ever like, inappropriate? Is that why you moved out?"

Evan curled her nose as she frowned down at the glass. "Nothing ever happened, but once in a while he'd come out with something that sounded like it could mean more than what he was saying," she said. "I always had a sense that there was something off-kilter in the back of his mind, some ideas he had that weren't quite polite, if you get my drift. Whether they were about me or Mom, I don't know, but either way I didn't want to find out."

"You look like her," Dion said. "It could have been both of you, warped as it sounds. He's never had any other women in his life that I remember. Or guys either, if he leans that way."

Evan took a swig of water and agreed.

"I've thought of that. It's one of the reasons I haven't minded working with him over the years, as long as he keeps a respectful distance. He's still family, and I'm not above giving him a focus for his fantasies or memories if it helps him get through the day, even if it might be creepy. It's not like any one of us is a saint."

Dion looked at the letter, asking if she had told their uncle or Lauda Aplikowski about Brillo's estate.

"No," Evan answered. "I wanted to show you first. Easy wasn't around. The boss was a little curious about why you and I were getting mail sent to the restaurant, but he didn't get nosy. He just told me not to be gone too long when I told him I was coming here."

She thought of something else. "Your grim cop was there too, and he did get nosy," she said. "He was talking to Lauda when the mail came, and then he stayed to talk to me. He figured out who we are, and I showed him the lawyer letter about Brillo's will."

A buzz erupted from atop the refrigerator. Dion rose from his chair to pull down his cell phone. He opened the arriving text message as he retook his seat. Evan leaned to look as the screen lit up with a headless photo of a woman in an unbuttoned oxford blouse.

"Hey now," she said.

Kady came back from the living room, carrying her jacket. Shiner was behind her, holding a puzzle book. Evan took the phone from Dion and held it up for the others to see.

"We must've started a trend," she said.

Kady looked at the image and then at Dion, asking whose phone she was examining. When he told her it was his, she answered with a slow nod.

"I see that I'll need to keep an eye on you."

Evan wanted to know who the woman was.

"You remember helping me send that goofy video of Honest Mike Walerius sitting under a hair dryer the other day?" Dion said.

"To his wife," Evan recalled.

He pointed at the photo.

"What does it mean?" Kady asked him.

"I couldn't tell you if I wanted to," Dion said. "This wasn't something I expected. Maybe it's her idea of a reward."

"I'd call it an invitation," Evan offered, admiring the shot. "Whichever, it's hard not to like her approach."

"I met her once, and I'm not sure I'd agree." Kady bent closer to the screen. "Nice bra, though."

"Nice cleavage," Evan added.

"Nice ring," Shiner said.

The others looked at her.

Kady pulled her jacket on, saying she needed to get back to work. Evan said that she did too, suggesting that they all converge later at the Matterhorn to celebrate the inheritance news. Shiner clucked. Evan promised that chicken wings would be ordered.

Kady gestured toward the phone, the text image still aglow with skin.

"Anything we need to worry about?" she asked Dion.

"No," he said with a yawn. "I'll deal with this, whatever it is."

She encouraged him to go back to bed. He looked from the phone to the letter and gave a chuckle at her idea that his circling thoughts might subside to the point of sleep.

When Shiner clucked again, he clucked back.

- 73 -

The back hallway of the Matterhorn at suppertime smelled to Arno St. Albans like dryer lint, the wood-paneled walls a smudged filter soured by tipsy decades of human passage immune to half-hearted applications of disinfectant cleansers.

"I don't need to be here," the sergeant complained as he followed Honest Mike Walerius in from the rear parking lot. "Lauda Aplikowski is not going to let you get the better of him, with or without me."

A speaker nestled in the ceiling between the dim recessed lights quavered out a syrupy orchestration of a big-band anthem with brassy underscore fills suggestive of a nagging sinus inflammation.

"It is evident that I still suffer your pique from earlier today," replied the councilman. "The sentiment is shared, if I am to be truthful, but even a feeble display of strength will register in the perception of such an adversary as we find here, and since I believe that I now possess an incentive for his capitulation that he will find difficult to refute, I shall value your witness to it."

"What did you come up with?" St. Albans asked.

Honest Mike stopped near the restrooms and unbuttoned his overcoat to reveal a suit that matched the pale-blue tint of his eyeglass lenses, its narrow stripes accenting the sheen of his silvery curls in the weak halo of light from a fixture above.

"A rigorous review of city ordinances pertaining to holders of liquor licenses," replied the councilman, "whereby I confirmed a personal recollection of a recent council hearing and the pertinence of City code that clarifies license parameters and prohibits any singular party from interest in multiple licensee entities."

"Better spell that out for me."

Honest Mike held up a hand as though about to count his fingers.

"A restaurant group or partnership may hold licenses to sell alcohol for consumption on site for only a prescribed number of locations within our jurisdiction," he said. "Call to your mind franchise outlets, or umbrella corporations formed to operate small chains of sister establishments."

"Okay. So?"

"So, our rules to discourage monopolized markets do not allow you or I as individuals to participate as owner-members of more than one such organization," the councilman continued. "Therefore, the arrangement between Lauda Aplikowski and my sweet Corinne, at present, cannot be justified or legally sustained. Either their hospitality endeavors must be incorporated as a merged business or registered with the secretary of state's office as an actual partnership, with resultant revenue and tax ramifications, or the pair must divest themselves of their association. At present, of the two he, with his finger in two pies as per your previous inelegant description, is in violation of the law."

The sergeant had to laugh out loud at that.

"And you really think he cares?" he said.

The councilman nodded confidently, saying, "I am sure he will understand that while public disclosure of his position might create some political turmoil for myself and discomfort for my wife, it would certainly expose him to unpleasant legal sanctions he could find indefensible and daunting, such as fines and suspension of his business operations."

"That would put a hit on his checkbook," St. Albans granted.

Honest Mike finished by declaring, "I expect his recognition of the benefit to him of simply forfeiting whatever might be the current balance of Corinne's financial obligation."

A shadow approached from down the hall, and they both looked to see a man whose uneasy, shambling advance indicated he was coming from the lounge rather than the dining room.

"Speaking of liquor," said St. Albans.

They squeezed themselves closer to the wall to let the man pass on his way to the twin restrooms. Another figure, a young blond woman making noises, followed behind him with the same apparent destination. As she came closer, the sergeant noticed a mangled white scar on her left temple, and he remembered seeing her behind the service counter during his first visit to the police impound lot. She looked at them as she reached the restroom doors, hesitating as she scanned their faces before her eyes found his and she smiled widely, as though to signify that she felt pleased with herself for remembering too.

"I am the egg man," she exclaimed.

She opened a door and went through. As it closed be-

hind her, Honest Mike frowned, saying he'd failed to cata-
logue the young woman's identity as an acolyte.

"I am the confused man," he said.

"I know you are," St. Albans said. "But what am I?"

The councilman shook his head in mild exasperation.

"Relax," said the sergeant. "If I'm guessing right, once
we finish harassing Aplikowski, we can take a peek to see
who's in the piano bar and that girl will make sense."

When he finished speaking, the background music
from the overhead speaker faded, and, in the pause between songs, muted cackles like a parody of domestic fowl
wafted from inside the restroom. Honest Mike cocked an
ear toward the sound, his frown deepening.

"Is she calling us chicken?" he wondered.

- 74 -

Shiner stared intently at the cribbage board between Evan and Kady, a peg between her thumb and finger hovering over a line of holes.

"Five spots, sweetie," Evan directed from behind the lounge bar, pointing to the appropriate spot on the board while she swept away a basket of denuded poultry bones.

Shiner pushed the peg home and sat back on her barstool with her hands folded over her lap to await the next count. Dion looked on from the stool beside her. Kady, sitting at her opposite shoulder, mumbled at an array of standard playing cards with no risqué adornments turned face up alongside the board, calculating their value as a hand.

Dion swiveled to peer across the mostly empty tables as Easy prepared for the evening set, the musician positioning ring binders of song arrangement sheets atop his piano up on the stage in the glare of the single spotlight.

"The old boy doesn't look any worse off for getting arrested again this morning," Dion said to Evan. "What did he have to say when you guys picked him up?"

Evan lifted a glass of wine and sipped.

"He started out by ranting about how he was being harassed for his civil claim against the cops, but he quieted down pretty quick," she answered. "I think he knows that he screwed up. He'll probably lose a year of driving once the courts are finished with him."

Kady showed Shiner the next peg to move, telling the others not to forget about his likely insurance rates once he was legally back behind the wheel.

"You might be carting him around in Brillo Ziemer's van for a while," Dion teased Evan.

"Christ," she muttered.

He asked her to refill his water glass, then shushed out a loud mock whisper when Easy stepped down from the stage and walked within earshot.

"Quiet, here he comes."

"Smart-ass," Easy said as he came over and slapped a palm onto the bar. "I'm facing the same kind of juvenile nonsense from your damn city attorney people."

"They don't want to settle?"

"They want to insult me by saying that my injuries show embellishment after the fact," Easy said. "My lawyer countered with your deposition testifying that when you bailed me out, I looked like I'd been roughed up while in police custody and my face was out to here."

He held his left hand six inches from his cheek. Dion glanced at his sister. She looked away. Easy looked at Shiner and then seemed to notice Kady for the first time.

"The cops know damn well they broke my jaw, and that's all I'm going to say in front of present company," he said.

Kady shifted her cards as she responded.

"Don't mind me," she offered breezily. "I'm not really listening."

Easy scoffed and swiped a hand over his nose, asking Evan for a diet soda in a glass with a straw. Dion watched as his sister scooped ice and was surprised to feel his throat slowly thickening against a thought, his chest tight as the thought became an argument that sounded like his voice.

"She might not be listening, but I am," he said. "And I don't hear anyone saying a damn thing. Nobody ever says anything around here, at least not anything important."

Evan had stopped what she was doing to look at him, and he could sense Kady looking too, the dull patter of the few customers around the lounge not as loud as the vibrations that had settled upon his ears, his breaths heating up and quickening.

"Two times this week the cops pick you up near the scene of the crime or trying to get there," he said to his uncle. "I'll listen to you talk all night about what that might mean. After waiting twenty years, a couple more minutes won't matter."

Easy had both his palms spread on the bar, his fingers beginning to flex tensely.

"There's nothing to say," he replied flatly. "Just let it go."

Evan shook the glass, and the ice sounded like chain links landing on stone.

"No, little brother, don't let it go," she said to Dion. "Let it out."

For a moment, Dion remembered her as a formidable teenager, tough and standing firm in her own space, with him wishing he knew how she did it so he could do it too, now feeling vaguely frightened that perhaps he was experiencing a flicker of that power for himself without knowing how to use it.

"You kids don't understand," Easy said.

"Never have," Dion agreed, the words coming out dry. "Whose fault is that?"

Easy didn't answer. Dion could see the old man's wired jaw pulsating, swallowing a response.

"We also don't understand why Brillo Ziemer left his house and all of his stuff to the two of us," Evan said.

"What?" Easy said with clear surprise.

"You heard right," Evan told him.

Easy stared toward the wall behind her. Evan poured some soda and handed him the glass. He turned and walked off toward the dining room without saying more.

"That shut him up," Kady said.

"I thought you weren't listening," Evan said.

Kady reached across Shiner's back to give Dion a squeeze on his shoulder, telling him that he was brave and asking if he was okay. He realized that he had been shivering, but he wasn't cold.

"I'm really tired," he said.

Evan told him to go get some sleep, that the women would get Shiner home in an hour or so.

"It's a slow night," she said. "The boss can cover the end of my shift for me."

Dion asked Kady if that worked for her.

"I'm good," she said as she gathered the playing cards for a shuffle. "I'll be better after I figure out this game."

As he climbed off his stool, Dion saw Lauda Aplikowski at the lounge entryway where Easy swerved out of sight around the corner. Dion went over.

"What's wrong with Easy?" Lauda asked. "He looked shook."

"Family issues on his mind," Dion answered. "Like why he can't stay away from my father's crime scene these days, and why Brillo Ziemer left his house and all his stuff to my sister and me. Bringing it up must have hit a nerve."

He pointed a finger at Lauda's suddenly unsettled facial response.

"Like that," Dion added.

Lauda turned his gaze toward the lights of the bar, and Dion looked also, Shiner cackling there at Evan with two straws tucked into her upper lip like tusks. The old man appeared to be seeing something beyond them in the distance.

"It's not a nerve with me," he said. "What I've got is a headache that won't go away."

Then his expression changed. Turning toward Dion again, he said, "Brillo? For real?"

"More like unreal," Dion said, walking away and zipping his jacket as he moved past the restrooms and out the rear entrance, the dark evening air cold at his neck as he made his way across the parking lot toward his car, sidestepping thin ice patches on the asphalt that reflected mist dripping from the light poles.

Tires crunched slowly toward him, the front-side passenger window of a familiar white sedan cranking down as it rolled close by. Dion stooped to see Honest Mike Walerius behind the wheel, braking the car and leaning to speak past his sergeant beside him.

"I am informed that you are the notable demon recently corrupted by the conniving of my vindictive spouse."

Dion blinked at the two men, confused, while the car engine wheezed in the wet air like it was on life support.

"Demon?" he said after a pause.

He thought back to his first meeting with Corinne Nasseff in her office and her reaction to the muffled voice of Hefty Von Hanson beckoning to him from outside the closed door. His laugh echoed over the parked vehicles.

"If that's what everyone heard, I guess that's what I am."

The councilman nodded to the rear seat.

"You had best get in, then."

Dion got in.

- 75 -

They didn't drive far. Honest Mike Walerius pulled the sedan into an opening two spaces away and let the car idle. Dion sat behind Arno St. Albans, who reached to the front dashboard to turn up the heat with the window still down. The councilman's overcoat rustled as he jostled himself on the front seat, making himself bigger. His voice came out threatening and thin.

"I have been advised that you are not of a deferential nature," he said. "I would caution you that I am not this evening of a mind to entertain affronts."

Dion draped his arm across the rear seatback, trying to look casual.

"What did you mean about me being corrupted by your wife?" he asked, a bit worried as he thought of the photo Corinne Nasseff had texted to him of her unbuttoned blouse.

"I should think you would find that obvious," Honest Mike said. "To be precise, your role in her production of that most disrespectful video in which I am the unsuspecting protagonist. Such conduct conflicts with the unstated obligations incumbent upon your municipal position. Must I remind you as to who is the party responsible for your civic appointment?"

"You," replied Dion. "Through Lauda Aplikowski and your wife and their connection with the restaurant and tavern people."

"Quite so. And as tribute to my intercession with our human resources and civil service officials on your behalf, might you recall that you assumed a responsibility not directly stipulated in the summary of your assigned duties?"

Dion took a slow breath.

"I am the egg man," he said.

"Again, quite so," Honest Mike said. "You acquitted yourself most favorably in the covert extrication of my impounded city vehicle, so you must now surely understand my bafflement at finding you to be an accessory to my wife's conspiracy to cast me in an unflattering light."

Dion thought of the photo again, and of the look she had given him while tapping her toe on his outside the cantina.

"She can be persuasive," he said.

He heard movement in the front seat and turned to see the two men glance at each other.

"He got that description from me," St. Albans said.

Honest Mike's head tilted as he stared out through the windshield.

"It could have just as readily been me," he admitted. "I harbor no illusions regarding the ability of my sweet Corinne to inspire an impulse of misguided cooperation from an associate."

He asked what she had offered as an enticement. Dion gave him half an answer.

"I'm not sure we ever got that far in the negotiation."

The sergeant chuckled.

"Welcome to West Seventh Street," he said, pulling off his sunglasses. "Where the natives know what they know, and never let you know."

Dion gazed out the rear window, his sister's bicycle chained to a bollard beside the building entrance, Lauda Aplikowsi's shining old Chrysler parked nearby. Up in the black sky, beyond the haze from the parking lot lights floated a thumbnail of moon and a dim star beside it, the distance between measured as both a factor of illumined velocity and the width of his fist, with the time it took for him to think of it that way calculated as a divisible ratio of the human experience, the wonder of what over why.

He reached to scratch his nose. His knuckle smelled like chicken grease.

"What did you want me to let you know?" he asked St. Albans.

The sergeant put his sunglasses back on as he answered.

"Why you didn't think you could tell me who you are," he said. "If it wasn't for your sister, I still wouldn't know."

"She told me about you figuring it out," Dion said. "I was just trying to keep my advantage for as long as I could."

St. Albans nodded as he went on, saying, "I'd also like to know what you and your partner are working at. Or if you even know yourself."

Dion saw the councilman's eyes grow suspicious in the rearview mirror.

"Might I interrupt to be briefed upon the identity of our young friend here?" Honest Mike said.

This time Dion spoke before the sergeant could.

"Call me the second coming of Cullen Arcade."

"The bartender we saw in there is Arcade's daughter," St. Albans added, pointing first toward the building and then to the back seat. "This is his son."

Honest Mike turned to regard Dion.

"The case records removed from this vehicle during its incarceration," the councilman pieced together aloud. "It was by your design, to protect Aplikowski? Was it not made clear to you by my sergeant here that I wanted that file?"

"I wanted it worse," Dion said. "And I'm not protecting anybody."

Honest Mike's mouth moved like he was chewing on something tasteless.

"Including yourself, it would seem," he said. "The sergeant has indicated that he has been unable to discern your intentions, so I will augment his curiosity with my own. What say you?"

Dion said he wasn't sure what that meant.

"He wants to know what you're up to," St. Albans said.

Dion replayed in his mind the hours of the previous days, of the case file and ballistic reports dedicated to his father's killing, of the aloof reticence of his uncle, of Brillo Ziemer's perplexing bequest, of exposed skin shared as cell phone pixels and shared live between bedsheets, and finally, of his introduction to Honest Mike's wife at the cantina and her approval of his capacity for listening while making him twirl for her.

"My ears," he said with a yawn he didn't realize he had been fighting. "I'm up to my ears."

The sergeant gave a short laugh. Honest Mike held up a hand to quash it.

"Do not encourage this blithe insubordination," he told him. "I find myself increasingly annoyed."

"I know you are," Dion said. "But what am I?"

He could feel a fuzz around his eyes fueled by fatigue as he fingered a hole in the seat fabric.

"Anybody else think it smells like gunshots in here?"

"We are not amused," Honest Mike huffed.

Dion sat slowly upright and leaned forward, gripping the backrest of the front seat between the two men.

"You really want me to tell you something I know?" he said tiredly. "How about this? It was his own gun."

"We already knew that," the sergeant replied. "Corinne admitted it to me, and I told the boss here."

Dion said that he wasn't talking about the bullet holes in the car.

"I'm talking about my dad."

The councilman turned his chin to speak across the seat.

"No weapon was ever discovered," he said. "Nor actual murder scene. By what alchemy do you feel emboldened to make this claim?"

Dion felt a soft smile spread over his teeth as he thought of something Kady had said to him the day they shared lunch downtown.

"Because the girl cop is magic," he said.

The two older men traded a look. The car heater hissed air that tasted like galvanized nails.

"Such response suggests that our young investigator has merited your regard for her potential," Honest Mike said to St. Albans.

The sergeant gestured with his head toward Dion behind them, saying, "His too, from the sound of it."

Dion sank back into his seat, closing his eyes. He could hear the others talking low in front of him, the words losing shape as his mind flitted on the edges of a doze. His eyes opened when he sensed the sergeant addressing him.

"What?"

"I asked if there's more to the story than just the gun," St. Albans said. "I won't insist on details."

Dion told him that there wasn't anything yet, that piecing together the information regarding the weapon had been complicated enough.

"Kind of like everything else in my life," he added.

The sergeant surprised him then by suggesting that it was possible to see that changing for the better.

"Partnered up with the officer, you might get a different outlook," St. Albans observed. "I can say she's given me some things to think about for myself the past few days."

The councilman huffed again, saying, "I fail to fathom this embrace of our young investigator as some feminine sage. If the rumors of her social proclivities accommodate any element of accuracy, I concede that while she may have, in fact, provided some prolific number of her colleagues fodder for thought, any enlightenment to be gleaned from their assignations would be less mindfully empowering than decidedly libidinous. By all accounts, the nymphet has suffered more mountings than a carousel pony."

"The kid doesn't need to hear this," St. Albans said.

Honest Mike twisted on the seat to look back at Dion. "You think me to be speaking out of turn?" he asked, his tone a little mean.

"It's your car," Dion said. "You can take as many turns as you want, but I'm still getting where I'm going, and if you're trying to say that she has a history, tell me who doesn't. I've got my own, and now you guys are in it. I wish you weren't, but here we all are."

The councilman blinked and faced the windshield again.

Dion felt his eyelids drooping again in the hush of the others' voices falling dryly silent. He remembered something he had heard just a few hours before but hadn't totally appreciated at the time. He repeated it aloud.

"Damaged people find each other."

He saw Honest Mike's eyes on him once more in the mirror.

"I decline to accept my insertion into assessments of yourself or your compatriots," the councilman admonished haughtily. "I reject any presumption that I contend with preternatural flaws in either myself or those close to me."

"Oh, yeah?" Dion sniffed and reached into his jacket. He pulled out his cell phone and rested it on his thigh, the screen facing the car roof, the sergeant turning to watch. As Dion scrolled to the text from Corinne and the image of her bare navel came into view, he was startled when the sergeant's hand reached over from the front seat to cover it.

"No," St. Albans said gravely. "That's not what friends do."

Dion felt instantly small as he angled the phone out of sight and sighed an apology.

"My head is just kind of fried right now."

"There's a lot of that going around," St. Albans nodded.

Dion wondered something as the image timed out and the screen went dark against his knee.

"How do you know what this is?"

"How do you think?"

"So, it's not just me," Dion said slowly.

"I'm having that exact same thought," St. Albans told him.

Dion squinted at the sergeant for a minute, remembering seeing him with Corinne at her cantina. Honest Mike cut in with a growl.

"If you have concluded this privileged discussion of what I imagine must be further discomfiting video evidence of my hair-salon encounter, I should desire more specifics of your progress on the Cullen Arcade investigation."

"Maybe some other night," Dion said as he reached for the door handle. "I'm going home to bed."

"But I have not dismissed you," Honest Mike scolded.

"If you believe that," Dion muttered, "then you haven't been listening to yourself."

The sergeant told Dion to just go, that otherwise somebody was going to end up being insulted. Dion opened the door, saying that somebody already had been.

"Thanks for the ride," he said, waving goodbye at them with his phone. "Next time, I think I'd rather walk."

- 76 -

Dion was not walking when his cell phone waved hello to him later, floating mystically through the darkness of his bedroom after waking him up with a chime and a glowing display to announce the receipt of a new text message.

"It's Tico," Shiner whispered as she set the phone near his pillow before padding barefoot back to the corner to retake her seat on the chair in the corner.

Dion was surprised to feel knees folded in behind his own and a petite arm warming his ribcage, Kady spooned tight and clinging, crowding him on his side at the edge of the bed, her breaths falling cool on his shoulder while her spiky hair tormented a ticklish patch of skin at the base of his ear.

He snaked his fingers slowly to reach the phone, trying to not rouse her or lose the body contact, but his subtle motion rippled in a wave across the mattress as he shifted, her hand rising for a moment in response before it dropped tighter into his chest hairs, the wave then spreading beyond her to trigger a reaction from the farther side of the bed. A rustle of blankets there released a hand that passed over her to hook itself into his elbow, and a solid calf that slid across her to crimp itself over his shins and lock him stationary against the sheets while sending his mind vastly adrift.

Dion heard Kady ease a contented moan into his back

that was seconded by another from Evan beyond, his sister so close as to leave no space for secrets or pretense, the three of them braided as one and sharing air on what felt to him like an eerie descent into the unexplored depths of an uncharted idea, his chest with each passing second growing tighter against the pressure of the dive.

The phone screen dimmed while his eyes stayed fixed on a memory of his sister reassuringly enfolded with him in the sleep of his youth, not so strong anymore in his old belief of her trying to protect him and thinking with dismay of the implications suggested by alternate interpretations. On his side there in the bed, her limbs resting on him in a reminder of how safe but confused she had made him feel back then, and was making him feel now, with Kady snuggled warmly in between to confuse him even more, he wondered which of the three of them most needed protecting right then, eventually deciding that it was probably him.

With some effort he slid his legs out and rolled free, sitting up as he fingered the phone to read the message. He pushed himself to his feet to the sound of Shiner bundling his clothes on the chair. She held them out to him as he rounded the end of the bed, and she patted him on the hip as he took them from her and headed toward the door.

He paused when he got there, stopped first by a soft rumble of bedding that carried across the blackness of the room, then by a single timid voice sleepily registering his flight, others soon conjoining in demure protest, a hotly alluring collective entreaty that formed a nearly irresistible harmony with the conflicted voice of his mind.

Don't go.

- 77 -

Tico Tocopilla was confused as he aimed his flashlight toward the back door of Brillo Ziemer's house.

"You're telling us that you and your sister own this place now?"

Dion worked a picking tool into the deadbolt lock, his hands chilled in the breeze coming from the river valley.

"Not yet," Dion replied. "Sometime after the attorney straightens out all the legal stuff, I guess. We need to call and see what happens next, but I didn't want you breaking anything trying to get in, leaving me with something that I'd end up having to fix."

The occasional whine of a vehicle passing on the river parkway was interspersed with footsteps in the dark, boots crunching on the knobby dormant grass of the backyard as Hefty Von Hanson tidied up by kicking sticks toward the low flagstone wall that surrounded the spindly lilac bush in the corner.

"Maybe we should just wait then, huh?" the big kid suggested. "For when we can't get into trouble."

The lock yielded as Dion answered.

"If we get caught, I've got the letter from the lawyer, so I don't think too much could happen," he said. "And I'd just as soon know for sure if there's really anything valuable here before we clue my sister in. I don't want to get her hopes up for no reason."

"So whatever we find, she's in on a four-way cut?" Tico asked.

"Make it three," Dion offered, picking up the canvas bag that held his inherited burglary tools. "I'll split my share with her. You guys deserve the rest for coming up with the idea to look for cash in the walls."

"Three wouldn't be fair to her or you," Tico said as Hefty nodded in agreement. "So, we'll stick with four."

With the door open, they followed each other inside to the kitchen.

"I thought about bringing her along," Dion told them wistfully, the heated aura he had awakened to still simmering in his mind. "But she was wrapped up in something."

He turned on the ceiling light, but Tico quickly switched it off, saying they shouldn't get cocky. They followed his flashlight beam to the stairway and went up.

"Why do you suppose Brillo left everything to you guys?" Tico wondered.

Dion told him that it was a good question with no good answer. At the bedroom door, Hefty took in a loud hacking breath.

"Smells like he's still in here, you know?"

Tico said he was okay with turning on the lamp on the bedside table, so Hefty hit the switch and the bulb colored the room in a weary amber glow that made all the furniture look sorry to be there. Dion set the bag down and opened the closet door. He pulled a large hammer from the bag. Tico came over and took it from him.

Dion moved to the bed and began paging through the photo albums still spread open atop the blankets, thinking he might come across another old picture that included his father. He was distracted when several loud, rapid blows ruptured the quiet, each strike chorused by the thump of plaster and drywall chunks dropping to the floor and the skittle of debris shards cascading down inside the wall like pebbles in a chute. After half a dozen swings, Dion heard a sound like a plastic trash bag being twisted, and then a laugh.

"My dad wasn't lying," Tico chortled as he pulled a shiny dark sack through the hole he had made. "These old outlaw paint and drywall guys were all like pirates, burying their treasure."

Streaks of white wall dust billowed from the sides of the bag as he placed it on the floor and knelt to unwind the twine that held it closed. Hefty took a knee beside him to watch.

"I'm supposed to be excited about this, right?" the big kid asked.

"Just keep your fingers crossed," Tico told him.

Tico opened the bag and turned it over. Short stacks of paper currency swaddled in rubber bands spilled out onto the rug at the foot of the bed, along with a few coins that Hefty corralled with his hand to keep from rolling away, then held up to the light to squint at the engravings.

"Is Krugerrand somewhere in the Bahamas?"

Tico rolled his eyes, then shook the bag as more bills fell out alongside a yellowed packet of stapled pages that landed flat like a folded newspaper.

"What is that?" Dion asked, pointing.

Tico partly unfolded it, saying it looked like a set of project prints.

"Prints?"

"Plans," Tico explained. "The kind of thing my dad works

off of for his bigger painting jobs, or my crews use for restoration work in the sewer tunnels. Brillo must have thought they were either worth something, or worth saving."

He pointed at the first page.

"The title sheet says it's for some old cleanup at the Matterhorn."

Dion came over and knelt with the others.

"Let me see," he said.

Tico handed him the plans. Dion spread them open on the floor, scanning the bid quantity and detail pages that followed the title sheet, eventually finding the scale drawings and schematics showing the layout of the Matterhorn lounge with the bar and stage in their respective places. Plan notes outlining the work were amended by penciled notations of field revisions and material adjustments. A prominent arrow, scribbled wide and darker than the other jottings and circled several times, pointed to the wall behind the stage but wasn't tied to any written explanation that Dion could find.

As the others began counting the money out loud together in voices growing more pleased with each partial tally, Dion could hear only the silence of the arrow. When he looked up past Tico to the closet and the battered opening in the wall, the dark hole seemed like a reflection of himself truer than a mirror, and the aged texture of the paper against his fingertips sent a charge up his arms.

"Still with us over there, D-man?" Tico asked, as though he could hear the fallout. "You look a little lost."

"I'm here," Dion answered with a thoughtful nod, eyes on the arrow again, not saying that for all the years he had felt adrift, he had never expected that the possibility of regaining his bearings might depend on the discovery of a pirate's treasure map.

- 78 -

The quiet in the darkened Matterhorn lounge fell deeper, well after closing time, when Dion finally clanged a small crowbar into the canvas tool bag beside him on the stage. The spotlight focused over the piano carved a white circle from the room. Chairs with legs skyward atop the tables spread shadow lines across the room like monuments in a cemetery. He picked up a bar towel from the floor and wiped plaster dust from his hands, dabbing at blood from a small cut on one knuckle as he sat down on the piano bench. The alarm from the security keypads near the front and rear entrances continued a tiresome bleat, with a voice warning that law enforcement had been notified of a system breach.

The threatened police response materialized as he rested on the bench. The alarm went quiet, and he heard the rattle of keys in the rear hallway, then footsteps accentuated with the unmistakable squeak of a heavy leather utility belt and holster jostling against the movements of an armed uniformed officer.

"I'm in here, and I surrender," Dion called out, and soon the cop appeared, tentatively peeking from the archway between the lounge and the dining room, staring at him warily through the dimness from beneath the short, glossy visor of her oversized hat.

Lauda Aplikowski was at her shoulder, the old man sockless in loafers and wearing a trench coat over tiger-stripe pajamas. Dion watched him take a long gaze at the new hole in the wall at the back of the stage.

"Thanks for your help, officer, but I guess we're okay here," Lauda told her. "He's one of mine."

She looked relieved as she turned to head away. When Dion heard the rear door close behind her, he began to unwrap a crusty paint rag bundled at his hip on the bench. Lauda didn't seem to notice.

"What the hell is this about?" the old man grumbled as he shuffled into the room, fists in the pockets of his coat.

"This," Dion answered, pausing halfway through the thought, "is about deciding who I should be mad at first."

"The line for being angry starts behind me," Lauda argued. "I'm the one who got woken up by the alarm company in the middle of the goddamn night. If your sister gave you a key to get in, why didn't she give you the security code?"

"I didn't use a key," Dion said. "And I didn't really think about the alarm until I got inside. Then I decided that the worst that could happen if the cops showed up would be that you'd have to vouch for me, and if you didn't want to, Honest Mike Walerius would."

"The walrus sent you?"

"Brillo Ziemer sent me," Dion said, bending to reach into the tool bag for the old restoration plans and holding them up. "Seen something like these before?"

Lauda stopped a few feet from the stage, his waxy head sinking lower into the collar of his pajamas and coat as he looked from the papers to the canvas tool bag, grimacing like he had spotted a fresh scratch on his Chrysler.

"I have," he said. "Back from after the electrical fire in the circuit box there. Brillo and your dad patched the wall."

Dion dropped the plans into the bag and unfurled the paint rag to free a blue steel pistol that he lifted toward the spotlight.

"One of them patched this into the wall," he said, his voice edgy. "Between the two, who do you suppose was the most likely candidate? The one who was still alive, or the one who wasn't?"

When the old man didn't answer, Dion suggested that maybe they could still catch the police officer before she drove off, to ask how she might vote. Lauda pulled a chair from atop the nearest table, set it upright on the dance floor, and sank heavily onto the seat as he began to speak.

"You know how in the movies there's a fight, and some- body gets between the guys to break it up but they're the one that gets nailed?" he said. "It was pretty much exactly like that."

Dion took a slow breath. "So it happened here?"

"After hours, like tonight," Lauda said quietly. "Easy and Ellie were working on some music arrangements at the piano. Brillo was supposed to come in and work on the wall. When he showed up, your dad was with him. I think they'd been out on some escapade your mother didn't ap- prove of, and your dad was supposed to be home with you kids."

"Wait a minute," Dion said, his face growing suddenly warm. "My folks were both here?"

Lauda looked down at his knees, one hand massaging his forehead as he nodded and went on.

"Your dad got loud when she started in on him."

"That sounds like what I remember of how things were."

"He always complained that she spent too much of her time down here," Lauda said. "But if she did, she had her reasons. I suppose you were too young to understand, but your dad was an immature, insecure man, and it didn't help that she was attractive and popular. He thought she had something going on with someone here, usually me, and he wasn't shy about saying so."

Dion licked the open wound on his finger, saying, "But that wasn't true, about you?"

"Only in my dreams," Lauda told him.

"So, if it wasn't you?"

Lauda responded by pointing at the hole in the wall and ignoring the question.

"Brillo would never tell me what happened to the gun," he remarked. "I think it was his trump card for if I ever turned on him."

Dion was about to repeat the question, but the old man was rolling with the memory.

"Easy and Brillo were up on the stage. Ellie was on the dance floor with Cullen, between him and the others. The one in the middle, like I said. She and your dad were arguing, which was nothing new. They'd been together forever and bickering for about as long."

"High school sweetheart syndrome," Dion said. "At least that's what Evangeline says her therapist calls it. I can't really say much about what they were like, you know? Most of what I remember about them now is from what I've heard. Or haven't heard. So, fill me in on what I don't know."

Lauda sucked in his flabby cheeks and asked if Dion didn't already know and did he really want to hear more, because the details weren't pretty. Dion said that thinking he knew something wasn't the same as being sure.

"I've gotten this far," he sighed, resting the gun on his thigh. "If she's really gone, like people always figured, then she's gone. It's time to finish this. I've had enough."

Lauda nodded and went on.

"Brillo and Easy were staying out of the fight. I was over by the bar. Your dad said something to your mom on the dance floor, and Easy heard it and said something back at him that your dad didn't like. Next thing I see, Cullen has that pistol raised in his hand and Easy is coming down off the stage toward him."

He shook his head at the memory.

"I'm moving too, trying to get over there. Your mom has got her hands on Easy's chest, trying to push him back. Then there's a shot, loud as hell, and your mom is staggering away from them, toward me, blood running down her shoulder. She drops to one knee, then both knees, and she keels over onto the floor. I grab a towel from the bar to put pressure on the wound, on her neck just below her hairline. While I'm holding it on her, Cullen is watching, like in shock, and I hear Brillo tell him to let go of the gun. Not to drop the gun or give him the gun, but to just let go of it."

"What's the difference?"

"The difference is that a couple of seconds later there's another blast and your dad hits the floor face down. When I look over, I see more blood and an open space in the back of his head and the gun smoking on the floor, with Easy and Brillo standing over him."

Dion looked down from the stage, the pistol heavy and lifeless in his grip as he tried to imagine the scene.

"So you couldn't tell who did it."

"Not then and not now, and that's the God's honest truth," Lauda said. "I do know what I'd say today to Honest Mike Walerius or any judge who wants to put me under oath, though."

"Brillo," Dion said with a knowing nod. "Because there's nothing they can do to him, and it lets everyone else off the hook."

He sat for a while thinking about time and secrets, wondering if gaining knowledge that he had long striven for and dreaded should have brought a sense of satisfaction that he just didn't seem to be feeling.

"Tell me where she is," he said.

The old man shifted noisily on the chair.

"Ellie was probably about gone before she got to me, I think," Lauda recalled sadly. "It hurts me to remember it. Blood everywhere between her and your dad, Easy and Brillo practically crying on each other's shoulders, just totally shook. I thought about calling the cops, but with two people shot from behind, saying it was a domestic murder and suicide thing wasn't going to fly."

"So, what did you do?"

"Brillo was driving a big panel truck back then. He finally calmed down and said he had an idea, so we helped him wrap the bodies in his tarps and load them into the truck, and he left. Easy and I stayed behind to clean up, and that's when we figured out that the gun was gone, that Brillo must have taken it. I guess he dropped it into the wall at some point."

"But where is she?" Dion repeated.

"I asked Brillo that," Lauda said. "When the newspapers said that the cops found your dad."

"And?"

The old man shrugged, saying that Brillo would never tell him.

"Another hold over me, I guess," he said. "It never made sense to me why he didn't want them found together. I think Brillo had a thing for your mom, like a lot of us guys did, so maybe he just couldn't stand the thought of leaving her in a ditch in the snow."

Dion heard a mild gasp and looked to see Lauda staring at the hole in the wall.

"This is all that was there, boss," Dion said, showing him the gun.

"Sorry," Lauda said, shaking his shoulders like he had chills. "My thinking is a little screwy right now. Hearing myself going on about this is tough. I've kept it quiet forever."

Dion dropped the pistol into the tool bag and stood, his legs heavy under him, his heart heavier inside. As he squeezed out a sigh, he heard Lauda talking softly to himself.

"No, baby, no."

"What?"

"The last thing she said when she was holding Easy back," the old man recalled quietly. "No, baby, no. And then she never knew what hit her, never saw the shot."

Dion frowned, thinking about the revelation, then saw that Lauda was frowning too, for a different reason.

"This hole you just chopped into my wall," Lauda said,

pointing a yellow finger that shone hairy in the spotlight. "What are we going to do about fixing it now that Brillo isn't around?"

Dion looked, his mother's last words reverberating in his mind.

"Call Tico's dad," he said. "Tell him I said you should pay him three times whatever he asks."

He picked up the tool bag. Lauda asked what he intended to do with the gun.

"I'm going to bring it with me when I turn myself in for breaking and entering," Dion answered, taking a last serious glance at the hole.

"To your new lady cop friend?" Lauda asked with a worried tug on the belt of his trench coat. "Where will that leave me with Honest Mike Walerius?"

"Depends on what I say, I guess."

The old man cast a thoughtful gaze toward the floor for a few seconds before offering a suggestion.

"What would you say to a partnership?"

- 79 -

The muffled breakfast-crowd noises filtering into the office of the Amor Abrasadora cantina sounded to Dion like the ethereal chanting of lost souls. No, baby, no. When the deadbolt on the door suddenly twisted, he welcomed the harsh immediacy of its metallic squeal. Then the door opened, and Corinne Nasseff burst through to find him reclining on her green leather love seat amid bunched mounds of her workout clothes; and the chants were drowned and gone.

"Kiddo," she exclaimed when she saw him, her keys jangling in her fist. "With you around, I don't know why I bother with locks."

The door closed with a heavy thud, and she crossed the small room to impishly bump her gym bag against his foot.

"You look like you've been up forever," she said. "You said yesterday that you were going to get some sleep."

He told her he had tried, but things got in the way.

"Too much on your mind?" she suggested.

"Among other places," he said. "I had a couple of family things pressing on me."

Corinne set her bag on the floor and eased down the zipper of her hooded rain slicker, watching him watch her. "I thought I might hear from you last night, after I texted that picture."

"I got the picture," Dion replied, looking up at her. "But I'm not sure I get the picture."

She peeled the slicker off and dropped it on his lap. Underneath, she was wearing a sweatshirt over warm-up pants.

"What's to get?" she asked, standing close over him, her face shadowed against the bright ceiling light, her teeth shining in a half smile. "Haven't you ever been teased before?"

He pushed the slicker onto a low pile of her hats near his shoulder and admitted that he had been teased lots of times, but never, so far as he remembered, as part of a group. Her eyebrows crested.

"Damn, you're good," she cried. "How did you know I sent the picture to someone else?"

Dion told her that he had found out by accident, while considering weaponizing the photo against her husband during an argument.

"The sergeant talked me out of it," he said. "He protected you. Better than I was going to."

He lifted his hand and tapped his wounded finger lightly against her kneecap.

"So, I owe you one," he said. "And you owe him one."

Corinne bent her knee to mirror his touch. "I sent it to him to cheer him up," she said. "Then I sent it to you to cheer me up."

She bounced her toe softly against the love seat, asking him if he was aware that his sister had shown the sergeant a topless photo of herself, telling him it was where she'd gotten the idea. Dion said that he hadn't known, but that he wasn't surprised.

"It's been that kind of week," he said.

"Did you like my picture?"

"I did," he told her. "So did my sister."

Corinne shook her head and laughed.

"I can see that this day is starting with a bang," she said. "Are you here for a particular reason, or just to drive me batty?"

He pointed toward her desk.

"I come bearing a gift," he said. "Courtesy of Lauda Aplikowski."

"From Lauda?" she said, looking. "For me?"

"For me," Dion said.

Corinne stepped to the desk and picked up a folder. After she opened it and read through several of the sheets inside, she looked toward him with a confused smile.

"He signed over my promissory note and his interest in the cantina?" she said. "To you?"

Dion nodded as he pushed himself upright on the love seat and pulled his jacket on. His father's gun in the pocket landed heavily against his belly.

"It took most of the night and waking up an attorney and notary public, but I guess it's all the legal paperwork we need to register with the city licensing office and get Honest Mike to leave him alone," he said.

Corinne remarked that Lauda had refused to buy her husband off, saying, "What have you got on him where he'll pay you, but he won't give in to the walrus?"

"More than either of us wants."

She regarded him seriously for a few seconds, then set the papers down. "You're a puzzle, kiddo," she said.

"So's my life."

Pointing toward the clothes beside him, Corinne asked him to toss her a T-shirt, saying she was going for a run. Dion picked one up and flung it underhanded across the room. She gripped the hem of her sweatshirt, ready to pull it off.

"You know, I'm thinking this new deal could work out really well," she said. "A smart kid like you can learn on the job while still being useful. Now, turn around."

Dion stood and stretched, telling her that they had already done that dance, that he was leading this time.

"You turn around."

She grinned and faced the desk, showing him her back.

"You want my hands up too, like I made you do for me?" she giggled as she raised her arms toward the ceiling, wrists crossed as though cinched by the T-shirt she held.

"I was only playing it safe that day," Dion said. "I thought you might still have had a gun around."

"Ahh," she murmured over her shoulder. "Like, is that a pistol in your pocket or are you just glad to see me?"

Her warm-up pants rippled tight creases along her hips. Dion fingered the handgun in his jacket, his brain pulsing with jolts of static.

"Unreal," he breathed out slowly.

"My ass?"

"My ears."

He found the door, saying he would see her later.

- 80 -

What Dion Drury saw sooner was a unit of forensic technicians wearing police coveralls as they scanned Brillo Ziemer's backyard with ground-penetrating radar equipment, their inspection of the basement floor suspended just after lunch to bring the search outside beneath low clouds in biting early-spring breezes. The metallic sky drooled sporadic veils of mist that jeweled the new grass.

Watching from the kitchen window as the crew probed, he could hear footsteps creaking above him and garbled voices from the second floor. His ears caught the sound of someone coming down the stairs as he sat at the table. Arno St. Albans came through from the living room a few seconds later and leaned one hand against the refrigerator, stroking his forehead with the other as he peered out the window to the yard.

"Lousy weather day for this," he said.

"Kind of fits the mood," replied Dion.

The team outside was converging on the raised soil in the corner of the yard where the overgrown lilac bush bobbed in the heavy breezes. Someone was shouting toward the street, calling for a chainsaw.

"The technicians say there's only a couple of feet of dirt over the bedrock down here along the river bluff," St. Albans said. "It's why the basement walls are just carved limestone. That planting bed is about the only place in the yard where the topsoil has any depth."

Dion didn't respond, imagining Brillo Ziemer twenty years earlier, in a panic, the barely thawed shallow earth inhospitable to excavation. He'd hastily settled upon the elevated flagstone planter.

"Are you okay, watching this?" the sergeant asked him.

Dion shrugged and said he wasn't sure what he was feeling.

"It's like being in a weird dream."

"One where you and your pals bash a closet wall digging for cash and a gun drops out," St. Albans said. "It must have been a shock when you figured out that you found the murder weapon."

Dion pressed his tongue against the roof of his mouth, thinking before he said, "I'd say it knocked me about halfway up West Seventh Street."

Two newcomers appeared outside in the yard, coming around the side of the house to stop near the back stairs.

"That looks like your sister," St. Albans said.

"She brought my uncle."

"Your mother's twin from the lounge act?"

Dion nodded. "They weren't really twins, but I guess they felt like they were. I thought he should be here if your theory holds up."

"You uncovering the gun here was a big break," the sergeant said. "A search for her remains is the logical next step. I apologize if that sounds insensitive."

As Dion said he was beginning to see that twenty years had dulled his sensitivity to most everything anyone said to him, a screaming buzz rose from across the yard, the chainsaw fully revved and dismembering the lilac bush branch by branch. He looked over at the older man and noticed something.

"You lost your sunglasses."

"Yeah, I think my face muscles are finally making a comeback," St. Albans said, sounding pleased as he fingered his cheek. "I even blinked this morning."

Dion gazed out at Easy Andrews huddled in a thin overcoat at the edge of the yard, the old man's hair flapping in the wind, face as flat as the sky, and made an oblique confession that the sergeant did not react to.

"So did I."

The chainsaw eventually whined to an idle and died. People began pointing and calling to one another. St. Albans said it looked like they were moving to erect a tent over the planting bed.

"This could mean something," he said as crossed the room and went out the back door.

More footsteps descended from upstairs, bringing movement into the living room. Honest Mike Walerius walked into the kitchen with Kady just behind him. They crowded against the table to peer out the window.

"Looks like maybe we'll know soon," Dion told them.

"It shall be gratifying to me personally to see a resolution to this troublesome episode." The councilman rubbed his palms together as he rocked slowly on the soles of his wing-tip shoes. "The two of you are to be commended for your persistence and ingenuity in bringing to light this new avenue of inquiry. I should also make clear my regret that the surviving parties will likely find small solace in a verification of the full nature of their tragic loss, so long delayed."

Dion was about to say that he doubted any of the surviving parties gave a rat's ass if Honest Mike felt regret or not, but Kady voiced a feeling of her own first.

"I get it that the ballistics check out, and that the gun was found here in Ziemer's house," she said, digging her fists into the pockets of her police windbreaker. "So, I'm not against pinning the blame on him, but I'd be more comfortable if I were seeing an obvious motive somewhere."

Honest Mike dropped his hands to drum his fingers on the tabletop as he gave his opinion on how to look at it.

"You have successfully created a circumstantial line of connection between the known victim, the weapon, and the related business associate. If, as we may soon confirm, there exists a second known victim, also of close association, we must satisfy ourselves, without the benefit of witness accounts to provide insight into the particulars of the criminal behavior, to simply attribute the intent of the perpetrator as indeterminate but in some way influenced by the dynamics of the triad."

Kady agreed reluctantly. "We could, for sure, close the file based on the evidence we have so far if we want to, but the *why* of all this will still bug me."

Dion looked out at his sister beside Easy Andrews in the yard, bent against the breeze, and thought about attribution and blame, and the lamentable misfortune of adults who navigate their entire lives from the childish perspective of self as the sole reality, unable to either think beyond the limits of their emotional fears and defenses, or to experience family and the greater world as anything but perpetually exasperating challenges to the harrowing task of getting through each day without being revealed as a pathetic, ineffectual fraud.

"Love," he said. "That's the *why*."

"What?"

"Like in a triangle," he explained. "With broken corners."

Kady looked at him, the lenses of her eyeglasses reflecting his face, and said she didn't understand. Honest Mike surprised him by saying that he did.

"Damaged people find each other," the councilman proclaimed, turning up the collar of his overcoat against the weather as he opened the back door, giving Dion a grudging nod before going out. "Or so I have been told."

Dion rubbed his eyes sleepily as he watched Honest Mike cross the yard. Kady pulled out a chair and sat down next to him.

"His damaged people thing come from you?" she said.

"It came from you," Dion answered.

Kady looked out the window for a minute before musing absently that she wasn't sure how she was going to write a final report that anyone would believe.

"You probably can't," Dion said.

He felt her hand on his knee.

"Did you ever manage to sleep somewhere last night?" she asked. "You look a little strung out."

"I was afraid to try," he said. "I wasn't sure who I might wake up with."

Kady's mouth went flat as she shook her head.

"I'm embarrassed," she said. "I always do this to myself. Your sister thought it would be funny, both of us climb into bed with you and see how you react when we wake you up, but now I'm thinking that it was just a way for her to get closer to me. I should've seen through it."

"She can be persuasive."

"When she said maybe we shouldn't wake you up after all, I was stuck there, between the two of you."

He saw her eyes growing earnest.

"I don't know what you're going to think of me, but I really liked it," she said. "Warm and cozy, like a little kid. I zonked out in a couple of minutes."

"I liked it too," Dion said, draping his hand over hers. "That's why I left."

He could see that the forensic crew outside had raised a canopy over the planting bed and digging tools were being handed out, the sergeant and the councilman off to one side watching, his sister still standing near the back stairs while Easy circled slowly over the grass, arms folded and his gaze low, like a football coach pacing the sidelines with his team down three scores.

"You know, I used to have this idea that if the real truth about my folks ever came out, maybe I'd be different," Dion said. "Now I'm pretty sure that I'll always just be me."

Kady brought down her other hand to sandwich over his.

"That doesn't have to be a bad thing," she told him. "My therapist can help, and I can help too. Just tell me how, and I'm there."

Staring through the cold mist outside, her breath sweet at his shoulder, his mind sifted through memories of his misguided past romances, of conquests and calculated misconceptions, of intensely immediate and casually clueless mismatches between drifting souls attempting in their desperate animal grappling to claim some rhapsodized share of human connection—and now, here was the elusive prospect of a better forever confronting him once more, teased out by an affectionate touch, tenuous hope somehow still enduring against the backdrop of a haunted, sad house where every room smelled like old sour varnish.

"Call me baby sometimes," he said carefully.

"Baby?"

"To let me know I'm in your heart."

He went on, feeling a strange openness coursing through the words as they came to him.

"Squeeze my ass in public once in a while."

"In public?"

"To let me know I'm in your head."

His final thought left him with a sense of serenity he could not recall ever feeling before, and that he had not seen coming.

"Touch your nipples to mine in bed now and then."

"In bed?"

"To let me know you're happy."

When he took a heavy breath and turned to Kady, she was blinking back tears.

Voices rose outside. Dion could see the technicians hoisting fabric walls around the tent canopy, a supervisor out talking with Honest Mike and St. Albans, the three nodding soberly. Easy was watching them, his body soon shuddering, hand over his face, overcome. Then Dion spied his sister moving through the gloom with hesitant steps, merely to stand near their uncle at first, and then resting a cautious arm across the old man's shoulders.

Dion felt his jaw begin to quiver as he rose slowly to his feet, Kady gently steering him toward the door.

"Go, baby," she whispered. "Go."

- 81 -

So it turned out that the editors of the Saint Paul daily newspaper had commissioned a feature highlighting the two-decade anniversary of the unsolved Cullen Arcade case after all. The discovery of the murder weapon and the skeletal remains of the victim's wife, along with the cinematic details of the friend and probable killer's fatal burglary-tumble down an ancient sewer shaft, provided a fortuitously lurid epilogue to the story. Dion had read the account, unsurprised that Honest Mike Walerius managed to claim the most direct quotes of anyone interviewed, and when he encountered it again a few weeks later on news-print wadded around a stoneware serving platter he could not envision ever using, he was glad for everyone to be finally moving on.

Other dishes wedged into a cardboard packing carton on the open tailgate of Tico Tocopilla's municipal pickup truck rattled when Dion lifted the box, prompting Kady to call out to him from across the driveway outside Brillo Ziemer's old garage.

"Be careful with those," she directed as she tugged an armful of police livery on hangers from the rear hatch of her car, her uniform hat cockeyed on top of the pile.

"They come from your grandmother or something?"

"No, but they're nicer than yours or your sister's."

Behind the car, Hefty Von Hanson helped Evan Arcade

slide a mattress off the deck of his flatbed truck, her face wet and shiny in the warm overhead sun. She puffed quick breaths as she pulled at a ribbed edge.

"You sure you're okay?" Hefty asked her.

Evan eased her end of the mattress to the ground and shook her head, saying she didn't know why she was so hot, and snapping her sweaty softball jersey away from her chest.

"Could be your new meds," Kady suggested. "The change can cause weird reactions."

"Like your night terrors?" Evan smirked.

Kady stepped over and dabbed the other woman's face with the sleeve of a pressed blouse from the bundle of police clothes while giggling and calling her a snarky bitch.

"Maybe you ladies should stick to drinking, huh?" Hefty said.

He hoisted the mattress and shuffled toward the house, while Evan walked the other way to Brillo's old van and pulled from the open side door a large plastic wastebasket loaded with brooms and mops that she set on the driveway before unloading her bicycle and rolling it toward the garage.

Dion followed Hefty and Kady up the uneven sidewalk tiles that snaked through the weedy lawn and reached the front stairs to the sounds of birdsong and fluttering leaves. Trees along the river parkway whirled in breezes that eddied up the navigation channel and smelled alive.

Tico came out the front door, swiping at his cell phone while standing aside to let the others pass.

"My dad says to call if you want to know his trick for stripping wallpaper," he said to Dion.

At the side of the stairs, Shiner, wearing shorts beneath a crisp food-service smock from the Kittsondale Treatment Center next door, knelt with small gardening tools near a clearing of fresh potting soil on the ground, sorting impatiens from a tray.

She squinted up at Dion, one hand shading her eyes against the burnished overhead sky, her hair a shade paler than the sun and the starburst scar at her temple the color of lightning.

"Think we should we plant some in the backyard too?" Dion asked her. "Around the old lilac bush?"

"Would she like that?"

Dion admitted that he didn't really know. "I guess maybe I'd like it," he said.

When he came back outside after leaving the box in the kitchen, with the voices of Kady and Hefty filtering from the open windows on the second floor, Dion saw that another vehicle had crammed itself onto the driveway. Arno St. Albans was already out from behind the wheel of his unmarked police sedan. He was gesturing.

"Please tell me that this truck isn't on city time," the sergeant was saying to Tico, who was standing in the bed of the pickup as Dion walked over to them.

"See, here's the deal on that," Tico said. "I'm on city time right now too, so it's all good."

"So is this car," Corinne Nasseff announced as she climbed out from the passenger side of the sedan. "And so is the driver, so don't let him give you any grief."

She opened the rear door of the car and waved Dion over, asking for a hand. As she was lifting flat pizza boxes with the logo of her cantina printed across their lids, Dion stood behind her and listened to St. Albans joking with Tico.

"It's good to hear the tough cop happy again," Corinne said. "That frozen face thing was a scare."

"Your cell phone picture cured it, I think," Dion told her. "Bare female skin works wonders on a guy."

Corinne put the boxes in his arms and grinned, tapping the toe of her sneaker on his.

"Don't tell the walrus, or he'll want some too," she said. "And don't tell him that I got talked into delivering pizzas. He already doesn't know what to make of you and me."

As Dion turned, Tico was climbing down from the truck while St. Albans gazed toward the house and said he was sorry he hadn't been there to see the reaction of the three younger men when they had smashed up the bedroom closet and accidently found the gun.

Tico looked at him blankly. "What gun?"

The sergeant shook his head admiringly. "You neighborhood guys never change, do you?" he said.

Evan came from the garage, heading toward the van for more of her things. St. Albans asked her how everyone was holding up in the aftermath of all that had happened. She answered that he could see for himself how she and her brother were doing, and that Lauda Aplikowski planned to bring Easy Andrews over later if the sergeant wanted to hang around to see her uncle too.

"The boss said he's bringing beer for when we're done," she said. "Easy has another couple of weeks of having his jaw wired shut, and he's pissed off that the city isn't budging on their settlement offer, but that's kept his mind occupied, which is good. The graveside service for our mom was a little tough on us all, but with him it's always been hard to tell where his brain is at. He doesn't say a whole lot."

She swept her arm toward the yard, where Tico was carrying two lamps up the sidewalk while Kady and Hefty were coming out of the house.

"I know he thinks this is kind of crazy."

Dion carried the pizzas to Tico's truck. Soon after he stopped there, he felt insistent fingers furrowing down the back pocket of his pants, Kady up close now and stretching into him.

"Hungry?" he asked her.

"I know you are," she said, her spiky hair nuzzling his shoulder. "But what am I?"

Corinne brought out paper plates and cantina napkins and breathed a soft whistle when she spied Kady's feet.

"I love your sandals, kiddo," she exclaimed. "You'll have to tell me your secret for always finding such nice stuff."

Kady began setting out the pizza boxes on the tailgate, giving Dion a sideways smile.

"Do I have secrets, D-man?"

Dion tasted a sweet rivulet of perspiration salting the corner of his mesmerized grin.

"I forget," he said.

Hefty strode up, the back of his loose T-shirt dark with a damp stain roughly the shape of Minnesota. When he noticed St. Albans, he went over and opened the cab of the flatbed, pulling out a pristine toilet plunger with a painted handle and a fresh tag from the hardware store. He held it up to salute the sergeant before spearing it into the waste-basket with Evan's brooms and mops.

"There you go," St. Albans said. "Now we're ready for anything."

Evan told Hefty to remind her to pay him back for whatever he had spent.

"You okay with Krugerrands?" she asked with a wry chuckle.

He told her not to worry, to think of it as a housewarming gift thanks to his windfall from Brillo.

"You were in Ziemer's will?" St. Albans asked him, surprised.

Hefty answered after a jovial shake of his head.

"I was in his wall."

Tico came out for another load, wiping his eyebrows on the sleeve of his work shirt. The others told him to take a break for lunch. Dion went up the walk to fetch Shiner. She had a small hole ready for one of the flowers and said she wanted to finish planting it, so he sat down on the stairs to wait.

Shiner hummed a melody like something from a nursery rhyme as she worked, and Dion drifted into faded memories, his parents and early years scarcely real anymore in his mind. He was beginning to consider the insights of his sister and Kady, that the gnawing ingrained sense of unworthiness and disconnection that had tarnished his life had hardly been his fault and had never even been about him. He had gotten things all wrong—it had been the flawed adults around him who in their neglectful impropriety and guilt had cast him off, unfairly adrift and profoundly abandoned to navigate alone the tempestuous currents of time.

He turned his face toward the sky, the sun undeniable and cleansing, its infinite heat searing the present everlasting moment into his awareness as surely as the scent of the spring flowers and the scraping of Shiner's planting tools over the soil.

From the driveway drifted the amiable low chatter of the others, and he drew in a long breath as though to fill himself with the sound. When he followed it with a hopeful sigh, Shiner asked if he was falling asleep. He smiled and rubbed his eyes as he stood.

"I'll sleep tonight," he told her.

She tilted her face as she looked up at him, shaking her head. Dion asked her why she didn't think so, and she told him.

"Evan and Kady were saying that you're going to be busy tonight."

He swallowed a short tingling breath, then reached down to help her to her feet. She reached up and handed him some woody cool dirt that oozed damply over his palm.

Then she laughed, and he had to laugh too.

ABOUT THE AUTHOR

Pete Gallagher is a native of Saint Paul, Minnesota. He resides in Ramsey County.